JACK BALLAS

IRON HORSE WARRIOR

Hunting for his brother's killer, Chance Tenery takes a job on the Union Pacific Railroad and begins a long fight for his honor, his life, and the woman he comes to love . . .

ANGEL FIRE

When Kurt Buckner agrees to escort a woman to the Colorado Territory, he finds that hostile Indians are no danger—compared to the three men who want her dead . . .

POWDER RIVER

Case Gentry is no longer a Texas Ranger. But the night a two-bit gunhand rides up to his cabin, he has to bring back every instinct to survive . . .

GUN BOSS

Raised by an Apache tribe, Trace Gundy never forgot his lessons in survival. Now, to avenge the loss of his beloved wife, he must call upon the fighting spirit he learned as a boy . . .

THE HARD LAND

JACK BALLAS

B
BERKLEY BOOKS, NEW YORK

THE HARD LAND

A Berkley Book / published by arrangement with
the author

PRINTING HISTORY
Berkley edition / October 1996

The Putnam Berkley World Wide Web site address is
http://www.berkley.com/berkley

ISBN: 0-425-15519-6

BERKLEY®
Berkley Books are published by The Berkley Publishing Group,
200 Madison Avenue, New York, New York 10016.
BERKLEY and the "B" design
are trademarks belonging to Berkley Publishing Corporation.

PRINTED IN THE UNITED STATES OF AMERICA

10 9 8 7 6 5 4 3 2 1

THE HARD LAND

1

JESS SANFORD, SHIRT soaked, sweat streaking his face, slammed the posthole digger to the bottom of the hole. The blades hit another rock. The handles vibrated. His hands stung. A glance down the fencerow showed only six postholes for two days' work. A glance at the field of cornstalks, less than waist-high, burned brown by the midsummer Tennessee sun, brought angry bile to his throat. His shoulders slumped, his gut knotted. If it wasn't for Ma and Pa—and even with him being broke—he'd leave this man-killing few acres of his parents. Hoofbeats sounded from back in the trees.

Sanford squinted between sweat-laden lashes. Simon Bauman. His anger pushed a red haze behind his eyes. All he needed now was that pompous, arrogant bastard to watch him vainly try to scratch out a living in this quarter section of sorry land.

Sanford stood looking at the spoiled young man, a man who'd lorded it over him since they were small boys. Even then he'd avoided trouble with Simon Bauman for fear of what the spiteful, wealthy Bauman family might do to his mother and father.

Bauman pulled his gelding to a stop, dismounted, looked

at the six holes, and kicked rocks back into two of them with a look that dared Sanford to say something. His mouth twisted in a contemptuous grin. "You white trash're determined to scratch out three meals a day on this hardscrabble farm. Why don't you deed it to my pa and move on?" He walked to another of the holes and kicked dirt into it. His grin widened. "Pa might even get real generous and give your folks a little something just to get rid of them. He could be raising horses on this land."

The anger in Sanford's throat bubbled higher, but he wanted to avoid trouble. "Bauman, I ain't botherin' you. You've already pushed rocks in those holes it took me two days to dig. Climb back on that horse o' yours an' leave, an' I'll forget you come here lookin' for trouble. Now get along, leave, before I . . . I . . ."

Bauman's face hardened, his fists clenched. "Before you do what, white trash?"

Sanford's anger pushed blood up behind his eyes and into his brain, then the fire in him turned to cold fury. "Leave now, Bauman, before I give you the beatin' your pa shoulda done years ago."

The expression on Bauman's aristocratic features changed from contempt to wonder. His eyes widened. "You'd hit *me*? Why, I'd have the sheriff run you out of this country."

Bauman's threat penetrated Sanford's anger. The Bauman plantation measured up there with the largest in the county and the man facing him with cool contempt could carry out his threat.

Despite his enemy being an inch or two taller than his own six feet one and probably twenty pounds heavier, Sanford grinned, dropped his hands to his side to take his enemy off guard, then stepped close to the man who had been taunting him and brought a right up from his waist, catching Bauman a glancing blow to the chin.

The big man staggered back a couple of steps and hit the ground on his back. Before his enemy regained his feet, insane fury blinding him, Sanford kicked Bauman in the side, jumped on top of him, and swung vicious, driving blows to his face, his chest, then grabbed his hair and pounded his head against the rocky ground. Bauman rolled to the side, struggled from under Sanford, and crawled to his feet.

Sanford stood and ran at his birth enemy. Bauman looped a right to the side of his head. Bright lights flashed behind his eyelids, an explosion went off in his skull. He fell, saw Bauman's foot swing toward him, and rolled away from it. The side of the big man's riding boot raked his ribs, making them burn like the fires of hell.

Sanford rolled to his knees and stood. Simon ran at him. Sanford swung from the ground and caught Bauman under his heart. The spoiled bastard stopped dead still, eyes wide, face pasty, and sucked for air. Before he could get his breath, Sanford hit him again, high on his cheek. It split, gushed blood, and Sanford hit him with a left that drew blood above his right eye. Bauman swiped at his face with the back of his hand, held the hand down, and stared at the blood smeared across it. He whimpered, looked wildly about and grabbed the posthole digger. He swung it at Sanford, the blades catching him on his left shoulder, numbing it. He fell.

Bauman ran at him, holding the posthole digger straight in front like a spear. Blindly, he stabbed it at Sanford. Flat of his back, Sanford rolled away from the attack. His shoulder felt broken. His wind came in gasps, but Bauman's breath sounded worse. Sanford kicked straight out from where he lay and caught Simon on the kneecap. He fell, grabbed his knee, moaned.

Sanford rolled over, and from his knees launched himself at his enemy, landed on top, and swung wildly at his face. Right, left, right, left. Every time he swung with his left, his shoulder felt at though it would tear from its socket. Still, he pounded at the pulpy face until he could hardly lift *either* arm. Hatred born of a lifetime of verbal abuse went into each blow.

He sat astraddle Bauman's chest, his fist drawn back. He blinked, squeezed his eyes shut to rid them of sweat, then opened them wide to stare down at the battered hulk. He swung his cocked fist one more time. His enemy's nose slanted to the side, spurting blood.

Strength, along with the insane rage, drained from Sanford. He stood, walked to a pine stump, and sat looking at the unmoving beaten body. A hot, metallic smell rose from the sunbaked earth, reminding him his work, his rage, didn't count for much. He continued to stare.

After several moments—or was it hours?—it dawned on him that he'd seen Bauman move only once, and then with only a twitch of his right leg. Had he killed the man? Not wanting to find out, he sat there.

Finally, knowing he could put it off no longer, and not sure his cut and bruised fists could feel anything, he stood, went to his hated enemy's side, stooped, and felt for a heartbeat. Nothing. He pushed his trembling hand harder against Bauman's chest. Still no pulsing under his touch. He put his ear to the man's mouth. No breath warmed his skin. He straightened, not breaking his gaze from the still body.

He'd killed a man.

He disliked Bauman from the bottom of his gut, but he'd not wished him dead. He walked back to the stump to ponder what to do. He couldn't stay here, he'd be imprisoned and hanged. He'd thought long about leaving, heading west. Now the decision was made for him.

He had no money, no weapons, no horse. He looked at the beautiful Tennessee walking horse Bauman had ridden, felt greed, desire, pull at him, but shook his head. Horse stealing wasn't another crime he'd add to his list. He considered searching Bauman's pockets for money, but decided against that idea, too. He'd never stolen anything in his life and wouldn't start now. The clothes on his back were all he had to face the world with, but so be it.

The country beyond the Mississippi drew him, but the Bauman plantation stood between him and the direction he must travel. Sanford gnawed at the problem, but the sickness in his stomach kept pushing into his thoughts. Killing a man, even Bauman, hit him harder than he believed possible.

Where would the law look for him? What was the best way to get where he wanted? Where would he be most likely to find work? He had to have money, had to get clothes, had to eat. Should he take a chance and go home to tell his folks and pick up his other shirt and jeans? He shook his head. He'd best leave life as he knew it behind— a clean break.

A wide swath of timber ran along the south side of the Bauman place, and after studying on it, Sanford decided the law would never expect him to head toward the family of the man he had just killed. He stood, looked again at the unmoving body of his enemy, and turned toward the setting sun. God. What would happen to Ma and Pa without him to help out? What misery would his crime bring down on their shoulders? But—seeing him hanged would be worse.

*   *   *

Simon Bauman watched Sanford through swollen, slitted lids. As much as he loathed anything by the name of Sanford, and as much as he'd wanted to kill Jess, the gnawing, gut-tearing fear of further beating overcame his hate. If he stayed still maybe he could avoid it. He'd been unconscious for a spell. The shadows from the trees at the edge of the clearing now stretched long toward the east, and it had been only a little after noon when Sanford attacked him. Not until his enemy stood and disappeared into the trees did Bauman try to move.

He stifled a moan. He'd never been hit before, never been hurt in any way. Now every muscle in his body screamed in agony. His face felt twice its normal size, like it should be even larger to hold the throbbing, pounding drums inside his skull. His ribs stabbed pain through his chest, and his knee throbbed with each heartbeat. He tried again to move, gasped, and lay still.

After a while, not wanting to lie there through the night, and thinking if he was to get home by dark he'd better get moving, he rolled to his side, moaned, whimpered, his sobs choking him.

Almost passing out twice, he pushed to his one good knee and gained his feet. His gelding stood at the edge of the clearing cropping grass. With every step, his knee buckled, feeling torn apart, causing him to come down hard on his right foot, jarring the tortures of hell through his chest and head.

He staggered to his horse, grasped the saddle horn, and tried to mount. The first pull on the saddle horn, and he again fell. He lay there a few moments, thinking not to try again, but now hate took charge. He had to get home, had to get the sheriff on Jess Sanford. Inch by inch he climbed to his feet, and again grasped his saddle horn. This time he pulled himself onto his horse and sat, fighting back nausea and a feeling that he was about to faint.

The hour it took Bauman to ride to his big antebellum home seemed like years. With every step of his horse, pain shot through his knee, head, and battered muscles. The only times he didn't hurt was when he grew faint trying to slip into unconsciousness.

Long after dark, lights shone from the myriad windows in the mansion at the top of a hill. The gelding walked to the steps leading to the wide multicolumned veranda and stopped, Bauman slumped against the cantle, hurting too much to move.

After what seemed a lifetime of torturous waiting, Tom, one of his family's liveried servants, ran to the side of the gelding. "Lordy, Mr. Simon, what done happen to you? You git throwed by this heah horse?"

"Don't stand there asking stupid questions, you old fool. Get me off this horse. Get me in the house, then find my father."

"Yes, suh. Git you right off'n that saddle." Tom stretched to take Bauman by the waist as he swung his leg across the horse's rump, then all Bauman's weight sagged onto the old man's frail body and he fell with him.

"Damned clumsy fool, get up, help me. Do something to earn your keep. Get me in the house." Then Simon realized the darky couldn't move with him lying on top of him. He rolled to the side, freeing the old man.

"Yes, suh, yes, suh, jest tryin' to git that job done." Tom stood and helped pull Bauman to his feet. Staggering under the leaden weight of his young master, Tom helped him up the steps and into the foyer, helped him stretch out on one of the long settees along the walls, then ran from the room yelling, "Mistuh Bauman, Mistuh Bauman, Mistuh Simon's done got hisself hurt somethin' awful. Come quick.''

Soon a half-dozen servants along with Simon's parents stood around him clucking their tongues, sponging his bruised face, holding cold cloths to his brow, and in general giving him the care he thought he deserved.

While they hovered over him he told his father that Jess Sanford attacked him without provocation, and left him lying in the clearing. ''He just turned and walked toward the shack they live in. Didn't care that I might be hurt bad. I want a warrant sworn out for his arrest come daylight; that, or I'll take my shotgun and kill 'im.''

His father studied him a moment, frowned. ''Didn't you try to defend yourself? You outweigh him by thirty pounds. You shoulda whipped him.''

''I tried, Papa, but he hit me with a posthole digger. I didn't have a chance.''

''*Hit you with a posthole digger?* No. I'll not wait 'til morning, I'm riding to town now. The likes of him won't get away with beating my son.'' He looked at Tom. ''Have one of the men saddle my horse. You get Mr. Simon to bed.''

Sanford stayed to the deep woods, making little sound. Most of his life had been spent hunting and fishing, and even though now only twenty years of age, he'd considered himself a man for several years. He didn't look back. He'd hear pursuit long before he could see it.

The thick canopy of limbs all but shut out the sun, letting only enough light through to set the sun's position at about three o'clock. Here, under the trees, a thick matting of leaves cushioned his feet. The thin light and leaf cover stifled any brush or plant life. He walked to a fallen tree and sat.

He patted his pockets, knowing little in them would help him along his way. The outline of his pocketknife came under his hand, then the feel of his corncob pipe, an oilskin of lucifers, and a small twist of rough-cut tobacco. He smiled, thinking how much hell his ma raised when she found he'd taken up smoking. Well, she wouldn't have to worry about that any longer.

A lump came to his throat when he thought of his mother, then his father. He missed them something awful, and they'd never know what happened to him, where he was, what he was doing. He would never dare write home. He was a wanted man, and the law could find him easy if they knew where his letters were posted.

He drew his pipe from his pocket, thinking to sit and rest awhile, maybe let some of his hurting soften. Bauman had given him a pretty good thrashing. Before cutting some of the tobacco into his pipe bowl, he stuffed the old corncob back into his shirt. He'd enjoy a smoke later.

If he expected to find a stream to make camp by for the night, he'd better get a move on. He might be able to get a couple of frogs for supper, or snare a rabbit. If he found nothing to eat? He shrugged. He'd been hungry before— many times.

Later that night Simon's father brought Sheriff Corcoran back with him. He questioned Simon and his father for over an hour, then said he would go to the Sanford farm and see what *that* young man had to say about the fight. Simon's father looked up from squatting at his son's side. "I'll go with you. You might have more trouble than you can handle."

Corcoran pinned him with a hard stare. "Mr. Bauman, I was elected to this job because I know how to handle it.

You'll stay right here. I'll not have interference in performing the duties of my office."

Mr. Bauman stammered a moment, then nodded. "All right, Sheriff, but I'm filing charges against Jess Sanford in the morning."

Corcoran tipped his hat. "That's your privilege. I'll see you tomorrow."

Although late, the sheriff knocked on the Sanfords' door and identified himself. Tom Sanford, Jess's father, answered. "Come in, sheriff. Ain't nothin' happened to Jess, has it? We been worried sick about him. He ain't come home since goin' to dig postholes on that field I got over east of here."

Corcoran squinted into the lamplight. "Don't know, Tom. What I do know is, he and Bauman's boy had a fight. Simon's beat might nigh to a pulp. Ain't seen Jess. 'Fraid I'm gonna have to look for him come daylight."

"You reckon he's hurt, Sheriff? Ain't like him to not come home."

"Tom, we're just gonna have to wait and see." He nodded. "See you when I find out anything."

The next morning, early, Corcoran had Simon describe where they'd had the fight. He went to the site alone, studied it, saw the scuffed-up ground, searched the area, then headed to the Bauman plantation. There, he didn't wait for blustering Mr. Bauman to say anything. "Gonna tell you something, Bauman. You can file charges against young Jess if you want, but he's disappeared, and if what's happened is like I think, I'll be finding his body. Then *I'll* be filing charges, murder charges, against Simon. I'll see *you* later." He walked heavy footed from the room.

Sanford trudged ever westward, staying to the woods, avoiding people and settlements, thinking the law must be not far behind. He trapped enough game to eat well if not often. Days passed, and every night he camped by a stream, he washed his clothes from the skin out. He kept himself as clean as lack of soap permitted. For two weeks he'd not talked to anyone, not been closer than a hundred yards to another human being. Looking down at his threadbare jeans and patched shirt, he realized he had to do something, had to have work of some kind, and even though it would be mighty chancy with the law looking for him, he had to get in among people somewhere. Squatting now in the brush on the banks of the Mississippi River downstream of Memphis, he scanned riverboats, cotton bales piled high on the wharf, and blacks and whites scurrying back and forth loading the boats. It looked to him like a man ought to be able to lose himself in all those people and find work doing something—anything.

Hearing leaves rustling in the brush behind, he spun to face the noise.

"Hi, Mistuh white man, whatcha doin' settin' heah looking at all them people down yonder?"

Sanford stared. The man he looked at was about as ragged as himself, stood six feet or more tall, had thick, ropy-muscled shoulders, and a lean waist—built like Sanford himself in almost every respect. If the stranger meant him harm, defending himself might be a day's work, even though his cuts and bruises from the Bauman fight had healed.

The darky looked and acted friendly, but Sanford didn't figure to turn his back to the man. He didn't think the stranger would know anything about him killing Bauman, not this far away, but there were many men out of work these days, and among them were those who would rob you. He had to squelch a grin. Anybody who robbed him would be sadly disappointed.

He pulled his old corncob pipe from his pocket, looked at the empty bowl, and remembered he'd smoked the last of his tobacco two days ago. He slid his pipe back in his pocket and cast the black man a guarded look. "Hi, you got some reason I shouldn't be settin' here lookin' down yonder?"

A wide grin split the stranger's face, showing even, snow-white teeth. He shook his head. "Jest thinkin'. You look 'bout lonesome as I feel. What's yo name, suh?"

Sanford nodded. "Reckon you're right, I'm lonesome. You're the first man I've talked to in far too long a time. Name's Sanford, Jess Sanford. What's yours?"

The black man's smile widened. "Reckon my name's Joe Bob Brown, least that's what they been callin' me most o' my life. 'Course they done called me other things when it figured I wuzn't workin' hard 'nuff." He frowned and nodded toward Sanford's pocket. "Notice you wanted a smoke, but put yore pipe back in yore pocket. You outta tobacco?"

Sanford nodded.

Joe Bob pulled a chunk, barely enough for one smoke, from his shirt. He held it toward Sanford. "I'd be obliged if you'd take this heah an' enjoy it."

Sanford looked from the small bit of tobacco to lock gazes with Joe Bob. "That all you got?"

The tall darky shuffled a foot through the weeds, studied the track he'd made in it a moment, then returned Sanford's look. "Yes, suh, but reckon I'm fixin' to get me some more when I get me a job."

A lump swelled in Sanford's throat. This man didn't know him, but was willing to share what little he had. On the basis of that small gesture, he gave Joe Bob his trust.

Sanford studied the darky a moment longer. "What you

doin' here 'longside the river, lookin' down at that town like I been doin'?''

Joe Bob frowned. "Reckon I wuz doin' the same thing you wuz. Jest wonderin' if maybe they's some work down yonder, payin' work. Mistuh Sanford, I need a job somethin' awful. When Mr. Lincoln give us our freedom, ain't nobody paid much 'tention to how we wuz gonna eat an' take care o' our needs when our masters quit doin' it. I been goin' through white folks' trash to find clothes, an' I'm pretty good in the woods, so I been eatin' sorta reg'lar. Reckon from the looks o' you, you hurtin' for them neecessities bad as I am.''

Sanford nodded. "My name's Jess Sanford. Call me Jess, an' yeah, reckon I need a job mighty bad.'' He couldn't help thinking that although not a slave, he'd probably worked as hard, and had had little more in the way of food and clothing.

"Well, Jess, don't suppose any work they got down yonder's gonna come 'long this here riverbank lookin' for *us*. Better get our lazy rear ends down where we can start askin'.''

Sanford grimaced. "Weeell, yeah. Might's well do it, gonna have to sooner or later.''

Joe Bob studied him a moment. "What's the matter, Jess, you runnin' from somethin'?''

Sanford went quiet inside, wary as a cornered coon. He pinned the black man with a hard look. "Don't reckon that's any o' your damned business.''

The big darky stepped back, a hurt look showing in his eyes. "Aw now, Jess, didn't mean to dig none. 'Course it wouldn't do no harm if I knew somethin' 'bout you, case you need help.''

Sanford felt shame. "That's all right, Joe Bob. Sorry I barked at you. Reckon if we stick together long, I'll tell

you 'bout it someday.'' He grinned. ''C'mon. Let's see if
there's a job waitin' for us down yonder.''

An hour later they wended their way through heavy-
muscled, sweaty men, hundreds of them, it seemed to Sanford, and from the smell of them, most hadn't bathed in a
goodly while. Every few steps he looked back to see if he'd
been recognized, or was being followed.

He'd never hunted a job before and he didn't know
where to start—who to ask. There was noise all around
him, men shouting, urging others to get a move on, and
those struggling under heavy loads grunted—or cursed.
He looked at Joe Bob. ''Reckon the ones makin' the most
noise're the ones to ask for work, Joe Bob Brown. What
you think?''

The black man pushed the frayed old straw hat back off
his forehead, wiped sweat, and nodded. ''Yeah. Good a
place to start as any. Let's try the loudest of 'em.''

Sanford sighted a man bellowing at the top of his lungs
at men to ''tote those bales,'' to move faster. Sanford
stepped toward him, but Joe Bob tugged on his shirtsleeve.
''That ain't no man we want to work for, Jess. One o'
us''—he grinned—''or maybe both o' us'd have to fight
'im fore dark, an' a darky ain't gonna make many friends
fightin' a white man, an' if you help me, somebody'd kill
you.''

Sanford shook his head, frowned. Even though the war
had ended seven years before, and the black man set free,
Negroes were still not treated well, and any white man who
befriended one was treated worse.

Sanford swept the dock area with a squinted glance. The
sun beat down with a brassy glare, and the smell of dirty
bodies and the stench of rotting garbage caused him to
breathe shallow breaths. His look stopped on the main deck
of the riverboat. ''You ever been on a boat before?'' Joe

Bob shook his head. "Me neither. Reckon we oughta make it a first time." He stepped toward the gangway, the big black man close behind.

He waited for a break in the traffic going on and off the boat, wedged himself between men carrying bales of cotton, and walked aboard.

At the top of the gangway, a man dressed in khaki directed the workers where to place the heavy loads they struggled under. His glance rested on Sanford. "What're you doing standing there? Get to work."

"They's two of us, mister, an' we ain't been hired yet. You puttin' us to work?"

The man's look raked them from head to toe. He nodded and said, "Go forward to the wheelhouse. Tell the man in there—his name's Rich—that Baldwin said to put you on the payroll—dollar two bits a day, feed ya twice a day, morning and night, you sleep on the boat, and when we get under way, you go with us. Pay's the same."

Sanford looked at Joe Bob, grinned, and headed forward. He had no idea what a wheelhouse looked like, but reckoned he could ask once he got to the *front* of the boat—or had the man called it forward.

2

SANFORD WALKED TO the bow, Joe Bob trailing right on his heels. He looked over the side, down at the swirling, muddy water—he'd never seen this much water in one place—then he looked at Joe Bob. "You see anything looked like a wheel?"

Joe Bob shook his head. "Only wheels I seen wuz them what wuz on the sides o' this here boat, an' they didn't have no house on 'em. Fact is, I ain't seen no house, nowhere. Reckon we wuzn't listenin' wid bofe ears." He again headed aft.

The first person they came to looked at them, frowning. "You men lose somethin'?"

Sanford grimaced. "Well, can't say we lost somethin' when we didn't know where it was to begin with."

"Where what was?"

Joe Bob, grinning like he found something funny about the way things were going, said, "We wuz sent *fohwahd* to find somethin' called the *wheelhouse*." He shrugged. "Ain't no wheel an' ain't no house where we been lookin'."

The stranger studied them a moment, frowning, but his mouth and eyes smiled. He pointed. "See that ladder?

Right there at the top of it, if you'll look, you can see the boat's wheel inside that glassed-in cabin. That cabin is the wheelhouse. The wheel's what we steer this contraption with. What you want to go up there for?''

Sanford sighed. ''This's a different world to us, stranger. That man back yonder by that plank we come aboard on, man by the name o' Baldwin, said to tell somebody in the wheelhouse to sign us on.''

The stranger nodded. ''Cap'n Rich, he runs this boat. He's up there, an' he's the one you need to see.''

Sanford nodded. ''Yeah, Rich was who he said to ask.''

The man cast Jess a kindly smile. ''Son, you better learn to put a handle to his name. He's *Cap'n* Rich, an' less'n you know who you're talkin' to other than him, put a 'sir' in front of your yeses an' noes.'' He grinned. ''Save you a lot o' trouble.''

''Yes, sir, reckon I was taught that way.''

Joe Bob cut in. ''Lordy, that ain't gonna be no trouble for a darky. I'm use to puttin' a 'ma'am' an' a 'sir' on danged near ever'thing—'cludin' the plow mules.''

In the wheelhouse, the captain scanned them from top to bottom. ''Well now, reckon I've seen some scruffy-lookin' characters in my time, but you two take the cake.'' There was a smile behind his voice. ''What you two men want?''

Joe Bob answered. ''Captain, sir, Mr. Baldwin, down yonder by that board we come over to get here, said as how you was to sign us on. Didn't say what we was to be doin', but he did say, sir, that y'all would feed us, an' we'd sleep on the boat, an' we'd go wherever the boat went.''

Captain Rich studied them a moment. ''When you ready to get to work?''

''Lordy, Cap'n, we'da gone to work weeks ago if we'da knowed 'bout this here boat. We ready right now.'' Joe Bob's words brought a smile to the captain's face.

"Where's your gear?"

Shame flooded Sanford. "Sir, we got no gear."

Rich reached in his pocket and pulled out a sawbuck. He studied them with a look Sanford would have bet would pierce a sheet of steel, then looked at the ten-dollar bill in his hand. "Reckon I can trust you. Want you to take this money, go ashore, buy yourselves at least one good change of clothes, soap, razor—hell, spend it on the things you figure you'll need 'til payday. I'll dock your first payday for this amount." He made as though to hand the money to Sanford, then handed it to Joe Bob, thus conveying trust in them both.

After giving Rich their names and being told to show up for work by daylight the next morning, they left the big side-wheeler and went to the business area in Memphis.

They stood at the corner of Poplar and Thomas, staring round-eyed at the bustling city. "Jess, you ever been in a place with this many folks 'fore?"

Sanford shook his head, a little scared and plenty nervous in the middle of this foreign environment. "Joe Bob Brown, soon's I get what I need to last me 'til payday, I'm gettin' myself back on that boat an' I ain't leavin' 'til somebody runs me off."

His eyes wide, the darky nodded. "Meee, too." He pulled the ten-dollar bill from his pocket and stared at it. "Ain't never seen, let alone had, this much money before."

Sanford put his mouth close to Joe Bob's ear. "Put that damned money back in your pocket. Hear tell they's them in these towns what would steal pennies off'n a dead man's eyes."

So fast Sanford hardly saw the movement, a black hand stuffed the bill back in his pocket. "Jest wanted to sort o' look at it. Sho is pretty, ain't it?"

Sanford grinned and nodded. "Shore is, an' jest 'tween

you an' me, *I* ain't never seen that much money before neither." Joe Bob shuffled his feet a moment. "Somethin' botherin' you, Joe Bob?"

The tall darky stared into Sanford's eyes. "Yes, suh. It ain't gonna do for a black man to show ten dollars around. Somebody's gonna figure I stole it." He pulled the sawbuck from his pocket and handed it to Sanford. "You better take care o' it an' pay for our stuff."

They bought the things they needed to keep themselves clean first, then looking at what they had left, checked the prices of jeans, shirts, long johns, and socks. They didn't have enough for shoes, which they agreed they needed, but Sanford said they could wait until payday to get them. It being summertime, they could go barefoot if they had to. Again Joe Bob agreed. Sanford suggested that being about the same size, they could buy a third set of jeans and shirt to share when the need arose. Joe Bob allowed as how that was a good idea, and said he'd never had so much *new* stuff in his life. They bought the third set of clothing and, after checking the change they had left, decided to buy some tobacco to share until payday, then headed back to their new home.

Sanford was quiet on the way back, his mind going over the past few hours. In only a few hours, far less than a full day he'd met a man, grown to like him, hired on to a job with him, and now they were going to share what clothing they had. His smile didn't show, but it was there inside his chest. He'd made a friend.

After stashing their gear, they reported to Mr. Baldwin, telling him that the captain said for them to go to work in the morning, but having nothing else to do, they'd like to get to work now.

He gave them plenty to do. The boilers used wood like they might quit growing trees on the morrow, so for their trip upriver they loaded firewood. Baldwin had also told them they would be stoking the firebox while under way.

Sanford wondered how anything could eat as much wood as they loaded, and was told that even though it seemed to him they had enough wood to burn forever, the boat would have to pull along the bank at selected places on the way to St. Louis and take on more fuel.

By sundown, the side-wheeler was loaded to the gunwales. Baldwin told Sanford he and Joe Bob better eat and get some sleep. At midnight they would have to begin stoking the firebox to build up steam. They'd be getting under way come daylight.

"Anywhere to take a bath on this boat, sir?" Sanford sighed, stretched his aching muscles, and smiled. "Sir, I sorta like to stay clean when I can."

"Don't apologize, young man. Most men who make their living on the water have a feeling for cleanliness. Back aft there's a place where you'll be able to shower. Take your own soap."

Sanford went to get clean clothes and soap. His new friend fell in beside him. "Was wonderin' wuz we gonna put on them clean, new clothes 'thout washin' our dirty bodies. If I hadn't seen no other way, Jess, I wuz gonna git in the river an' scrub up some."

Sanford dug through the parcels they'd bought only a few hours before. "Yeah, figured as much, Joe Bob. When I met you this mornin', I seen your clothes was clean even if they was mighty thin. We gonna get along right well."

After cleaning up and eating supper, they went to the crew's quarters on the main deck, aft of the boilers, and crawled in their bunks. Sanford, although used to hard work, couldn't remember being more tired. He worried awhile about how to do the job they were expected to do, then decided if there was much to it there would be someone to show them. He turned over and went to sleep.

Someone shook his shoulder. "Time to go to work, boy. Go to the boiler room. It's straight forward, just below the wheelhouse."

Sanford stifled a groan. He felt like he'd only closed his eyes for a second. He stretched to the next bunk to waken Joe Bob, but before he could touch him, the big black man whispered, "I heard the man, Jess. Looks to be a right long day." With that, he stood and started dressing.

A huge redheaded man stood by the wood stacked neatly in cords within easy reach of the round, open, glowing maw of the huge steel boiler. Sanford felt his gaze on the two of them as they walked up.

"Name's O'Malley, chief engineer." He said it as though chief engineer was part of his name. "Gonna first show you lads how to stoke this here furnace. When I think you got the swing of it, I'll show you how hot *not* to let it get. These boats blow up more often than I like to think about. Why, I've seen 'em scatter one o' these boats over a half mile o' water, break 'em into such small chunks you'd think somebody'd chopped a bunch o' kindling an' tossed it in the river." He pointed to a set of gages. "Them's the steam gages." He placed his finger on a red mark. "This here's where you don't want to never let the needle climb to. Past this red mark there's danger o' blowing the boilers.

"I'll be here with you, won't leave you alone, ever, until I know you know what to do. That time's quite a while off. They's a voice tube here where the skipper can talk to you. He does it with bells, too. I'll tell you 'bout them later. Okay, let's build a head o' steam."

Sanford bent, picked up a length of cord wood, and threw it to the back of the furnace, bent, picked up another, and repeated the action, realizing Joe Bob was duplicating his movements across the opening from him. After a while—it seemed like days, sweat streaming from every pore—he stood erect, flexed his back muscles, and bent to his work again.

When the gages showed a head of steam sufficient to turn the giant paddle wheels, O'Malley began talking to the captain on the voice tube, then did something with some knobs and handles. The deck shuddered under Sanford's feet and then throbbed a steady vibration.

"Well, lads, we're under way," O'Malley roared above the noise of the pounding engines and splash of the churning side wheels. "You lads worked hard, done a good job. Gonna tell the cap'n so, and ask for you to be assigned down here with me all the time."

Sanford had mixed emotions about that. He felt pride that on their first day they'd done what was expected of them, but he wasn't too sure he was pleased about being here in this heat all the time.

He'd noticed O'Malley writing something in a book every hour or so after reading the gages. "Mr. O'Malley, sir, is that somethin' I could do for you?"

O'Malley looked at him a moment. "What's that, lad?"

"I seen you writin' in that book after checkin' the gages, figured I might do that for you. I can read an' cipher."

"You sayin' you want me to show you what I'm doin' here?"

Sanford nodded. "Yessir. If you figure it ain't none o' my business, then I'm sorry I asked, just thought I might help."

O'Malley placed his hand on Sanford's shoulder. "Lad, you *can* help. They's a many a time I need to get some air. Ain't young as I used to be. I'll speak to the skipper 'bout it. Thanks." He looked toward the gages, then back to Sanford. "C'mere, I'll show you what I been doin'." He looked at Joe Bob. "You want to see, too?"

Joe Bob nodded. "Yes, suh, but I don't read much, never had no chance to learn."

Sanford cut in. "Sir, show 'im anyway. I'm gonna make sure he learns to read right well."

O'Malley only smiled, and pulled them close around him.

Noon of the first day brought a change in the watch. Sanford, so tired he could hardly lift his arms to throw more wood into the firebox, looked on his relief like he was an angel. Tired though he was, he assumed he and Joe Bob would man the boilers until the boat got where it was going. He looked at O'Malley. "Sir, what do we do now?"

O'Malley smiled, weariness causing his face to sag. "Lads, the both o' you get some sleep. You'll be back down here at midnight. We work twelve-hour shifts. You boys did a good job."

On the way to their bunks, Joe Bob tugged on Sanford's sleeve. "Jess, you mean it 'bout learnin' me to read an' cipher?"

Sanford studied Joe Bob's face a moment. "Yeah, I meant it. Don't you want to learn?"

The darky shook his head in wonder. "Jess, I never wanted nothin' so bad in my life." With those words, they came abreast of the paddle wheels churning the muddy water to a froth. They stared at them a moment, then Sanford shook his head. "You ever see the likes o' this, Joe Bob? Who'd ever think them wheels could push this boat through the water with all them cotton bales on it."

Joe Bob stood there shaking his head. Finally, he said, "Lordy, Lordy."

They watched awhile longer, and when the novelty wore off, Sanford said they'd better eat and get some sleep if they were going to get up in time for supper.

"Wanta ask you somethin', Jess. How'd you learn to read?"

Remembering his mother, warmth flooded Sanford's chest. He looked at his friend. Teaching him to read was something he fully intended to do.

He frowned as a picture of his mother pulling him to the floor beside her chair formed in his mind. Quietly he described how it had been at home. "Ma was a schoolmarm 'til she married Pa. She used to sit me at her knee after I done the chores an' read to me. Then, after I got older, she had me read to her. Pa would make me tell 'im the multiplication tables, then he'd make me add, subtract, divide 'til I could do most of it in my head. I sometimes bowed my back and got stubborn as a old mule, couldn't see no need for all that stuff if I was gonna be stuck on a farm all my life.

"Pa never let up on me. He showed me how he kept track of what the farm was doin'. Joe Bob, most o' what *he* showed me was cipherin'."

The tall darky shook his head. "Don't know 'bout that multiplication stuff, Jess. Maybe I'll jest learn to read."

"Nope, you gonna learn it all. You gonna be able to hold any job I can by the time we get through."

"Why you doin this, Jess? We don't hardly know each other."

Sanford smiled. "Well now, Joe Bob Brown, seems like we know each other pretty good if we gonna share tobacco, each other's clothes, an' work together . . . an' . . . well, seems we gonna do most things together. I figure we're partners."

Joe Bob's "Yes, suh!" came through a wide smile, but Jess would have sworn he saw a bit of moisture in his new friend's eyes.

True to his word, Sanford started his partner learning the

alphabet before they got to St. Louis, and there they bought a primer for Joe Bob to start identifying words, and some pencils and paper to write and cipher on.

They both were learning from O'Malley the controls and gages for the boilers and engines. But Sanford never lost his dream of heading west. One evening before going off watch, after about six months on the river, Sanford straightened his back, stretched, and looked the chief engineer in the eye. "Mr. O'Malley, sir, don't want you to believe I'm gonna be a riverboat man for too long a time. I'm figurin' to head west when I make enough to buy me a outfit. Don't know what Joe Bob Brown's gonna do. He might stay on the river. Seems he's taken to it pretty good."

Joe Bob tugged on Sanford's sleeve. "Thought we wuz partners. Jess, you go I go, less'n, o' course, you don't want me."

Sanford switched his attention to the big darky he'd grown to love as a brother. "Hopin' you'd say that, partner, but didn't want to push you into somethin' jest because I figured to do it."

Joe Bob's grin gave him his answer, but the darky's words put the icing on the cake. "Jess, I been thinkin' a pretty long time now, wherever you go I'll be taggin' along."

Sanford looked again at O'Malley. "There you have it, sir. But we ain't leavin' for quite a spell yet, less o' course you don't want us, but you been so good to me an' Joe Bob, I figured it was only right I should tell you. Figure to let the grass start greenin' out agin 'fore we cut out. Think that'll give you a chance to start teachin' somebody else the things you done taught us, an' me an' Joe Bob'll help teach 'em soon's you figure it's the right time."

O'Malley stared at them a moment, shook his head, and grimaced. "Knew it was too good to be true that you two would stay with me. You're both smart, learn quickly, work hard, don't gripe.'' He again shook his head. ''You're the best men I've had, and I'm gonna be sorry to lose you.'' He smiled. ''But heck, the grass greenin' up, as you put it, is still 'bout six months off. Maybe you'll change your minds.''

Simon Bauman hadn't changed *his* mind. He was the only one who knew he hadn't killed Jess Sanford and hidden the body, and ever since his beaten body had healed from Jess's treatment of him, he'd been consumed with hatred, determined to find the man who'd done to him what no other had, and blow his head off. He continued to stew about it, think about it, study about it until he decided his enemy headed west. He decided to find him if it took the rest of his life.

One morning, about six months after the fight, he looked across the breakfast table at his father. ''Pa, I'm leaving. Going in search of Jess Sanford. Everyone thinks I killed him. Now I'm gonna find him and make their suspicions come true. Been thinking about it a long time, so don't try to talk me outta it.''

His father looked at him a long moment, a cold smile breaking the hard planes of his face. ''Talk you out of it, boy? Hell, this's the first time you've made sense in months. No, I won't try to talk you out of it. Fact is, let me know where you are from time to time and I'll send money to carry you while you look.'' He stood, threw his napkin to the table alongside his plate and strode to the gun cabinet in the family room. ''Gonna give you a rifle an' money to buy a handgun. Take any horse you want from the stable. Be sure to take a warm coat, blanket, ground-sheet—oh, hell, get yourself outfitted for the long haul.

When you're ready to leave, come in and I'll fix you up
with money to carry you awhile.''

A couple hours later Simon again stood in front of his
father. ''Ready, sir.''

Bauman looked at his son. ''Got a few words of advice,
Simon. When you find Sanford, don't try it with fists again.
He whipped you soundly once; don't give him another
chance. Do it with firearms this time. Practice. Get good
with them, then challenge him where all can see—then kill
him. Gut-shoot him if you have the time.'' He placed his
hand on his son's shoulder. ''You're finally doing something to make me proud of you.''

Simon looked at his father, hoping his face didn't betray
his inner resolve. He would shoot Sanford from behind a
rock if he had to, anywhere so long as he didn't give him
a chance. He denied to himself that he was afraid of Sanford, but in the dark recesses of his mind he knew he was.

3

To O'MALLEY'S DISAPPOINTMENT, Sanford and Joe Bob did not change their minds. Almost six months to the day after their conversation about leaving when the grass greened up, they bought themselves an outfit in St. Louis and rode west.

Now, six years later, Sanford and Joe Bob sat their horses on the banks of the Pecos River. Sanford shoved his hat to the back of his head. "Well, partner, we're 'bout as far south as this here river runs in Texas. Any more an' we gonna be swimmin' the Rio Grande or sweatin' in Mexico."

"Ain't the rivuh I'm worried 'bout, Jess, it's them danged Comanches. We fight 'em 'bout as much as the Rangers do."

They talked in voices barely above a whisper. "Them tracks I seen a while back wasn't but five warriors, best I could figure." Sanford swept the area with a glance and urged his horse up the bank. He hadn't topped out at the river's edge when an arrow whirred past his side. "Take cover," he yelled, no need for quiet now. He dived off his horse, pulling his Henry from its scabbard as he fell. Joe Bob landed alongside just below the top of the riverbank.

"Look to our backside, Jess." Joe Bob eased his rifle forward, pointed toward the top of the bank.

Sanford rolled to his back. A shadowy form flitted from a pile of brush downstream and dived behind another. He held his fire hoping for a better shot, his gaze glued to the spot but giving the surrounding area a glance every few seconds. "Them Comanche cain't see us real good from where they are. This deadfall'll hide us pretty good."

Joe Bob's grunt signaled he agreed. They lay still. A half hour passed, then an hour. Early spring though it was, the temperature hovered close to a hundred degrees.

Sweat ran into Sanford's eyes. He wanted to wipe his forehead, but movement of any kind could give away their hiding place. The pile of brush he'd had his sights upon trembled, and a few branches parted. Sanford moved the barrel of his Henry a hair and squeezed the trigger. A slim warrior straightened, clutched his chest, blood oozed between his fingers, and he fell across the pile of brush. Joe Bob's rifle sounded almost in Sanford's ear. "Reckon that leaves three," Joe Bob whispered.

Sanford checked their position. "They know now where we holed up. See if they're anywhere else'd give us better cover." An arrow whirred into the brush and buried itself in the bank at the side of his head. His gut muscles tightened. He cursed. "Arrows don't give 'em away like powder smoke would. Don't know where that one come from."

They lay still. Another half hour passed. Sanford swept the far bank and up and down the bank on his side for hiding places. There were too many to count. He kept his eyes moving, searching. "Keep lookin', pard, they's still three o' them devils hereabouts. They get close, they gonna want to use knives. Keep yours handy."

Yells blended with his last word. One Comanche came from his right and two came over the riverbank above Joe

Bob. Sanford rolled to his feet, fired his rifle into one, but didn't put him down. He dropped the Henry and pulled his bowie knife. He didn't have to look to know Joe Bob stood at his back.

The warrior he faced stood only about five feet eight inches, wiry, deadly—and bleeding from a hole in his side. Sanford had to make short work of this one; Joe Bob would need help.

His Comanche darted in, swung at Sanford's chest, and faded back out of reach. Sanford followed, sliced at the Indian's arm, felt his knife bite flesh, pulled hard on the handle to deepen the cut, and stepped back. The wiry warrior held his arm against his chest. Blood came in spurts from the gash Sanford had pulled his knife through. He wanted to wait, let the artery and the side wound bleed the Indian dry, but didn't dare. He stepped toward the warrior, danced to the side, then darted straight in. His blade slipped under the slim Indian's ribs and didn't stop until Sanford felt it strike backbone.

He jerked his bowie free and spun to help Joe Bob. The tall, powerful Negro had both warriors bleeding, but a glance told Sanford neither was hurt bad. He stepped to his partner's side. These Comanche would not quit. The odds now even, they'd fight till dead.

"Make 'em separate, pard. I'll take the one on my side." He moved toward the taller of the two, then slipped to the side away from Joe Bob. The Comanche turned to keep him covered. Sanford circled farther, enough to see Joe Bob had accomplished the same thing, then he glided toward the red man. The warrior sliced at his arm, missed, and his knife slipped along Sanford's ribs. Only a scratch. He danced back out of the way and waited for the Indian to attack. They circled a moment, then the warrior leaped in, swung his knife, and stepped back. Sanford followed close, and when the Comanche landed on his feet, Sanford swung his blade. Only the tip caught the Indian, not enough to do much harm, but enough to bring a steady flow of blood. Sanford glided back as soon as he swung—and just missed getting gutted.

The Comanche's blade sliced through his shirt. The warrior's swing turned him sideways to Sanford. Jess stepped in and pushed his blade into the tall redman's chest. He tugged at its handle and pulled again, trying to free his blade. The Comanche died spitted on the bowie. Sanford jerked around in time to see Joe Bob's adversary fall.

The big darkie looked at him. "Why you always give me the most to fight?" He grinned. "Ah, I know, 'cause I'm the best."

Sanford studied him a moment, knowing from the past they always joked after any dangerous event. It was their way of relieving tension. "Well, if you really figure that, I'll scout us up 'nother bunch right sudden an' take twice what you take." He said it deadpan, and for a moment thought Joe Bob believed him, until his partner smiled.

"If you was a complete damned fool, Jess, I might believe you. You don't want no more o' these hellions than I do, an' I'm here to tell you I don't want no more o' 'em, not today, no way."

Sanford looked at his partner, letting pride show through. "Don't reckon we gotta worry 'bout no more o' them right soon, but let's sit tight for another few minutes. See if they's more of 'em out there. By then, the shakes might have a chance to leave us, then we'll find a good place to camp an' figure what we gonna do next."

Joe Bob squatted right where he stood, just below the riverbank. "You right 'bout one thing, Jess, I'm gonna sit right here a bit an' give my knees a chance to quit knockin' together.'' He grinned. ''I notice you ain't standin' too steady on them legs o' yourn.''

Without a word, Sanford slid down the bank to sit beside his partner. They sat still, letting the hot sun cook into them. The sky, not even a puffball of cloud, was almost a white blue, with only a soaring eagle breaking its spotless expanse. Jess sat breathing deeply for several minutes when he felt Joe Bob's gaze upon him. ''What's the matter, old friend, I do somethin' wrong?''

Joe Bob only shook his head. ''Nope. Jest wonderin'. You reckon a man ever gits used to the idea of dyin', 'specially when he has to face up to it sometimes several times durin' the same day?''

Sanford, using a small twig drew lines in the sand, studied them a moment, then shook his head. ''Don't reckon long's a man's got any sense he's ever gonna stop bein' scared. Yeah, he's gonna keep on doin' what he's gotta do without wettin' his britches, an' sometimes he's gonna do damn-fool things, things that'd make him a hero in most eyes, but I'm here to tell you, Joe Bob, I don't figure any man in his right mind ever put his life on the line without bein' scared.''

Joe Bob nodded. ''Think you right, leastways that's the way I figure it. Now, if your knees done quit shakin', an' if you figure we waited long 'nuff to see if they wuz any more o' them varmints out there, let's find a campsite an' fix a pot o' coffee.''

A couple hours later they sat by a small, smokeless fire built under a cutbank. A roasting jackrabbit dripped fat into the flames. The coffeepot sat on the coals at the fire's edge.

Sanford looked from Joe Bob to the rabbit. ''Joe Bob Brown, I figure we gettin' to the point o' hoppin' 'stead o' walkin'. Reckon it'll take only one or two more rabbits to get us to that stage.''

"Jess, we done eat worse'n that. Fact is they's many a time you an' me would've been mighty happy to see one o' them long-eared sons o' guns come under our sights." Joe Bob stood, poured himself a cup of coffee, and looked questioningly at Sanford.

"Still got some. Sit down, we gotta figure what we gonna do next. It's been nigh onto six years since we left that riverboat at St. Louis, an' we gotta figure out what we gonna do with the rest o' our lives. We cain't drift forever."

Joe Bob stared toward the fire. "Yeah, an' in them years we done give minin' a shot, worked for the railroad a mite, lumberjacked, cowboyed, been on two trail drives, even took on bein' lawmen. An' mostly we done seen the big warriors o' the Comanche, Kiowa, Cheyenne, an' Sioux killed or tamed. These here Injuns we fightin' now are just renegades. Hell, Jess, we 'bout done it all. What you want to do now?"

Sanford thought a moment, opened his mouth to answer, stopped, and held his hand out for silence. He cocked his head, listened, grinned, and shook his head. "Nothin'. Just some animal settlin' in for the night." He frowned. "Reckon your question deserves a answer, partner. Yep, we just about done it all, 'cept one thing. We ain't never gone into business for ourselves."

"Aw now, Jess. I ain't cut out to be no storekeeper, an' neither are you."

"Ain't talkin' 'bout storekeepin', talkin' 'bout ranchin'." He stood and sliced one side of the hindquarter from the rabbit onto his plate, poured himself a cup of coffee, and filled Joe Bob's cup while he was up.

"Jess, we got no money to start ranchin' with."

Sanford pushed his hat to the back of his head. "Think 'bout it a minute. You an' me, ain't neither o' us hell-raisers. We done all the things you said a while ago, an' we ain't spent much more'n it took to keep us in tobacco, a occasional drink, warm clothes on our backs, shells for our weapons, an' ever'where we worked we got our sleepin' and eatin' as part o' the pay. Some o' that time we drew top-hand wages. Why I'll bet 'tween you an' me we got nigh onto four thousand dollars.''

"Jess, that ain't gonna buy land, cows, eats for the winter. Hell, it ain't gonna—''

"Now wait a minute, partner, hear me out. I been thinkin'. The last time we took a trail herd up to Cheyenne for Mr. Charley Goodnight, we left him there an' went up into the Sioux country, up yonder to the Powder River. Man, that's lonesome land, a *hard* land. Ain't *nobody* around. That land's just sittin' there waitin' for us to come take it.''

Joe Bob looked at Sanford, a worried frown creasing his brow. "Jess, you done gone slam crazy. You think them Sioux gonna sit there an' let us squat on their huntin' grounds?''

Sanford blew on the coffee in his cup. "Ain't worried 'bout the Sioux. Probably ain't more'n one more good fight left in 'em. If we got a worry, it'd be the weather more'n anythin', an' next to them is outlaws. Hear tell that Montana country's full o' them what's been run outta every town in the West. Right now, they ain't much law in that country, an' 'till there is them outlaws gonna keep flockin' up there. They're the ones we gonna have to fight.''

Joe Bob twisted and pulled his Henry from its scabbard. He shook it. It rattled. "These old rifles 'bout wore out, Jess.'' He shook his head. "Reckon if we goin' to that country you talkin' 'bout, we better each get a new outfit, an' that means new six-shooter an' rifle. I been hankerin' for one o' them .44-40 Winchesters—a rifle, not a carbine—'cause of the twenty-four-inch barrel. 'Sides that it holds fifteen cartridges, three more'n the carbine."

Sanford sipped his coffee. " 'Nother good reason, Joe Bob, it an' Sam Colt makes a revolver uses the same size cartridge. Yeah, we better get ourselves a complete new outfit." He pulled his old Henry to his side. "But in the meanwhile we better clean these weapons we got or they ain't gonna last 'til we get somewhere to buy new ones." He grinned. "An' we won't neither."

Joe Bob leered from under his hat brim. "That somewhere to buy 'em gonna be Del Rio, or Fort Stockton?"

"Del Rio's closer. Less'n a day's ride, Stockton's 'bout three days' ride, but it's the direction we wanta go. Might see if they's anybody gonna head a bunch o' cows north, maybe tie on with the outfit."

They finished their coffee, cleaned six-shooters and rifles, and went to sleep.

Three days after Sanford and Joe Bob decided to head for Fort Stockton, Tom Bishop and Gant Langford stood at the bar of that town's best saloon—its only saloon. Langford knocked back the shot of whiskey he'd had in front of him, shuddered, walked to the front window, stared down the road a moment, and asked over his shoulder, "Boss, you still looking for hands?"

Bishop nodded. "Yeah, long's they're good ones. Why?"

Langford continued looking at the street. "Two men just hitched across the street at the café, both well set up, salty looking, one a Nigra, the other a white man. Figure if they're riding together, they might be what you're looking for. You want to find out?"

Bishop stared at Langford's back. It always irked him when his foreman enunciated his words so precisely—but what the hell, Gant Langford was a top hand. He couldn't help being a Yankee. "Langford, I'm sure them men'll come over here after they stuff their stomachs. Bein's 'bout half our crew's darkies, I figure they'll fit right nice."

A rangy hard case standing down the bar frowned, reached down, and settled his holster more comfortably against his side, obviously not agreeing with the words of the two ranchers a few feet from him.

Across the street, Sanford and Joe Bob had the small café to themselves, it being the middle of the afternoon. They ate, and when they left, Sanford said he thought a beer would taste good. Joe Bob nodded. "We ain't wet our whistle for over a month. Reckon a brew would taste mighty fine." He hesitated, frowned, and said, "Jess, maybe we shouldn't oughta go in there. These folks 'round heah don't cotton to no darkies eatin', drinkin', or nothin' else where white folks is at."

Sanford's gut muscles tightened. "Reckon we gonna go in there and find out about their feelin's." His face stiffened. "Joe Bob Brown, I'm gonna have a beer. An' I'm gonna drink it with my partner come hell or high water. If they's somebody in there wants trouble, reckon you an' me can carry it to 'em. C'mon, you an' me're Southern as any we'll find anywhere."

Out on the street they spotted an adobe building across the dusty road. The sign hanging above the door said SA-LOON. They stopped at the hitch rack, climbed aboard their horses, angled across the street toward the watering hole, stopped in the middle of the road to let a wagon pass, pulled rein at the hitch rack in front of the saloon, dismounted, and again stopped. They petted a stray dog that came to them, tail wagging.

Figuring the pup would break his tail off, hard as he wagged it, they sent him on his way and stepped up on the boardwalk. Before pushing through the batwing doors, Sanford slipped the thong from the hammer of his Colt.

He wanted trouble from no one. If it came he'd take care of it with his fists—if they'd have it that way; if not, he could hit what he shot at without spraying bullets all over the countryside like some of the fast guns were known to do.

After the bright sun outside, the saloon was dark. The two of them stood just inside the door long enough for objects to come into focus. There were only three men in the room other than the bartender. Sanford, Joe Bob trailing him, walked to the corner of the bar where it curved into the wall. Sanford pulled a two-bit piece from his pocket. "Two cold beers."

"Don't serve niggers in heah." The rangy puncher down the bar from the other two spoke quietly. "Leastways, I don't drink with 'em."

Sanford placed his .44 on the counter in front of him. "First thing you gotta learn is, they ain't no niggers in here. My friend here is a Nigra. Second thing is, if you don't drink with Nigras, ain't nobody holdin' you. Leave." Still holding his gaze on the tough-looking gun hand, Sanford said to the bartender, "Put a beer in front o' us right damned quick bartender or you won't be servin' nobody." Despite trying to squelch it, Jess's anger had a firm hold on him.

A man about at the middle of the bar laughed. "Spicer, you better get the man a beer. He sounds like a Reb to me and don't like to be told what to do. 'Sides that, that .44 he got out right slick makes a pretty good argument."

The tall rangy man standing the other side of the two cowmen stepped away from the bar. "I don't reckon that six-shooter puts up no argument I cain't handle, Bishop."

He looked toward Sanford. "Holster your six-shooter an' we'll see if you get your beer."

Sanford measured the man from head to toe, tall, raw-boned, and lean as whang leather. He was tempted to let it be guns. The man looked to be one tough customer, and whipping him would be a day's work. To fight him with handguns didn't look too good either. He wore his revolver in a holster on his left side, at waist level, grip slanting toward his belt buckle. A right handy setup for a cross draw.

Joe Bob tugged at Sanford's sleeve. "Jess, I done lost my taste for beer. Let's go. We don't need no trouble."

A little fear caused Sanford's gut to roll, and a whole lot of anger pushed bitter bile into his throat. "Mister, we neither one o' us is lookin' for trouble, but this man an' me done shared cold, hunger, trail drives, fought Injuns, an' even wore each other's clothes for several years now. Reckon we gonna share a couple o' beers."

"Not in this town, you ain't."

Hot blood pushed into Sanford's head, making him forget the butterflies in his stomach. "How you want it—fists, guns, or knives? Makes me no nevermind."

A confident twist to his lips, the man slowly moved his hand to his belt buckle and dropped his gun belt along with his knife to the floor.

Bishop spoke up. "Son, I don't know that man yonder very well, but he's talked about. He goes by the name o' Banack, a right slick gunfighter, an' to top it off he's been known to cripple men in a knuckle-an-skull fistfight. You better make it knives if you're any good with 'em." He shrugged. "Whatever way you choose, you're likely to lose."

Without looking at the grizzled old rancher, Sanford said, "Done give 'im his choice." He wished he could back out without getting the name *coward* plastered on him, but there was no way. He handed his gun belt to Joe Bob. He'd been in barroom brawls before, knuckle-and-skull, no holds barred. This fight would be that way, and with this man he needed an edge.

Banack held his fists out in a fighter's stance and walked careful like toward Sanford. The talking was over.

Sanford held his fists down about his waist. Banack walked into range and Sanford let fly his right. It caught the tall man on his left cheekbone. Blood flowed from the cut. He staggered, gained his balance, and again advanced. Sanford tried the same tactic again. Banack whistled a right inside of Sanford's left. It caught him in his ribs. He gasped, sucked for air, and moved out of range. The raw-boned man bored in swinging. A right caught Sanford alongside his head. He went down, rolled away from a kick, and aimed his own foot at Banack's crotch. It connected.

The brawler doubled over, grabbed himself, and tried to move back. Sanford gained his feet and shuffled in, swinging. He caught the gunfighter with a right, a left, and a right, all to the head. Each blow opened a cut, one above each eyebrow and one at the corner of Banack's mouth, blood oozing from each cut. He wouldn't go down. From his crouch, he swung a long uppercut to Sanford's chin. Jess again hit the floor, rolled, and came to his feet—his eyes blurry, his breath coming in gasps.

He shook his head, trying to clear his sight. His head hurt like it had been stomped. Banack hit him again, this time over his heart. He couldn't get his breath. Pain shot through his chest all the way to his back. He felt he was going to die.

He gasped and kicked Banack in the shins, then waded in swinging. The Negro hater kicked his foot behind Sanford's leg and tripped him. He fell on his back, saw a foot coming at him, grabbed it, and twisted. The bully went down, rolled, tried to stand, but his leg gave way under him. He hit the floor on his side, clutching his knee.

Sanford staggered to his feet, backed up to the bar, gasped for breath, feeling warm blood running down his neck from a chin cut. He didn't know if he could last much longer. His fists felt like lead weights at the end of his arms. His ribs hurt. His head hurt. The rawboned man again climbed to his feet and limped toward him. Jess sucked in a breath and stepped forward. This punch had better be good. He swung with all the strength left in him. His right landed flush on the Negro hater's chin. He stopped dead in his tracks, his eyes glassy. He turned his back to Sanford, took a couple of steps on rubbery legs, and fell.

Bishop spoke from behind Jess. "Reckon you better draw two cold beers, Spicer. Set 'em in front of those two gentlemen, an' give me an' Langford a bourbon and branchwater. I'm buying."

The bartender put the beers in front of Joe Bob at the bar, all the time staring at the prone body of Banack, as though fearful when he gained his feet, the fight would progress to guns.

Bishop took a swallow of his drink, walked down the bar, and stood next to the two of them. "That was one helluva fight, young man. Long's I've been hearin' 'bout Banack, never knowed 'im to get whipped—guns, knives, or fists. Where you men headed? Lookin' for a job?"

Joe Bob shook his head. "Don't rightly know, suh. If'n my partner don't git us killed first, we been talkin' 'bout headin' up Montana way." He pulled one of Sanford's battered fists from the polished surface and looked at it, then back to Bishop. "This here's my partner, Jess Sanford. I'm Joe Bob Brown, an' we already know you're Mr. Bishop."

Bishop nodded at the introduction and asked, "What in

the name of old ned you goin' up to that cold country for?''

Sanford had his breath back. "We figure they's a lot o' land up yonder a man can build a ranch on if he's got the stomach for fightin'. We figure to see if we got the stomach for it."

"You gonna need cows, an' all the other things it takes to set up a ranch, son. You thought of that?"

"Yes, sir, but we'll get it done." He hadn't thought of cattle, but he'd give it some thought, maybe come back down here and get some of those mavericks wandering around in the chaparral after they built a living place.

Bishop frowned, obviously thinking hard on something, then he turned his back to the bar, pushed his elbows back to rest on its polished surface, and faced the two of them. "Men, this's not the time o' year to track north. By the time you got there, cold weather would be settin' in. You wouldn't get much done."

He again faced the bar, picked up his drink, sipped, and put it down. "Tell you what, you men come to work for me through the winter. Come spring, I'll be putting a herd together to deliver to a man outside o' Cheyenne. I heard you say you'd been on trail drives afore. If the man you drove cows for on any of those drives was Charley Goodnight, I want you on mine."

Before he could say more, Langford drew their attention. "You an' your partner drink anywhere you want, and I'll back your right to do it. But any fight you had with Banack isn't over. He's got a 'get even' sort of mind. He won't forget."

Bishop looked at Langford. "Slide down the bar, I want you to meet Jess Sanford and Joe Bob Brown. Jess's the one what done the fightin', an' Joe Bob's the one what the fight was about."

Langford pinned Joe Bob with a look, accompanied by

a grin. "Howdy, Joe Bob. Just want you to know, half my
crew is made up of darkies, about half of them ex–buffalo
soldiers—all good fighting men, not to mention their being
good with cows. Didn't take sides in your fight. I had to
see how the two of you stacked up, see if you'd fight for
each other." His eyes twinkled. "I sure as hell found out
all I need to know."

Bishop cut in. "You see, men, Langford's foreman o'
one of my ranches. We come in town today lookin' for
hands. We seen the two o' you come outta that café, figured
right then to see if you was lookin' for work. Our crew's
made up o' darkies, Yankees, Mexicans, an' Johnnie Rebs,
and we don't stand for no fightin' amongst our men." He
scratched his head. "Yeah, we have fights amongst the
boys, but ain't none o' those fights caused by a man's
color." It was then they heard Banack groan. All three pairs
of eyes turned to look at him. He rolled to his side and
pushed to his feet.

Legs wobbly, he walked to stand in front of Sanford.
"Cowboy, you and your nigger drink your beers—this
time. Next time you cross my trail, remember it ain't over.
It'll be guns then." His picked up his gun belt, staggered,
caught himself, and headed for the door.

4

BISHOP BOUGHT TWO more rounds, said he had some shopping to do and for Sandford and Joe Bob to get anything they might be short of before riding out to the Circle B. "Soon's we clear the edge o' town, we'll be on my place, but headquarters is on out 'bout twenty miles. You'll have a chance to come to town every two or three weeks."

"That ain't gonna bother Joe Bob an' me none, Mr. Bishop. These three beers is more'n either o' us ever drunk at one sittin' 'fore."

Bishop studied them a moment. "Reckon we gonna get along right well." He looked at Langford. "Gonna leave in 'bout half a hour. Stay if you want. I'll take these men out an' get 'em known about the place."

Langford smiled, then grimaced. "If Ginny'll see me after my standing her up last time I came to town, reckon I'll ride out in the mornin'."

Bishop looked at Joe Bob. "Meet you boys in front of the general store."

Before meeting Bishop, Sanford and Joe Bob stocked up on pipe tobacco, soap, looked at some rifles and handguns, then stood by their horses waiting for their new boss.

The ride to the ranch gave them a chance to get better

acquainted. Sanford had long ago told Joe Bob why he'd left home, but they didn't mention it to Bishop, and *he* wouldn't ask where they'd been—or anything about their past. In the West, a man's past was his business. Men were judged by the way they did their job, and how they stood up to hard situations.

They pulled their horses in in front of the bunkhouse. Inside, by lantern light, Bishop introduced them to the men who worked close to headquarters. "When we rotate the men out at the line shacks, you'll meet the others. C'mon up to the house an' meet Ma, an' my daughter, Hope, see if they kept supper warm."

Sanford and Joe Bob washed up before going to the kitchen. There, Bishop introduced them.

Mrs. Bishop was a pretty woman, about fifty years old, Sanford guessed. He didn't know what he expected Hope to be like. She had her mother's beauty, but her features were almost too strong to be termed truly beautiful. An almost masculine strength showed in her green, penetrating eyes, accented by blue-black hair, and a deeply tanned complexion. Tall for a woman, she had nice shoulders and a slim waist, flaring into feminine hips. All in all, a lot of woman showed through the rough ranch garb she wore. Even though it was unheard of in those days, she wore jeans, and they looked to be well work-worn.

"Shore nice to meet you ladies, both o' you mighty pretty." Sanford felt his face turn red. He wasn't used to talking with women, and didn't know why he said it, but it needed saying.

Hope smiled. "Why, thank you, Mr. Sanford, but that hogwash won't even get you an extra piece of pie."

"Ma'am, don't know why I said it, 'ceptin' it's true. I ain't used to talkin' with ladies." His face still felt like it was on fire.

"Stop ridin' the man, Hope. Can't you see you've embarrassed him," Mrs. Bishop cut in. "Now, you menfolks sit and we'll put some victuals on the table while you have a cup of coffee."

Over supper, Bishop said he'd show them around the ranch the next day and draw a map of where the streams, along with prominent landmarks, line shacks, and boundaries were. "Runnin' cows on close to a million acres, so ain't gonna try to show you all of it . . ."

"Pa, why don't you let me show them around and you can get on with the work."

Sanford slanted Hope a questioning look. By offering to show them around, she had placed trust in them, and when Bishop agreed, he knew they had been accepted. He frowned. "Ma'am, don't y'all never have Comanche trouble around here? Seems like you'll be takin' a chance out yonder with only two o' us."

"Mr. Sanford, ah reckon"—her exaggerated drawl surprised him—"they's gonna be three pretty good rifles pointed at any who have an idea about harming us. That is, if *y'all* can shoot."

Sanford knew he'd touched a sore spot, and his face again reddened. "Ma'am, we're both better'n passable with any kind o' shootin' irons. Wuz just thinkin' we might want to be careful out yonder."

Hope pinned him with a straight-on look. "Sir, I'm here to tell you, I'm *always* careful."

Mrs. Bishop poured each another cup of coffee before this confrontation could go further. Looking over the rim of his cup, Bishop asked, "Know you been up the trail, know drovers work, but have you worked a ranch before?"

"Mr. Bishop, me an' Jess done done it all. We drawed top-hand wages the last three, maybe four years. Worked for Mr. Goodnight on his Bosque Grande ranch over in the

New Mexico Territory. It was there he promoted both o'
us to top hands.''

Bishop stared into his cup a moment. ''Why didn't you
tell me you were top hands?''

Sanford grinned. ''Figured to let you make up yore own
mind on that, sir. You was good 'nuff to give us a job.
Figure we better see can we swing our own weight in your
mind.''

''You're mighty trustin' men, cowboy. It might take Pa
a long time to break loose with more money.'' Hope looked
at her father, a devil lurking behind her eyes. ''Why, look
at the way he makes me dress, like his lowest-paid hand.''

Bishop sputtered. ''Gosh ding it, Hope, your ma an' me
been tryin' to get you in a dress for ten years now. Ain't
no self-respectin' woman dresses the way you do.''

She laughed. A deep-chested happy sound. A laugh that
said she teased her father more often than not. ''Knew I'd
get your goat on that one, Pa.''

They finished supper and coffee while Bishop asked
pointed questions about their experiences with Goodnight.
On the way to the bunkhouse, Joe Bob glanced sidewise at
Sanford. ''You get the idea Mr. Bishop knows 'bout as
much 'bout us as we do?''

''All 'cept one thing, Joe Bob. He don't know yet we
can *both* read, write, an' cipher. Figure when he learns that,
we gonna climb a little higher in the way he looks at us.''

Joe Bob was quiet for a few more steps, then said, ''Jess,
I reckon if you don't never do nothin' else for me, learnin'
me them things sorta put the whole world in my lap.'' He
chuckled. ''How you figure a pore cotton-field darky ever
got so lucky as to partner up with the likes o' you.''

Sanford dug his elbow into Joe Bob's ribs. ''Well, way
I figure it, partner, if you didn't have *that* kind o' bad luck,
you wouldn't have no luck atall.''

"Jess, if you don't git me killed on some sunbaked hillside someday, reckon I can stand the kind o' bad luck you brung me for the rest o' my born days."

Hope watched Sanford and Joe Bob push their way out the screen door and felt her mother looking at her. She glanced at her. "Why're you lookin' at me like that, Ma?"

Her mother smiled. "He's right handsome, ain't he, daughter?"

Hope blushed. "Yeah, Ma, he surely is, but better'n that, he was clean; both of them were. Ain't many strays Pa brings home you can get that close to for the smell they bring with 'em." She fiddled with her apron belt. "That partner of his is kinda quiet, but I got the feelin' their minds worked along the same trail the whole while. Think maybe Pa got himself two good men there."

Her mother studied her a moment. "Why'd you offer to show them around tomorrow? Never knowed you to do such before."

Hope pulled the bow loose on her apron. She frowned. "Ma, I don't rightly know. Think maybe I want to see how he handles his horse; whether he has the kind o' manners you taught me a man ought to have; how he looks out across the waving grass. And if he has to, if he can handle a rifle." She sighed. "Just plain don't know, 'cept it seems important."

Her mother placed an arm across her shoulders. "Hope, if you got that kind o' feelin, somehow I b'lieve it *is* important. You've always had good judgment." She smiled. "Let me know your thinkin' when you get back tomorrow."

With the sun just a silver above the eastern horizon, Sanford had just finished saddling his horse when Hope walked up. "Ah, I see you already saddled my mare." She glanced at him. "How'd you know which horse I'd ride?"

He pushed his hat to the back of his head. "Mornin', ma'am. To answer yore question—I asked the men in yonder." He flicked a thumb at the grub shack. "They said put a saddle on the chestnut mare." He grinned. "Bein' this's the only horse in the corral meets that description, I didn't have too much problem figurin' out this must be the one."

Hope placed her hands on her hips and nodded. "Smart, real smart, Jess. With that kind o' thinkin', I reckon you'll go far in this world." She took the bar off the gate. "You men ready to ride?"

They nodded, and Sanford stepped to the side of her horse, took her elbow, and helped her into the saddle. "Didn't reckon you needed that, ma'am, but Ma taught me to be polite around ladies."

Hope chuckled. "Cowboy, there's a whole bunch o' men around here think I'm more cowboy than cowgirl—but thanks."

Sanford wondered who in his right mind would think of this woman as anything but a lady. Then, too, he felt pleased at the way she'd poked fun at him. Looked like they were going to be friends.

As soon as they crossed the brow of the first hill, the ranch buildings dropped from sight. An undulating sea of grass, still a bright, early-spring green, mixed with prickly pear, ocotillo, creosote bush, and Spanish dagger, stretched as far as Sanford could see, with a brisk wind singing its way across the distance. That, and the swishing sound of their horses hooves, was the only sound to break the stillness. Sanford pulled in his horse, sucked a deep breath of the fragrant new-growth grass into his lungs, and stared across the distance. "Now, that's got to be 'bout the prettiest sight a man could lay eyes to.'' He wasn't aware he uttered his thoughts above a whisper.

"Cowboy, if there's anything more beautiful, I don't even want to see it. This's good enough for me. Oughta be enough for anybody.''

He brought his gaze from afar to look at Hope—and again said words that came without thinking. ''Ma'am, this land ain't the only thing out here that's purely beautiful. Reckon a woman like you b'longs to this land.''

Her face flushed red through its tan. She kept her eyes locked on his. Sanford lowered his look from hers, wondering what she must think of him, not to mention what Joe Bob must be thinking. ''Again, ma'am, reckon I'm used to being around men and sayin' what comes to mind. Hope you don't take no offense. Didn't mean none.''

She smiled. ''I don't see how any woman could take offense at such. Thank you, Mr. Sanford, I think that's the nicest thing anyone could say to me.''

''Ma'am, I shorely would take it as a favor if you'd call me Jess.''

She nodded.

They rode in silence another mile or two. Again Sanford reined in and glanced at them. ''Stay where you are.'' He squatted by several pony tracks, ran his fingers around the edge of several, then, without looking up, said, ''Joe Bob, step down an' take a gander at these.'' The big Negro was at his side before he finished speaking.

Brown went through the same routine as had Sanford. '' 'Bout a hour old, way I figure it.''

Sanford nodded. ''Me, too.'' He looked at Hope. ''Reckon we better head for the ranch, ma'am. No point in gettin' us killed or hurt. They's other days to see the ranch.'' He again glanced at the tracks. ''At least five of them, an' I don't see nowhere to fort up.''

She nodded. "If we run onto 'em right soon, there's a pile of boulders the other side of that landswell."

Joe Bob looked over his shoulder. "Comanche," he yelled. "Find them rocks."

They kneed their horses into a belly-to-the-ground run. Sanford, a brassy taste of fear for Hope in his throat, took care to stay between her and the Indians.

At the top of the hill, she pointed to the side of the next rise and urged her horse faster.

Joe Bob dropped back to side his partner. A look over his shoulder showed Sanford the band holding their own, but not gaining.

Hope reached the boulders, dismounted on the run, and pulled her horse to the ground alongside her. Sanford and Brown hit the ground running, right behind her, each pulling his horse to lie flat beside him. From the way Hope reacted, Sanford knew she had faced similar situations before. He glanced at her and saw no fear. This woman would do to ride the river with.

Behind the rock of his choice, Sanford drew his sights on the lead Comanche, still far out of range. He held his fire. His scalp tingled and his chest muscles tightened. The thrill of the fight took hold of him, clouded by fear for Hope. He wished now he'd taken time while in town to buy the new weapons he and Joe Bob had talked about.

Neither of his companions fired. He waited, still keeping his sights on the Indian.

Finally, he judged he'd have about a two-hundred-yard shot and squeezed off his round. The warrior threw up his hands and fell from the saddle. He felt Hope look at him. He jacked another shell into the chamber. Before he could squeeze off another shot, Joe Bob and Hope fired, their shots sounding almost as one. A horse fell with his rider. Sanford fired again and watched the rider fall alongside his crippled horse. The remaining three Indians wheeled their ponies, withdrew out of range, and sat there, obviously studying whether to continue the fight. The Comanches liked a good fight—but didn't like losing men. Jess hoped they'd figure the odds were not with them and would go back where they came from.

After only a second the Indians dug heels into their horses' sides and came at them again. Sanford glanced at his companions. "Don't fire 'til I do. Gonna let 'em get right close this time. Miss Bishop, take the one on the left, Joe Bob take the right, I got the center."

Sanford waited until he could see sweat beading the Comanche's greasy body. He squeezed off his shot, saw a black hole dot the warrior's face, and shifted his rifle to take the one he'd assigned to Hope. Her rifle spit fire at the instant he drew a bead on her target. The Indian threw up his hands and slid back over the rump of his pony. Joe Bob's shot followed Hope's, but just as he fired, the warrior jumped his horse to clear the boulder in front. Joe Bob's shot missed.

Seeing the Comanche pull his slim-bladed weapon while leaving his horse's back, Sanford pulled his bowie knife.

"Y'all stand clear." Jess's voice came out calmly, quietly.

The red man he faced stood about five feet eight inches, with heavy shoulders, chest, and legs. They stood still a moment, each taking the other's measure. The Comanche then circled to his right, away from Sanford's hand holding the heavy, twelve-inch-bladed bowie. Then, quick as a mountain cat, he darted toward Sanford, swung his knife, and retreated out of reach just as quickly.

Sanford made no aggressive move, he had his work cut out for him. He circled, making sure of perfect balance on his toes, his movements slow, methodical, studied. The Indian again attacked, swung his blade, his knife found Sanford's left shoulder, bit deep enough that Sanford sucked in a breath. His gut muscles tightened. Fear welled into his throat. Again the Comanche faded out of reach, then darted in swinging his blade.

Sanford caught his enemy's wrist and thrust his own blade. The powerful warrior grabbed Sanford's wrist. They stood chest to chest, straining, sweat pouring from their bodies. The rancid smell of bear grease pushed its way into Sanford's nostrils.

Abruptly, still holding the Comanche's wrist with the knife, Sanford threw himself to his back and catapulted the Comanche over his body, breaking the warrior's hold on his knife hand. He rolled to his feet in time to face the Indian again. The warrior darted in, thrusting his blade at Sanford's gut. Sanford sucked in his stomach only a few inches, felt the knife slide along his side, the sharp sting of it telling him the Indian had again scored. He thrust his own weapon and missed. The Indian grabbed his wrist again, he grabbed the Comanche's knife hand at the same time. They stood there, face-to-face.

Abruptly, Sanford let his right arm yield to the strength of the red man, then brought his arm around in a circle and felt his blade sink to the hilt in the warrior. He still held a tight grip on the Comanche's knife hand. They stared into each other's eyes.

The warrior showed no fear, only hate, and something else—respect. "You fight well, white man. You have killed me." Those words were his last. He sagged against Sanford's knife, then fell. Sanford drew his blade from the Indian's body. He glanced at Hope. She stood wide-eyed, staring at his shoulder.

"You're hurt, Jess. Let me look at it."

"No, ma'am. Gonna get you to the ranch 'fore we look

at it. Might be more o' them devils about. Let's go." He pulled his neckerchief from about his neck and pushed it inside his shirt to cover the cut, mounted, and led them from the boulders.

They were silent during the ride to the ranch, but Sanford felt Hope's eyes on him much of the way, and when they rode to the hitching rack, he made two attempts before getting his leg over his horse's rump. When he did, Hope stood ready to help him inside.

Ma Bishop pushed the screen door open and, clucking like a mother hen, helped Sanford to the kitchen. "Ma'am, I been hurt worse'n this many times. I can walk alone." He said it, but didn't feel like it. The ground seemed to be rolling like waves on the sea.

"Not in this house, young man. Me an' Hope'll take care of you. Now sit there at the table while I heat some water."

Jess sat, his head swimming, feeling as though he'd pass out any moment. Sweat poured from him, yet he felt cold. Lord, he thought, please don't let me act like a boy with no backbone right here in front of these two ladies. He pulled air into his lungs, wanting to put his head between his knees and maybe get blood back to his head, but didn't dare, not with Hope standing there watching. Finally, the spinning in his head slowed—stopped.

5

HOPE AND HER mother stripped off Sanford's shirt, and with water, now hot, Hope sponged blood still welling slowly but steadily from the cut. "Ma'am, you don't need to go to all this trouble," Sanford said. "I can take care of it in the bunkhouse."

"No such thing, young'un. Me an' Hope'll take care of you right here." She stood back and raked his chest and arms with a hard, studied look. She shook her head. "My, my, you ain't much of a stranger to trouble, are you? Look at all them scars. Why I've seen old he-coons with less."

Sanford wanted to shrink down in the chair until invisible. He couldn't do that, nor could he escape the kitchen. Hope and her mother had him hemmed in. He crossed his arms over his chest. Hope laughed.

"Jess, that's about the same kind o' move I'da made if I was bare to the waist."

Sanford's face felt like flames engulfed it. It just flat wasn't decent to even *think* of her bare to the waist. "Aw now, I ain't used to sittin' almost naked 'fore women." He looked at them, his eyes pleading. "Let me an' Joe Bob go to the bunkhouse. He can take care o' me. He took care of most o' these other scratches I got."

Hope's voice came at him, no give in it. "Not in this life, cowboy. You just sit still while Mama and me take care of you. No tellin' where that Indian's knife was before he took a slice at you."

They made the two men stay after Ma Bishop packed a smelly salve into Sanford's cut, explaining it would keep down "festering." Still acting the mother hen, hovering over him, she told Hope to pour a couple cups of coffee. "An' cut a couple healthy slices of that blackberry pie. Get some for yourself, too. These men look hungry."

Ma Bishop kept them in the kitchen until they each finished two slices of pie and a couple more cups of coffee. "Now I want the two o' you to go to the bunkhouse. You see that Jess crawls in his bunk an' stays there, Joe Bob. Don't need to start that cut to bleedin' again. I'll tell Mr. Bishop what happened when he gets home tonight."

Sanford pinned her with a "no argument" look. "Ma-'am, I'll do like you say, but Mr. Bishop ain't startin' my pay 'til I get back outside and start earnin' my keep. 'Sides that, I ain't never been babied so much in my life." He and Joe Bob each tipped their hat when they headed for the bunkhouse.

Hope stared at Sanford until he rounded the corner of the house. Her mother touched her arm. "Daughter, that man's gonna be here the rest of the summer, all winter, and on into spring. You don't need to let your eyes eat 'im up all in one gobble. I'll bet if he could see that look you just give 'im, he'd crawl on that big buckskin gelding he rides an' git slam outta the country. You'd scare *him* more'n you do me. I ain't never seen you look at *any* man that way."

Hope looked her mother in the eyes. "Ma, if you coulda been with him today, despite bein' married to Pa, you'd be lookin' at him the same way."

Ma Bishop smiled. "Hope, I'm mighty happy with your pa, have been for nigh onto thirty years now, but yeah, if I was a young'un, an' single, I reckon I'd fight for a man like Jess Sanford."

"Ma, he was polite, like you always told me a gentleman ought to be. An', Ma, he can shoot that rifle like it was part of him, an' he fought that Indian with his bowie knife, an' won. An' all the while we was bein' chased he stayed between the Comanche an' me." She still stared at the screen door Sanford had departed through. "Ma, I figure he's like Pa was a few years ago."

"Daughter, that ain't no reason to go moonin' around like a sick calf. Ain't no reason for you to think of him as anything but a good man, a man what did what any man would do. Wait awhile 'fore you start thinkin' man-woman thoughts about 'im."

"Oh, Ma, I ain't thinkin' about him *that* way."

"Hmmph! I hope not, daughter. He may be all right, but so far he's been a wanderin' man. 'Course, now he says he's gonna build hisself a ranch. Let's see how he does with those thoughts. Now, help me get supper started. Your pa's gonna be a hungry man when he gets home. He's been helpin' move that herd from the west range in closer to home."

Daylight faded to shades of red, pink, orange, and violet, and those colors all melted to a deep purple, then velvety black before Bishop rode in, tired, sweaty, and hungry. Ma Bishop and Hope waited supper for him.

Sitting with their coffee in front of them after eating, Bishop cocked an eye at Hope. "Well, young miss, did you show the new hands the ranch? Ain't heard nothin' outta you on that score."

Hope knew she'd have to tell him about their run-in with the Comanche, but wished she didn't have to, because it would mean he'd keep her in close to headquarters. He always did when the Comanche got too bold. They wouldn't attack the ranch. There were too many fighting men on it, but they'd use hit-and-run tactics, what Pa called nuisance raids. She took a deep breath. Might as well get on with it. She told him the whole story—including her opinion of both Sanford and Joe Bob.

Bishop stared into his cup a long while, then looked at her. "Hope, sounds like you figure these here men are among the best I ever hired."

Her father had always considered her judgment valuable. She could ride, rope, brand, and shoot with the best, and he took pride in her opinion. She thought about her answer awhile before speaking.

Then, looking at him straight on, she said, "Pa, you're wrong. Those two ain't *among* the best you ever hired. They stand alone as *the* best."

Bishop looked in his cup, then asked his wife to pour him a refill. "Hope, them words are mighty high praise. Comin' from *anyone* they would be, but from you . . ." He shook his head. "Never heard you speak such 'bout anyone before."

"I ain't ever seen anyone who deserved such before, Pa, but let's wait an' see how they handle cows. If they're as good as I figure they gonna be, then words aren't good enough to describe 'em."

"Reckon we'll start findin' out tomorrow. We got a lot o' work in close to the house here."

Ma Bishop cut in. "Mr. Bishop, you're not gonna work that young man tomorrow. Give his shoulder a chance to heal." Bishop's given name was Thaddeus, but in all their married years she'd never addressed him other than Mr. Bishop.

He cocked an eye at her. "Ma, sounds kinda like you're

taken with him, too.'' He frowned. ''Shore hope he's as good as the two o' you figure. I need a man like that—badly.'' He grinned. ''That is, if I don't get too jealous.''

Ma poked him in the ribs. ''As if you had anything to worry about.''

At sunup the next morning, Sanford stood with the rest of the crew for his day's assignment. Bishop took care of all the men before he came to his tall new-hire. He scowled. ''Sanford, Ma and Hope think you might be hurtin' a mite an' should stay away from work today.''

''Mr. Bishop, I ain't never let nothin' stand in the way of me earnin' my keep. What you want me to do?''

Bishop's eyes and lips crinkled at the corners—almost a flat-out smile in Sanford's opinion. ''Son, sounds like you want Ma an' Hope to light right square on my shoulders. I was thinkin' of havin' you top off some o' them broncs, take the kinks outta them, but reckon the women folks are right. For today, an' maybe tomorrow, chase strays outta the chaparral. You got a good set of chaps?''

''I got 'em.''

Bishop nodded. ''Good, get after it.''

Days and weeks passed, during which Sanford and Joe Bob proved beyond a doubt they were top hands on anybody's ranch. Bishop raised their pay to sixty dollars a month and found. Then, on a cold, bleak day in mid-January, Bishop held them at the ranch, said he wanted to talk.

They sat in the kitchen close to the cookstove, drinking coffee. Bishop from studying the grounds in his coffee cup, finally looked up. ''Men, come spring I'm gonna put a herd together, want the two of you to drive 'em to Cheyenne. You both been up the trail with Charley Goodnight, and I want you to take my herd on the same route. Charley was right in taking them through New Mexico Territory; all the other trails been grazed off 'til a herd would get to market with little meat on their bones. Will you take on the job? Cheyenne's a goodly way toward where you want to find land o' your own.''

Sanford glanced at Joe Bob, then back to Bishop. ''Only got one burr under my saddle about it. We been talkin' over the winter about gatherin' a bunch o' them mavericks down below Marfa an' makin' a drive of our own. Reckon if we took off now, we could hire us a crew and put together a fair-sized herd by May—then we could drive yours an' ours in one drive.''

Bishop nodded. ''Don't see nothin' wrong with that. If it wasn't for the likelihood of hard weather yet, I'd let you take some o' my crew for your gather, but don't see no sensible way to do that.''

Joe Bob cut in. ''Ain't no problem, boss. The men we use to gather our herd we figure to keep with us for our regular crew. Me an' Jess been savin' our money, figure we can hire a crew down Marfa way. I hear they ain't near 'bout got all the longhorns outta that brush down yonder.''

Sanford gazed at the cherry-red sides of the stove, scooted a little closer to it, then said, ''One thing, Mr. Bishop, I'm gonna draw up a chuck wagon like Mr. Goodnight had. While we're down yonder, want you to get one o' them Conestoga wagons, or even better, a Army ambulance, an' have it rebuilt to the drawin's I make. Figure it'll cost 'bout seventy-five or eighty dollars. I'll pay for it 'cause after we sell your herd, I figure to take my cows an' head for Montana Territory. I'll need that wagon then.''

Bishop shook his head. ''I'll pay half the cost and the wagon's yours once we get to Cheyenne.''

Sanford grinned. ''Nope. You pay twenty-five dollars on it, the wagons mine, an' we take it after you don't need it no more.''

Bishop nodded. "We'll do it your way. You men leave anytime you figure the weather'll let you, an' I'll start our gather about the middle of March."

During the discussion about the trail drive, Hope said nothing. In the months Sanford and Joe Bob had been with Bishop, she had attached herself to Sanford's side like a cocklebur. She rode with him to work cattle, she helped set fence posts, she even topped off a few horses when he had that task. When the talk was over she left the room with him. "We gotta talk, Jess."

He glanced at her. "Figured as much. What you got to say?"

"Well, we been workin' together for some little while now, an' you know I can swing my own weight with any cowboy on the ranch." She hesitated. "Well, 'cept I ain't *quite* as good as you an' Joe Bob—but almost."

Sanford laughed. "Hope, I ain't so sure you cain't top us in 'bout any job needs doin'."

"Never mind the flattery, Jess Sanford. I don't reckon you nor Pa would let me go with you to round up those mavericks, but I'm here to tell you, I'm goin' on that trail drive."

"Aw hell, Hope, you don't want to do that. I been on a couple drives, an' they's Indians, stampedes, storms, dry camps . . . aw damn—it just ain't no place for a lady, 'specially a beautiful one like you."

She stood back and pinned him with those green eyes that looked right through a man. "Jess, that's the second time you said I was beautiful, know I ain't, but long's you think so, that's what counts."

Sanford wanted to pull her to him, hold her, kiss her, but he had work to do that couldn't include her, despite how good she was with a gun or cowboying—cowgirling, in her case. "Hope, I'm gonna go tell Joe Bob we're leavin' at sunup. I'll see you when I drive my herd in.''

He stepped back a pace to make sure he didn't reach for her like he yearned to do, then tipped his hat and headed for the bunkhouse. After he turned away, he would have sworn he heard her mutter, "Damn you, Jess Sanford." He shrugged. He must be wrong. Why would she say anything like that?

When the next morning dawned, gray and drizzly, Sanford and Joe Bob were already a couple of hours south of the ranch. Sanford figured on a three-day ride to Marfa, maybe two days in Marfa to find a crew, and then head for the chaparral.

About noon of the first day, the drizzle changed to freezing rain, then to sleet. Sanford had his sheepskin pulled up around his neck, his neckerchief tied over his ears, and his hat jammed down on top of the kerchief, even though it was a tight fit. Squinting against the ice pellets, he looked at Joe Bob. "Weather like this makes me wonder if Montana's where we want to set up ranchin'."

Joe Bob grinned through chattering teeth. "Jess, if we evuh gonna have our own place, it dang nigh has to be that Montana Territory. Ain't much free land nowhere else."

The afternoon of the third day, they rode down a frozen, rutted trail between gray, weathered, unpainted storefronts lining Marfa's one street. At this higher elevation, the sleet had changed to snow. The only way Sanford knew it must be afternoon was by his growling belly. They hadn't stopped for a nooning.

About a hundred yards ahead, a small, crude wooden sign nailed to the front of a clapboard shack told him the building housed a café. Before he could call his partner's attention to the sign, Joe Bob grunted from between the flaps of his coat collar, "We got a choice, Jess. A shot o' red-eye to warm our stomachs, or coffee with a steak an' some eggs, if they got any.''

''Let's eat first. Figure when we get in a saloon we'll start hirin' brushpoppers. We'll have a drink or two then.''

Joe Bob's wide grin told him he'd gone according to his partner's druthers.

In the café, they took a place at a long hand-hewn table as close to the big potbellied stove as they could sit. They cooked on one side and froze on the other. The proprietor, a man who looked like he ate everything he couldn't sell, waddled to their table. ''Whatcha have, gents?''

Sanford turned the collar of his coat down and looked at the man. ''Steak, biscuits, an' eggs, a half-dozen each if you got any. An' some information.''

''Got everything but the information. You rangers?''

Joe Bob shook his head. ''Nope. We lookin' to hire some hands.''

The proprietor frowned. ''There's a few riders hang out at the saloon across the street who ain't had work since they got laid off in the fall. Figure they stayed around, livin' off what they made during the summer, figuring to hire back on with the same outfits come spring, maybe get a permanent job that a way.''

Sanford nodded. ''That's the information we was lookin' for. Now rustle up the grub. We ain't et since breakfast, but bring coffee now. See if it won't thaw me from the inside out.''

Finished eating, Joe Bob paid for the meal. He always kept their money, because they figured it'd be safer with him. He paid the café man seventy cents for the two of them.

From the café, they went to the general mercantile store and bought the new weapons they'd talked of buying for several months, and along with them they bought ammunition.

Before heading across the street, Joe Bob looked at Sanford. "Jess, I better go to the outhouse and take a few cartwheels outta our money belt 'fore we go in that saloon. Might be safer if they don't know the size o' our poke."

Sanford nodded. "Go ahead. I'll see nobody bothers you."

Only a few minutes later they stood at the bar sipping straight whisky. Sanford studied the men lined up there. He watched those who drank like they had money, and those who seemed to be nursing their beer to make it last as long as possible so they wouldn't have to go back into the cold. When they came in, both Joe Bob and Sanford unbuttoned their sheepskins and pushed them back to hook behind their new Colt .44-40 six-shooters. Then, at the bar, they thumbed the thong off the hammer—just in case.

The man standing next to Sanford glanced at him. "Noticed you take the thong off'n yore six-shooter. You figuring on trouble?"

Sanford grinned. "Nope. Just bein' careful."

The puncher nodded. "Shore don't hurt none. A man tends to live longer thataway."

Sanford scanned the men at the bar. "Lookin' for a crew. Gonna round up some o' them mavericks. Reckon they's any here who want a job?"

The puncher nodded. "Dang near everybody in here does, but, mister, I gotta warn yu, ain't many of 'em'll take you up on it."

"That don't make sense."

The puncher nodded. "Yeah it does when ever' danged landgrabber around is claimin' all the cows, branded an' unbranded, on land he don't even own." He looked up from his beer. "An to make it worse, they're shootin' them who try to round 'em up."

Sanford glanced at the puncher's beer. "Want another? I'm buyin'."

The cowboy, a likable, reed-thin, redheaded man, downed the last swallow of his beer. "Never been known to turn down a free drink. If I'm gonna drink with you, seems like I oughta know your name." He stuck out his hand. "I'm Bob Twilley."

Shaking Twilley's hand, he said, "Jess Sanford here." He nodded toward the end of the bar. "An' that man yonder's my partner, Joe Bob Brown."

Sanford ordered each of them a drink and glanced to the end of the bar, where Joe Bob had stationed himself with his back to the wall. Joe Bob nodded and Sanford ordered him a drink, too, then turned his attention back to Twilley. "Knowin' what I'm figurin' on doin', you want to ride for me? Figure we'll be through by mid-April."

"Well, Mr. Sanford, I'm a fair-to-middlin' shot with six-shooter an' rifle, an' I ain't never turned down a good fight. Count me in."

"Tell Joe Bob yonder to write you in his book while I talk to the rest o' these men." Sanford turned his back to the bar. "Listen up, men, any o' you want a job helpin' round up them wild cows out yonder in the chaparral, I'm hirin'. Thirty a month an' found. You gotta have your own weapons. I furnish the ammunition."

Six of the fifteen or twenty men at the bar stepped forward. Sanford measured each one with a hard look. "Give the man down yonder at the end o' the bar your names. He's my partner, an' if any o' you got any feelin's 'bout workin' for a Negro, then back out now an' no hard feelin's." Every one of the six men left his position and headed for Joe Bob. One of the men left standing alone faced Sanford.

"Sounds like you're thinkin' of rustling some of my cattle." His voice came out soft. He stood about five feet ten inches, had wide shoulders, a lean—and mean-looking—hatchet face, eyes too close together, and a tight-lipped small mouth.

"Mister, I never rustled a cow in my life. Anybody says I have better be ready to back his words with his side gun. If you own the land them cows're grazin' on, *and* if they're branded, you ain't got nothin' to worry 'bout. If not, don't get in my way." Sanford's words came out like shards of ice. He was damned if he'd let anything stand in his way unless a man had an honest claim to the land and cattle. Nine chances to one the man he faced had gotten his land and cattle the same way almost every rancher in the West had gotten his. Those maverick longhorns had been breeding and running wild since before the war. They belonged to anyone strong enough to lay claim to them—and who would fight to keep them.

Sanford hooked his thumbs in his belt, only an inch or two from his Colt slung from his cartridge belt, butt forward on his left side, almost in front of his jeans pocket.

The man claiming the cows dropped his hand to his side, his fingers brushing the walnut grips of the six-shooter holstered in a tied-down rig. "Seems like if I stop you here and now, I won't have to round up my crew and blow you off my land."

The men lining the bar moved from behind the man facing Sanford.

Joe Bob said, "Don't none o' you even think 'bout takin' a hand in this, or this .44 in mah hand gonna start talkin'."

Sanford gave all his attention to the threat in front of him. He went quiet inside. His gut muscles tightened around the empty feeling in his stomach. He shut out all sound, all awareness of everything except the man in front of him.

Luke Short, who owned the White Elephant Saloon in Fort Worth, a man as good as any with a gun, had told Sanford most men who fancied themselves a fast gun wore low, tied-down holsters, but they seldom hit what they looked at with their first shot.

Sanford looked in the man's eyes. "Don't want no trouble, mister, but I *am* goin' after them cows. If you got other ideas, reckon you better start convincin' me right here."

Surprisingly, the man smiled. "Don't suppose we need have gunplay." He turned to face the bar. But as he did so his hand flashed to his side. His revolver had almost cleared leather when Sanford drew and fired. His slug caught the man in the chest, knocked him backward.

The man finished his draw and triggered a shot. It went into the ceiling. Sanford's second shot took the man in the throat. He fell, face buried in sawdust, now turning red with the gusher of blood spurting from his jugular—but he still tried to trigger a shot. He died straining at the trigger.

Sanford swallowed twice to rid himself of the urge to heave up his supper. Killing a man was a hard thing. He looked at the men who'd crowded together in the middle of the room, all talking and beginning to crowd back to the bar. "Any o' you got ideas 'bout takin' on his fight? I got four more shells in this here Colt, an' my partner's got six. Neither o' us misses very often."

A lanky puncher in front of the group shook his head. "I ain't, mister. I never seen a man get a six-shooter to smokin' fast as you did."

Sanford removed the spent shells from his six-shooter, shoved in a pair of new ones, and holstered his Colt. "Cowboy, you didn't see me draw, 'cause you were lookin' at the man on the floor. I ain't fast—just accurate.'' He spoke to the remainder of the bunch. "Any of you worked for the man who braced me, seems like you're out of a job. You want to work for me, give Joe Bob your name.''

Without looking at Joe Bob, he said, "Write down the caliber weapons each of our men have, partner. We need provisions an' a buckboard, too.'' He looked at Twilley. "We need four more riders, an' send somebody for the marshal. He'll wanta talk to me.''

6

$\mathbb{S}$ANFORD PICKED UP his drink, went to a table, and sat down to wait for the marshal. He had not long to wait.

The marshal, a tall, grizzled, weather-worn man of about forty summers, came through the doors and walked right to Sanford's table. "Tell yore side of it."

Sanford almost smiled. The man, a no-nonsense-looking gent, didn't waste words. "Marshal, I come in here to hire some o' these out-o'-work brushpoppers to round up some unbranded cows. The man lyin' yonder accused me of bein' a rustler. I said I wuz gonna get them cows if they wuz on land he didn't have title to an' if they wuzen't branded. He drew on me an' jest didn't shoot straight enough."

The lawman looked at the men gathered around. "That the way of it?" Without exception, they nodded. "Looks like a pure case of self-defense." He looked at the drink in front of Sanford.

"Let me buy you a drink, Marshal."

The grizzled man—Sanford figured he looked old for his age—shook his head, then apparently changed his mind. "Reckon I will. See if it'll take the chill outta my bones." Sanford signaled the bartender, and when their drinks came, the marshal drank a couple swallows of his, then eyed Sanford. "Mind me giving you some advice, son?"

"Don't mind, Marshal. I don't like it, I don't have to take it."

"First off, my name's Brownlee, an' what I got to tell you might save you a lot o' misery."

Sanford nodded. "Let's hear it."

The marshal took another swallow of his drink, packed his pipe, lit it, then looked straight on at Sanford. "They's a old man south o' here, name o' Senegal. Leave him an' his cows alone. He's got a whole army workin' for 'im. Good old man, but don't take nothin' off'n nobody an' he and his men can back his play to the hilt."

"How long's he been on his place, Brownlee?"

The lawman squinted into his drink, obviously thinking. "I'd say he's been there, first with his ma and pa, then with his wife an' sons, since 'bout the turn o' the century. His land an' whatever's on it b'longs to him—legally."

Sanford, smelling the rich aroma of the marshal's pipe tobacco, pulled his old corncob from his pocket. Before packing and lighting it, he looked Brownlee in the eye. "Sir, I didn't come down here to take nothin' that b'longs to somebody else. I ain't gonna bother Senegal." He grinned. "An' from the sound of it, I couldn't do more'n ruffle his feathers, but they's a many a cow runnin' 'round out yonder on land what ain't his. I aim to get my share."

Brownlee's face broke into patches of wrinkles that passed for a smile. "Don't blame you, boy. If I was a few years younger, I'd give it a stab myself. Where you figurin' on stakin' out some land?"

Sanford nodded toward Joe Bob. "That man yonder is my partner. We figure to drive our gather up to the Montana Territory; still a lot o' land up there what ain't taken. All we gotta do is fight the Sioux, an' maybe a couple big outfits what figure on movin' up there from down here. The

N-Bar, over yonder near El Paso, is one o' them, but I figure if I beat 'em up there, I'll be able to pick the land I want—if I can keep my scalp.''

The marshal relit his pipe and frowned. ''Don't reckon you gonna have much trouble keepin' your hair tied to yore head. Since Custer pulled his damn-fool stunt up yonder, they ain't been much Indian trouble, 'cept maybe a few renegades, an' they ain't lookin' for no fight 'less they're hungry. The gov'ments starvin' them pore devils to death.'' Brownlee reared back in his chair and knocked back the rest of his drink. ''Think you're doin' the right thing, son.''

Sanford looked at the marshal's glass. ''Want another?''

''Nope. Thanks, but one's enough.'' He stood. ''Reckon I'll git back to the office. Stop an' visit next time you come this way.''

''I'll do that, Marshal. Good luck.''

After seeing Marshal Brownlee, Sanford hired six more riders Twilley had rounded up and brought to the saloon. He scrubbed each of them down with a look that missed nothing. They all looked like they could handle themselves in hard situations. He made certain they understood what his mission was, that there might be shooting as a result of people taking exception to what they were doing, and to keep their weapons in good shape. He told them to be ready to ride at sunup. He then went to the general store.

After buying provisions and loading them in the wagon Joe Bob had bought, he and his partner went to the livery stable to get a night's sleep.

A couple hours before dawn, Sanford, Joe Bob, and the twelve men they'd hired squatted by a fire on the outskirts of town. Joe Bob cooked breakfast since they hadn't decided whose job it would be.

Sanford blew on his cup of coffee, then breathed in the smell of frying bacon, feeling his hunger juices flow under his tongue. Over the rim of his cup, he eyed the men with him. "Any o' you men ever cook for an outfit before?"

He got nothing but head shakes. "Well, let me put it another way—would one of you want to give it a whirl for a while, or you want to take turns?"

Ted Ransome, probably the oldest of the men he'd hired, looked at his partner, Jim Eli, chuckled, and said, "Well, Jess, I done et what Eli here cooked—*once't*. Ain't never gonna do that again. He cain't boil coffee water 'thout burnin' it. I'll cook 'til somebody gripes about it, then they got the job."

Sanford nodded. "Fair 'nuff."

It turned out, during the days and weeks of man-killing work, Ransome was a better-than-average cook. He even found time and the ingredients to fix doughnuts—good doughnuts. He won the hearts of all the men.

Each day the herd grew, some days with as few as ten head, and on good days they drove as many as fifty or sixty into the holding area, a canyon they closed in at one end with brush, mesquite trees, scrub oak, and prickly-pear cactus. By the end of March, Sanford and Joe Bob figured they had over twenty-five hundred head.

They'd had but one belligerent rancher contest their right to the cattle, a man by the name of Bill Tetlow. After Sanford read to him from the book, he pulled his men back and didn't bother him anymore—but Jess figured they weren't through with the man yet.

Tetlow didn't own his land, nor had he branded many of the cattle on it, but seemed to figure to squat and back up his play with guns. Sanford made sure whether he owned the land or not by sending one of his riders to Marfa to check on it. The cantankerous longhorns were trouble enough, but if Tetlow had a large enough crew to hit him once the drive started, the least he could expect would be a stampede.

Sitting by the fire during what Sanford figured was getting close to the end of their gather, he signaled his men around, except for the two he posted at the entrance to the canyon. "Men, I want 'bout five hundred more' o' these foul-humored, mean devils, then we gonna drive 'em to Bishop's Circle B outside o' Fort Stockton. Come May first, I'm headin 'em for Montana, along with 'bout the same number o' Bishop's cows, only we gonna lose him an' his cows in Cheyenne. Gonna need trail hands. Any o' you ever been up the trail 'fore?"

Seven men held up their hands. Sanford hadn't expected more than three, and he still had to check with the two men standing guard. He expressed his satisfaction with a grunt, then looked at the rest of them. "Any o' you want to come along? Gotta tell you, when we get there, I'll keep as many o' you as I'll need for the usual ranch work; the weather up yonder is colder'n anything you ever seen here in Texas. It'll freeze the horn off'n a anvil, so think about it awhile. An' another thing to think on, you men what ain't been on a cattle drive before will be ridin' drag most o' the way. Okay, startin' in the mornin', let's get them five hundred cows we need."

The next day, several of his riders told of seeing men scouting them—white men, not Indians. They'd seen them only from a distance, riding the ridgelines, and far out on level ground. They were there, and the only reason they had for being there was to look for the time and place to cause trouble. That night Sanford doubled the watch, and cautioned each man not to ride alone during the day.

Another three weeks and they had the gather complete—and now there were many more riders scouting them who didn't seem to care whether they were seen or not. They skylined themselves, and even rode close enough to be seen plainly, although out of rifle range.

Every time one of his men saw a strange rider, he asked Sanford or Joe Bob how about shooting him. "Cain't do that. They ain't done nothin' to us—yet. An' long's we tend our business, don't take no branded cows, or kill someone, Marshal Brownlee ain't gonna bother us. But if we cross the line, he's gonna have to do somethin' 'bout it.'' Both Sanford's and Joe Bob's answers were the same.

The morning they started the drive to Bishop's, Sanford told the men to drive the herd hard the first few days. He wanted to cover twenty to twenty-five miles a day, get the mavericks tired, get them trail-broke. "They's gonna be one hell of a lot o' bunch quitters at first, gotta take care we don't lose none o' them.''

They bedded the herd at the end of the second day outside of Marfa on the Alamito River. Sanford called Twilley to the fire. "Want you to take a couple o' men to town. See how many horses you can buy. I want them hammerheads with bottom, ones that can run day an' night. We'll need night horses, too, an' swimmin' horses. You might have to take a few head what ain't broke. We can take care o' that. When we leave Bishop's place, every rider's got to have at least ten horses. I'll need fifteen, so will Joe Bob. We'll be coverin' a lot more ground than you drovers. If you cain't git enough horses there, we'll have to get more in Fort Stockton, or maybe borry some from Bishop.''

He looked at the rest of the men. "Double the watch tonight. If we get a stampede on our hands, turn 'em soon's you can 'thout runnin' in front of the herd. Don't want none o' you hurt.'' He stood, signaling he was through. He got another cup of coffee and sidled over to Joe Bob. "How much money we got left?''

Worry lines creased Joe Bob's forehead. "Jess, 'tween

us we got 'bout thirty-five hundred dollars, with what we saved since workin' foah Mr. Bishop. You reckon it'll be 'nuff?''

Sanford grimaced. ''Gonna have to be, partner. To top that off, we better sell off a few hundred head o' steers when we get outside o' Denver, or Cheyenne. I figure to keep the bulls. We'll use what we get from them steers to pay our hands.''

He glanced to the northwest. ''Been seein' lightnin' over yonder on the horizon the last hour or so. Reckon it's heat lightnin', or a storm blowin' up?''

''My bet's on a storm, bein' the time o' year it is.'' Joe Bob shook his head. ''If it ain't gonna be Tetlow gets these cows up an' runnin', it'll be somethin' else.''

Sanford put his arm around his partner's shoulders. ''Quit worryin', old friend, we knowed this wasn't gonna be no picnic when we decided to do it, an' once we get 'em to Montana, we got a whole bunch more misery facin' us.''

Joe Bob slanted him a look. ''You reckon it'll be worth it, Jess?''

''Why, heck yeah.'' Sanford grinned. ''Think 'bout it, Joe Bob, if we wuzn't doin' it for *us,* we'd be doing it for somebody else. Now, tell the men to sleep in their clothes. I ain't got a doubt in my head we'll be up an' ridin' long 'fore daylight.''

When Sanford crawled between his blankets, his thoughts were the same as they'd been almost every night since he left Bishop's ranch. His thoughts centered on Hope. He missed her. In addition to being one helluva woman, she was a friend, a helpmate, a woman who could take on any job a man could do. The more he thought of her, the more determined he was to find out how she felt about him. And if she felt the way he did, he'd come back and get her after he got the herd to Montana, but only after he got the ranch on a paying basis.

He smiled into the night. She'd be so much more than a helpmate. He had a hunch she'd be a right fiery lover. "Hmmm," he muttered into his blankets, "That ain't all bad, then I'd have it all." He turned on his side and closed his eyes.

A low rumbling noise woke him. He lay still a moment listening. The thunder was closer, though still a distance away, and the sky came alive with flickering, dancing light. Nothing to worry about right now, but when the jagged, thunderous streaks lighted the clouds overhead, he and his men better be ready to ride. Even now he smelled the fresh scent of rain. He woke the men, then saddled his horse while Ransome threw wood on the fire and put coffee on.

They huddled close to the fire, tired, dirty, haggard, unshaven, drinking their coffee. One of the men, Tom Bean, glanced at the puncher next to him. "What you reckon the good Lord has agin us? Must be somethin' or he'da never saddled us with bein' a cowboy."

The puncher cast him a sour grin. "If you don't like it, you can always climb aboard that spavined thing you call a horse an' slope outta here." He shook his head. "But you ain't gonna do that, jest like none o' us will. Hell, Tom, you like these night rides we 'bout to take too much to do anything else." He took a swallow of his coffee and slanted Bean an innocent look. "'Sides that, you oughta know by now, the only thing dumber'n a cow is a cowboy. That's why we do this."

All he got out of Bean was a grunt, and a retort about his ancestry that didn't sound too complimentary. The storm moved closer.

The first clue Sanford had that the storm was upon them a blinding jagged streak came to earth, hit a giant cottonwood at the river's edge, split it down the middle, and sound exploded around him. "Let's ride, men."

The cattle were still climbing to their feet when he reached the bedding grounds. They were all bawling. Sound pounded his ears. The smell of brimstone burned his nostrils. A few cattle began to run, then the entire herd was on its feet, and lined out behind the front-runners. Sanford raced to the side of the herd away from the river. If he could keep them headed upstream, without turning toward him, the river would be better than riders on that side.

Sanford kicked his gelding into a flat-out run down the side of the herd. "String out along this side." His yell reached some of the punchers. He waved for two of them to stay with him, hoping three men would be enough to keep the leaders from turning away from the river. Joe Bob reached the lead cows first. He fired his six-shooter close to the side of the nearest steer, slapping him with his rope. The steer crowded close to him, the needlepoint horns swinging toward his horse. The big brindle longhorn tried to turn into Joe Bob. "Dammit, Brown, pull up, shoot 'im if you have to," Sanford yelled at his partner.

The left horn, close to Joe Bob's horse, hooked to the side, trying to gore the big horse. The steer swung his head again, this time catching the big bay along his withers. Sanford crowded close to his partner's horse, held his arm out, and yelled, "Grab. Swing on behind."

Joe Bob grabbed Sanford's arm, pulled his feet from the stirrups, and left the saddle. His feet hit the ground. He bounced and came up behind Sanford. With his gelding carrying double, other riders passed Jess. He yelled to each, "Stay with 'em. Let 'em run. Keep 'em 'longside the river."

Finally, the storm ran out of steam about the same time the cattle grew too tired to run.

The herd slowed to a walk. Not until then did Sanford and his men turn the herd into a milling, lowing bunch.

Jess kicked free of the stirrup on the left side and let Joe Bob dismount. "Find yore horse. Seen 'im swing away from the herd once you were outta the saddle. We may be able to doctor 'im. If not . . ." He let his words trail off, knowing his partner knew shooting was the only alternative.

When they gathered around the fire, Ransome had coffee brewing. One of the hands said, "Shore am glad we drove them cows hard the last couple o' days or they'd still be a-runnin'."

Twilley came and sat next to Sanford. "Boss, you reckon Tetlow'll be dumb 'nuff to try to run 'em agin tonight?"

Sanford frowned. "Jest wonderin' that myself, Bob." He blew on his coffee. "Way I figure it, he'll know them cows ain't gonna spook easy, tired as they are, so I b'lieve if he does anythin', he'll hit our camp." He nodded. "Yep, b'lieve that's what he'll do." He stood. "Men, ain't none o' us gonna sleep close to the fire tonight. Make your blankets look like they's somebody in 'em, then bed down outside o' the firelight with rifles an' handguns. Figure Tetlow's gonna pay us a little visit fore mornin'."

Joe Bob walked into camp just as Sanford finished his instructions. He shook his head. Sanford stared at him a moment. "We'll find that old nag o' yores come daylight. Now take cover 'til Tetlow gets here."

Each man put his possibles bag under his blankets, along with bunches of grass and brush they gathered from the riverbank, then they drifted away from the fire to find a place to hunker down and wait.

Sanford squatted behind the bole of a huge cottonwood. He glanced at the sky, the only reminder of the storm a few wispy clouds and a flicker of lightning on the eastern horizon. He looked at the Big Dipper. The time was about three o'clock. He figured if Tetlow was going to hit them, he'd do it before daylight, still about three hours away. He sat there until his knees stiffened and had it in mind to change positions when he thought he heard something.

A horse snuffled in the distance, not in the area where his wrangler held the remuda. He eased his rifle into firing position. Dark, shadowy forms drifted almost ghostlike between him and the fire. He locked his eyes on one he could see clearest. Instead of a rifle, the man held a six-shooter.

Abruptly, the gun in the bushwhacker's fist spit a streak of fire toward a form under the blankets. Sanford's rifle echoed the sound of the man's six-shooter. The shadowy form sank to the ground. Sanford levered another shell into the chamber and picked another target.

The brush and trees along the river came alive with powder flashes. In close to the camp, fire lanced toward the trees. Someone yelled, "The bastards tricked us. Let's get outta here." Before the words could be swallowed into the gunfire, a deafening quiet blanketed the area, and with the quiet, the man who'd shouted the words fell to the ground. Soon the pounding of horses' hooves broke the stillness.

"Y'all stay where you are." Sanford's words held his men where they were. "They mighta left a straggler to pick us off."

He kept his men from the fire for over a half hour. Several moans from the camp broke the stillness. Men were hurt out there, needed attention, and even though they attacked his camp, meaning harm, Sanford had all he could do to keep from seeing to them. After a while, figuring it safe to show himself, he stood. "All right, men, let's see what they left behind." A careful search found three men wounded and four dead. One of the dead was Tetlow. "Don't reckon he'll do much claimin' what ain't his no more." Try as he might, Sanford couldn't muster any sympathy for the man. If you gonna dance, you pay the fiddler. He had no other thoughts on the matter.

"Go through their pockets and see if they left anybody behind who we can tell what happened to 'em," Joe Bob told a couple of the riders. "When you get through, find a ravine an' dump 'em in. Push rocks over 'em so's wolves an' varmints don't feed on 'em."

Sanford and the rest of the crew set about straightening camp and taking care of the wounded. One waddy, not much more than eighteen or nineteen years old, with a bullet through his thigh, stared sullenly at those trying to help him. "What you gonna do with me?"

Tilley stared at him a moment. "Reckon after we get yore leg fixed up, we gonna leave you here. If they's one o' your outfit's horses around what joined up with our remuda, we'll leave 'im for you."

"You ain't gonna hang me?"

Twilley shrugged. "Got no reason to. You wasn't stealin' cows or horses."

The kid's face brightened. "You mean you gonna turn me loose?"

Twilley nodded.

The kid stammered a moment, looked down at his bandaged leg, glanced at his companions, then looked back at Twilley. "Don't reckon, now that I ain't got no job, yore boss'd take me on? I'm a fair-to-middlin' cowpoke." His voice was hopeful.

Twilley burst into a huge guffaw. "By damn, kid, you got nerve. A hour ago you was set on killin' us, now you ask for a job." He looked over his shoulder. "Hey, boss, c'mere. You gotta hear what this waddy just said."

Sanford handed the cowpoke squatted next to him a roll

of bandages and walked over. He looked from the kid to Twilley. "Let's hear it."

After he heard Twilley's story, he stared at the kid. "Boy, what makes you think I'd give you a job? You just tried to kill me an' my men."

The kid bristled. "First off, mister, I ain't no boy. I'm a full-growed man. Second, I ride for the brand. When I git a order from the boss, I try to do it, if it kills me."

Sanford grunted. "You can bet one danged thing, son, the last order yore boss give yu did almost get you killed." He stared at the youngster a few moments, pulled out his corncob, packed it with rough-cut tobacco, and put a light to it. He hid a grin. He liked this kid, liked his spunk and his honesty. Yeah, the boy had made a mistake, but in the long-ago so had he.

He took a few puffs on his pipe and took it from his mouth. "Tell you what I'll do. Ain't gonna pay you nothin' till yore leg gets well. After you get well, if you prove to me you want to learn to be a drover, you got a job. We goin' up the trail, where you'll ride drag the whole way. All right?" The kid nodded.

7

THE KID—IT turned out his name was Ben Quaid—said he'd ride anywhere so long as he had a job.

Seven extra horses, along with their Texas rigs, including Joe Bob's, stood with the remuda when Sanford checked it shortly after sunrise. He was not surprised. Horses, being social animals, tend to stay close to one another whenever possible. The raiders' horses had searched out their own kind and stayed with them.

"Strip these saddles and bridles, throw 'em in the buck-board, along with the kid, an' let's get them cows up an' head 'em out."

Riding out ahead of the point riders, Sanford and Joe Bob talked it over, and figured, barring trouble, they'd be back on Bishop's range in eight to ten days. Joe Bob grinned at his friend. "Jess, you ever wonder why ever' time we say some'n, we gotta add them words, 'barrin' trouble'?"

Sanford stared into the distance, frowned, pushed his hat back, and wiped sweat. "Partner, if we didn't have them two words, ain't nothin' we said would make sense, we jest flat wouldn't have nothin' to talk 'bout."

Joe Bob's grin widened. "Life sho is full o' misery, ain't

it, Jess? We could go back east aftuh we sell this herd and open a dry-goods store if'n this life's too hard on yuh.''

Sanford slowly turned his head to stare at his partner and, seeing the grin, raised an eyebrow, laughed, and slapped Joe Bob's gelding on the rump, causing him to jump, sunfish a couple of times, then settle down to run.

When Joe Bob got back, Jess told him to keep the riders on their toes, he was going to scout out ahead.

Every time Sanford rode alone, he felt like half of him was missing. He and Joe Bob had almost become part of one another, especially considering they had, between them, two pair of eyes and ears. Alone, he used extra care.

He'd not ridden fifteen minutes when the herd dropped from sight. The country he rode into, broken by dry washes, deep ravines, and landswells, all dotted with creosote bush, cactus, and yucca, was tailor-made for an ambush. Anywhere he looked could hide Comanche, comancheros, or outlaws. He skirted the hill ahead, stopped, and studied the skyline; the lips of ravines and dry washes, even a slight roll in the land, could hide Indians. Nothing showed reason for caution, but that meant nothing. There were myriads of places men could stay out of sight until the unwary rode up on them.

About two hours ahead of the point riders, his scalp tingled and a hard knot formed between his shoulder blades. He knew the feeling only too well—he was being watched. He pulled his buckskin close to a large boulder, dismounted, bent, picked up his horse's left front leg, and made a pretext of looking at the shoe nailed solidly to the hoof. From under the gelding's neck, he searched every rise, every piece of broken ground, then he walked to the other side, picked up the right leg, and repeated his search in the opposite direction.

He turned loose his horse's leg, thinking he might be

dodging shadows, when he saw the edge of the next rise change shape—only slightly, but something had moved. Careful not to make a sudden move, he took the bridle in hand, led the gelding behind the large rock, and pulled the Winchester from its scabbard. "All right, come out, or start shootin'."

A shot whined past his ear. He pulled the buckskin to the ground and threw himself flat at his horse's side. Black smoke drifted along the edge of the ridge. He lay still, watching the skyline, his gaze sweeping the rough land around him. Another shot pinged off the rock next to him. Black smoke again rose into his sight.

Comanche, he figured, still using black powder, and probably an old, ill-kept rifle. This thought didn't make him feel any better. Even with an ancient firearm, the sniper might get lucky. And—though he'd heard from only one, there might be more. He lay still.

The day had turned off warm. This time of year in Texas, a man could freeze or bake, all from one sunrise to the next. Jess lay in the sun, sweating, not daring to move, but his eyes were never still. Sweat trickled down his lip into his mouth. The salty taste, along with the dusty, coppery smell of baked earth, made him wish he had the canteen hanging from his saddle. It was within easy reach, if he wanted to stretch a bit, but he wouldn't move enough to unscrew the cap even if he had it. Sweat ran into his eyes. He squeezed his lids together to rid himself of the burning moisture.

Although he'd been called on for patience many times, he used more now than he thought he had. An Indian would wait what seemed like forever for a shot that wouldn't jeopardize his hide. If they could do it, so could he. He lay motionless. It paid off.

Very slowly, a crown of black, greasy hair rose above

the ridgeline, about ten feet from where Sanford had seen the powder smoke. Sanford moved his rifle barrel only an inch or two and waited. Two eyes rose into his view. He shifted his sights a hair to center between the hard, black eyes and squeezed off a round. Before the sharp sound of the shot died away, a small, black hole appeared, looking like a third eye between the ones the Indian was born with. The Comanche straightened, his knees folded, and he fell backward down the slight incline.

Sanford rolled to his back and levered another shell into the chamber. Brassy fear boiled to his throat. To his side, another Comanche stood, yelled a thin, high screech, fired his rifle, and pulled his knife. Jess squeezed off a shot into the warrior's chest, levered another round into the chamber, and put another shot in almost the same place as his first one. The Comanche stopped in his tracks, his yell squelched to a moan. He fell at Sanford's side, tried to thrust his knife into his chest, and went limp.

Sanford lay in the sweltering heat, smelling the rancid bear grease coating the Indian, and the acrid gun smoke hanging in the still air. He didn't move for another hour. The feeling wouldn't leave him there were more Indians.

He wondered if he could pull the buckskin to his feet and get in the saddle and away before he caught lead.

The midafternoon sun beat down. In another two or three hours, darkness would set in, and the raiding party—if there was one—could take him easily. He studied on it awhile. His gut muscles tightened around the empty void most called a stomach. Dead tonight, or dead now, what was the difference?

He moved his hand from across his horse's neck, grasped the reins in one hand up close to the bit, and pushed upward. Then he threw a leg across the saddle and settled into it when the gelding came to his feet. Simultaneously, he raked spurs along the buckskin's sides, urging it to a dead run. Angry yells sounded behind, shots sang by his head, but with each second the yells faded farther behind.

The war party stayed after him, firing an occasional shot, none coming close, until the boiling dust of the herd rose above the next hill. The Indians dropped farther behind.

Joe Bob and Twilley ran their horses to meet him about a quarter of a mile ahead of the herd. Sanford pulled his tired mustang around to ride alongside. "Keep Coyanosa Draw close on our left. They's some flat ground up ahead. We'll bed 'em down there. I want every horse in the remuda hobbled tonight. I figure them Comanche gonna try stealin' 'em, an' if they cain't get the horses, they'll prob'ly stampede the herd."

Twilley slanted him a look. "Boss, with the hosses hobbled, an' the herd runnin' like hell, how we gonna protect both?"

Sanford frowned, patted the buckskin on the neck, wiped his eyes with his neckerchief, then looked at Twilley. "Good question. Best I could count, they wuz only six of them devils, eight this mornin' 'fore I come up on 'em. Anyway, leave eight men with the remuda, Ransome an' the kid can stay with the buckboard, an' four o' us'll see can we head the herd. Usin' the draw on our left, I figure we can do it. Ain't none o' them savages got weapons good as ours." He grinned tiredly. "If they did have, I wouldn'ta come ridin' back this way."

Joe Bob shook his head. "The misery don't never leave us, do it, partner? Sometimes that dry-goods store back east looks pretty good."

Sanford dug him in the ribs. "Aw, come on, man. What kind o' excitement we gonna find sellin' them Easterners pants an' shirts? Partner, we'd dry up an' die o' boredom."

Joe Bob grinned, every tooth showing. "Bet you a

painted pony you'da traded some o' that fun you had this mornin' for a smidgen o' that boredom."

Sanford grimaced. "You'd win that bet hands down, old friend."

Sanford glanced at the sun. "Soon's we reach that flat ground, water the herd if they's water there, an' bed 'em down."

Ransome had supper fixed by the time the herd bedded. Jess and the crew ate, and sat around the fire drinking coffee by the time the sinking sun painted the sky rainbow colors in the west.

Sanford stood. "You men what ain't on remuda watch, keep yore horses saddled an' tie the reins to your wrist when you crawl in your blankets. You men with the remuda ain't gonna get relieved til after them Comanche try their luck. Every man here put a full load in your rifles an' handguns. Those of you who ain't assigned the remuda, get some rest."

Joe Bob walked to the fire and poured himself a cup of coffee, then sat by Sanford. "I'll stay with the horse cavvy, you take the herd." Sanford nodded, threw the dregs from his cup, and went to his blankets.

Even with trouble sitting on his shoulders, Sanford couldn't shake Hope from his mind. She edged her way into his thoughts more all the time. He smiled. "Shore am glad I didn't bring her on this gather," he mumbled to the stars overhead. "An' she'da been here if her pa an' me hadn't put our foot down." He turned on his side, thinking she'd have been a real addition to his crew. He moved a rock from under his hip and let exhaustion take him.

A shot brought him awake. His eyes scratchy from too little sleep, he pushed his legs under him, pulled his horse to his side, and hit the saddle running. In only a moment he was at the remuda.

Gunfire winked from every side. Indians yelled in a crescendo that vibrated his eardrums. Horses screamed in fear. Sanford pulled his Colt and waded into the melee. Gun flashes and sound told him where his targets were.

A redskin loomed out of the darkness. Sanford triggered a shot. The warrior slipped from his horse. Another came at him from the side, war club raised. Sanford pointed his .44, but before he triggered a shot, the Indian slipped to the side of his pony. Abruptly, the attack became a running gun battle headed for the herd a couple hundred yards to the north.

The Comanche could have saved themselves the trouble. The cattle were up and running before their horse-raid party got there, but their screams and yells urged the cows to greater fear.

Cows bawling, horns clattering, shots fired, and yells mixed with the acrid smell of gun smoke and lathered, hot horses, painted a nightmarish, ghostly scene.

A warrior loomed out of the dark at Sanford's side and swung his rifle, using it like a club, at his head. Jess ducked low over his horse's neck and triggered a shot into the Comanche's chest. As he did so a fleeting thought crossed his mind. The raiding party was low on ammunition or the Indian would've shot instead of clubbed. He shot another Indian from the back of his pony. About the same time the yells drew off to the side. The raiding party had more men than Sanford expected, and they'd lost too many of them.

They had not expected the drovers to be ready, Sanford thought. They'd wait for a better day to die.

The herd ran themselves down to a tired slow walk. The drovers started them milling, and finally got them, one by one, to bed down. Sanford left a couple of men for night herd. "They ain't gonna be back tonight, an' if they do you men can take care of 'em."

He took the rest back to camp. It'd take more than Indians or lightning to stampede the tired cattle again tonight.

A look at the Big Dipper showed they might as well have breakfast and start the day's drive.

Ransome had coffee boiling when they got back to camp, and on making sure they all had coffee, he started breakfast. The kid—Ben Quaid—hobbled to the fire. "Geeze, I'da hired on with this outfit sooner if I'd a knowed y'all had so much fun all the time." All he got for his comment was a bunch of sour looks, and a few comments as to where he could go. He slapped his hat on his leg and laughed until tears flowed down his cheeks.

A week later, they drove the herd onto Bishop's Circle B range. Sanford told Twilley to keep the herd loosely gathered until he could ask Bishop where he wanted them held. He and Joe Bob headed for headquarters.

Hope must have seen them from a distance, because she came hell-bent-for-election to the side of Sanford's horse, launched herself from the saddle, straddled his horse behind him, and squeezed a hug on him that almost crushed his chest. He grinned at her. "Damn, woman, what'd yore ma say if she coulda seen you actin' like a barroom huzzy? 'Sides that, you're dealin' with a mighty tired an' wore-out man."

"Oh, damn you, Jess Sanford, I don't care what Ma or Pa might say. You're just flat out a sight for sore eyes." Her eyes widened. She looked around. "Didn't you get any o' them longhorns you went after?"

Joe Bob sat his horse to the side, grinning like a mule eating briars. "No, ma'am, don't reckon we got many cows, so don't reckon we can go on that trail drive Mistuh Bishop wuz plannin' on." His grin widened. "Less'n, o' course, you figure thirty-two hundred head's worth messin' with.''

Hope's lips turned into an O, and her eyes opened even wider. "Joe Bob, you don't mean it. You mean y'all got that many cows?"

"Sho do, little missy, me an' Jess got us a herd for that Montana country. You oughta come 'long, see what pretty country we gonna be in."

Hope's face flamed. She slid from behind Sanford and climbed aboard her own horse. "Don't reckon it'd be lady-like to invite myself on a trail drive. O' course, if somebody was to ask me, well, I figure that'd be different."

Sanford set his face in a stubborn look. "Hope, it wouldn't be different, none atall. A woman's got no business on a trail drive, with Indians, outlaws, rivers outta their banks, an' Lord knows what else. A woman could get killed—or cause her man to get killed. I won't have it."

She looked at him, her expression stormy, face flushed, green eyes like arctic ice, and her jaw thrust forward. "First place, Jess Sanford, I got no man to get killed; second place, I won't ask you, I'll ask Papa; an' third place, a man ain't gonna have to nursemaid *me,* I can take care o' myself."

Jaw set in hard lines, Sanford didn't answer. He stared between his horse's ears, refusing to argue with the hard-headed female, maybe the hardest-headed one of all time. He grimaced. Besides, he knew *he'd* lose any argument they might have. With a grunt, he decided to turn the problem over to Bishop; he'd know how to handle it. They topped a knoll and the ranch buildings spread before them.

Joe Bob shook his head. "Mmm-mmm, ain't that a beautiful sight. Jess, we gonna sleep indoors tonight, an' we gonna eat cookin' what Ransome ain't servin' up, an' we can take a bath and put on clean clothes. Gracious good-

ness, you evuh see anything that'd beat what we lookin'
at?''

"Nope, Joe Bob, it's a right nice sight." Sanford's voice
came out hard and flat. It reflected the anger toward Hope,
still seething inside him. He looked at her. "Tell your pa
we'll be up to see 'im after supper. Me, Joe Bob, an' him
need to talk."

She stared at him a moment. "You want to tell my pa
anything, you tell 'im. I'm no messenger boy." She nudged
her horse to a trot and headed for the stable. Sanford and
Joe Bob put their horses in the corral, unsaddled, slung their
rigs across the top rail, then went to the horse trough to
clean up.

His face dripping, Joe Bob slanted Sanford a look.
"What for you get so mad at Miss Hope, Jess?"

" 'Cause she don't listen to reason. 'Cause she ain't figured out yet that she's a woman. 'Cause she don't draw a
line 'tween what's man work an' what she'll barge into the
middle of." Sanford toweled his face and tossed the flour
sack to his partner. "I got a hundred more reasons. You
want to hear 'em?"

Joe Bob shook his head, a frown breaking the smooth
lines of his forehead. "When you cool down a mite, an'
sit an' think on all them reasons you got, you gonna find
a whole lot o' them're the very reasons you like her so
much."

"You might be right 'bout that, but I'll tell you one
thing, she ain't goin' on no trail drive where you or me's
trail boss."

Joe Bob slipped into the clean shirt he'd taken from his
possibles bag. "Tell you somethin' right now, Jess. I ain't
gonna be no trail boss. I ain't seen nobody so far what
wasn't friendly with me, but when it comes to a colored
man bossin' whites, I jest flat don't b'lieve that old dog

would hunt. I know any o' the men, no matter what color, would follow you up the trail, so let's don't make trouble we don't need.''

Sanford studied on his partner's words awhile, then he looked at him straight on. ''You been givin' this some thought, ain't ya?'' Without waiting for an answer, he continued. ''We been partners so long, don't reckon I ever give consideration to the troubles you got, troubles I don't never have to think about.''

As he usually did when he was troubled, Sanford pulled out his old corncob, packed, and lit it. He sat there frowning, then, not looking at Joe Bob, he said, ''It ain't fair, old friend. You know cows an' horses well as I do. You can scout good as any. Hell, they ain't nothin' a white man in the cow business can do you cain't do as good—or better.'' He shook his head and said again, ''It just flat ain't fair.''

Joe Bob gave him that big grin that showed all his snow-white teeth. ''We ain't gonna worry 'bout it, Jess. You an' me, we know how things stack up, an' long's you boss that herd, I'll do any job that needs doin'.'' He shook his head. ''I jest cain't b'lieve I'm partners in a gonna-be ranch.''

Sanford threw an arm across Joe Bob's shoulders. ''That's one thing you an' me can always b'lieve. Now let's go get some grub. I'm hungry nuff to eat the south end of a northbound skunk.''

''Whoooeee. We better get you somethin' to eat right sudden.''

Supper over, Bishop walked to the bunkhouse. After a round of handshakes, he asked, ''Why didn't you come up to the house for supper? Didn't know you got back 'til I seen that buckskin o' yours in the corral.''

Sanford nodded. ''Yep. Joe Bob an' me rode in a couple hours ago. Left the boys holdin' our cows down yonder along that crick on the southeast side o' yore range.''

Bishop looked a question at him. ''Y'all get many head?''

Joe Bob answered, ''By our count, we got over three thousand head. We figure we done right well, an' we got a salty crew what'll ride into the fires o' hell for us.''

Bishop whistled. ''Mmm-mmm, you boys did it up right, didn't you. Come on up to the house. We got some plannin' to do.''

On the way to the house, Sanford asked, ''You find a old army ambulance to get made over?''

''Sure did. I'll show it to you in the morning. Right now I figure Hope's gonna be right proud to see you.''

Sanford frowned. ''Don't bet yore poke on it. She already seen us, an' rode off in a huff when I told 'er she wasn't goin' on the cattle drive.''

''Well, reckon she can jest stay in a huff, only it's gonna get worse when I tell 'er she danged sure ain't goin' nowhere when they ain't nothin' but a bunch o' men along. Wh-why, hell, it wouldn't be decent.''

Sanford pulled his pipe from his pocket, looked at Bishop, and sliced rough cut into the bowl. ''Mr. Bishop, trouble with her is, she don't see that she's a woman grown. She figures she's as much man as any o' us here. An' I ain't gonna argue the point she can do any job any of us can do, an' some a whole lot better'n us—but she *is,* any way you cut it, a woman, an' a danged beautiful one at that. She'd be trouble on a drive an' not even know she was the cause of it.''

Bishop nodded. ''Son, reckon you noticed her ma an' me worry 'bout her, try to get 'er to actin' like a woman, but, Sanford, she's got a head some little bit harder'n a anvil. We just ain't gettin' through to her.'' He sighed, waved his hand helplessly at his side, and said, ''I'll have a talk with her.''

8

SANFORD HUNG BACK, not wanting to face Hope, knowing she would not give up going on the trail drive, and knowing he'd not change his mind. All this anger tainted the joy of being back. Bishop grabbed Joe Bob's arm and pulled toward the door. "C'mon, men. We got a lot to talk about."

Before letting them start planning, Ma Bishop put hot coffee and a huge—to Sanford's thinking—bowl of dewberry cobbler in front of each of them. She looked at her husband and dimpled him a smile. "Mr. Bishop, you always said you could think better with my cobbler sittin' right comfortable in your stomach, and being that's where I think your brain is, reckon it's time to feed your thinkin' machine." She looked at Joe Bob and Sanford. "Reckon if it fixes him up thataway, it'll do the same for you two." Bishop growled at her comment, but it didn't stop him from digging in for his first bite.

"G-g-good gosh, ma'am, I never seen a man could eat that much at one sittin'." Joe Bob said it, but Sanford knew from experience his partner could eat every bite. Fact is he'd seen him eat twice as much and groan with the stomach hurt of it.

"Ma'am, don't let Joe Bob sway you. What he don't eat, I'll take care o' his leavin's." He grinned. "Only to keep you from havin' to throw it out, understand."

"Miz Bishop, if Jess reaches a spoon for my bowl, I'll crack his knuckles," Joe Bob said, bringing the first spoonful to his mouth.

Hope sat in stony silence while they joshed one another.

Ignoring her anger, Sanford asked Bishop if he had any druthers about the route the drive should take. "Know you said once you liked the New Mexico route, but thought I'd check again."

Bishop frowned and took a swallow of coffee. "You been up the trail a couple o' times, boy. I ain't got thoughts that would add anything to what your experience tells you. The only thing I want is my herd to get to Cheyenne in good shape."

Sanford shook his head and stared into the bottom of his empty cup. "Mr. Bishop, Cheyenne's a long way off. They's many a thing can happen to a trail crew and their herd twixt here an' there. I cain't *guarantee* gettin' the herd nowhere in good shape."

"Aw, son, I wasn't askin' you to guarantee nothin'. I was just sayin' that I figure with your experience, we got a better'n even chance our herds'll git there all right."

Sanford nodded, then glanced at Hope out of the corner of his eyes. She still sat staring straight ahead. He again turned his attention to Bishop. "Your three thousand head along with mine's gonna call for 'bout thirty drovers, three hundred twenty-five or thirty head o' horses, the chuck wagon you an' me bought, an' I figure another wagon to haul extry supplies. We gonna need each wagon to have a six-mule team along with a relief team for each." While he talked Ma Bishop went to the stove and picked up the coffeepot. Sanford held his cup out to her.

He frowned, took a pad of paper from his shirt, and wrote a list of the kinds of food they'd have to take in order to maintain good health. "A lot o' what we gonna need will have to be made and stored right here. We ain't gonna be able to buy much o' it from the general store."

"Why you figure that, boy?"

"Well, I seen it on the first drive I wuz on. Some o' the men come down with scurvy from not eatin' the right kind o' food, you know, vegetables and such. Just in case, I bought a book what tells all 'bout gettin' outfitted for travel in the wilderness."

Bishop snorted. "Who the hell knows more about this kind o' life than us? Some city man gonna tell us how to keep ourselves healthy out here?"

Sanford grinned and shook his head. "Ain't that way atall, sir. This man, a army captain by the name of Randolph B. Marcy, spent over twenty-five years on the frontier 'fore writin' his book, *The Prairie Traveler*. Me an' Joe Bob's done read every word o' it an' we ain't found nothin' he said that wasn't right.

"We bought our copy in Fort Worth some years back." He took another bite of cobbler. " 'Sides that, here on the ranch, Ma Bishop feeds y'all from the garden—you git the right things to eat. On the trail we won't, less'n we take the right stuff with us."

Bishop held up his hands in surrender and laughed. "All right, son, you're gonna be the one who has to live with it. If *you* think we gotta do what the man says, then we do it."

Sanford looked at Ma Bishop. "Ma'am, gettin' us ready is gonna put a right smart load on yore shoulders. We gonna need pemmican, a whole bunch of it. An' in Marcy's book, he talks 'bout somethin' called antiscorbutics. That's the sort o' stuff keeps men from gettin' scurvy. We can get them 'scorbutics by slicin' fresh vegetables into thin strips, smashin' all the juice outta them, pressin' them into blocks, then dryin' 'em in the oven. A slice o' this concoction about half the size of a man's hand, when boiled, swells up enough to fill a vegetable dish. It'll feed four men, an' I figure to take about one an' a half cubic yards of it. If you figure you cain't make it, the sutler at the fort might carry it. They's a outfit in New York what makes it for the army.''

Ma smiled. ''We can handle the pemmican all right, but let's see about *buyin'* those 'scorbutics you're talkin' about.''

Sanford finished eating his helping of cobbler, studied the bottom of his empty bowl, frowned, and looked at each of them, sliding past Hope's eyes as quickly as possible. ''They's a whole lot more we need to talk about, but we better save it 'til later.'' He stood. ''Reckon I better git back to our herd. Joe Bob can stay the night here if he wants, but I better get back. Long's you say where we got 'em is okay, Mr. Bishop, reckon we better make sure every head we got is branded. Ain't gonna trail-brand 'em seein' as how we only got two brands to worry 'bout.''

''What brand you an' Joe Bob settle on?''

Jess glanced at the women and flushed. ''We thought 'bout BS, decided that didn't sound good, then we looked at SB, an' that was even worse, but we decided on S-Bar-B, an' ain't nobody better rag us 'bout it.''

Bishop chuckled. ''Long's you don't bring it up, don't reckon nobody's gonna kid you 'bout it.''

Hope stared at Sanford's back until he disappeared from sight around the corner of the house.

''What's the matter, daughter? You an' Jess seem to be on the outs.''

Hope swung her attention to her mother. "Ma, we're not just on the outs, we're on the waaay outs. He said he's not takin' me on the cattle drive with him, an' no matter what he says—*I'm goin'*."

Bishop choked, coughed, and sputtered. "Y-y-you're what?"

"Pa, I said, I'm goin'. Ain't gonna be no argument 'bout it. There isn't a thing a man can do on that drive I can't do just as good."

"I—I'll be damned if you are. Yore ma an' me have put up with you dressin' like a man. We've been tola'ble with you workin' like the rest of the hands. We even didn't say nothin' when you an' the hands sat outside the bunkhouse on warm Sundays and played poker—but right here, right now, I draw the line. You ain't goin'."

She hoped the rock-hard, icy stare she gave him would give him the idea the subject wasn't closed. "We'll talk about it later, Pa."

She figured to give him time to get used to the idea before bringing the subject up again. She stood, cleared the table, and proceeded to wash the dishes. Standing there, her hands in warm dishwater soothed her nerves, quieted her anger. She questioned why going on the drive meant so much. She admitted to herself that part of it was her own hardheadedness, if for no other reason than to prove she could do anything a man could do, but aside from that, and despite her anger at him, she wasn't about to let Jess Sanford head for that Montana Territory without her.

She knew he saw her as a woman. He'd even said he thought her beautiful—he'd said it twice— and they were friends, or had been up until now, and they worked well together, and—and, well, come hell or high water, she was going to make him think more of her than just as a good ranch hand.

She wondered if he had thoughts about her after he crawled into his blankets at night like the ones she had about him.

Her face warmed, and turned red with the turn her thinking had taken. She shouldn't be dreaming things like that. Ma, and Pa, too, would pitch a fit if they had any idea she ever thought about any man like she thought about Jess.

They might not like the idea, but she was a woman grown, and thoughts of Jess made her warm all over, warmth such as she'd never known before, warmth she couldn't imagine feeling for any other man.

She smiled. Her pa and Jess hadn't seen anything yet. Her ma hadn't said anything, but Hope had a hunch she could claim her as an ally. After all, Ma had come west with Pa when this country had more Comanches than rattlesnakes, and they must have had such thoughts about each other—or *she* wouldn't be here.

She dried the last dish, deciding to bide her time, play it cool and calm, work with Jess like she had before, be friends again, and when she figured she had him off balance, she'd get him and Pa together and hit them with the idea again. She wasn't going to take no for an answer.

The next morning, sitting close to the cookfire to ward off the early chill, Sanford poured himself another cup of coffee and returned to his seat. He'd told the men to take it easy for a couple of days, the drive up from the other side of Marfa had been a hard one. He told them he could spare about half of them at a time to go into town, have a few drinks, find themselves a woman, play a little poker, and relax; then, when they returned, the other half could go. He heard a horse coming and glanced in its direction, only to see Hope barely within shouting distance.

Every muscle in his body tensed, his scalp tightened.

Was she bringing him more trouble? He hoped not, but knowing her, it was an eighty-twenty bet in favor of another argument.

"Hi, Jess, got more coffee?" Her words and her smile didn't show she'd ever had an angry word with him. He nodded, wary as an old brush-wise maverick facing its first horse.

"Yes'm, light and set a spell. I'll get you a cup." While going through his possibles bag for another cup, he studied her from the corners of his eyes. She looked friendly, didn't seem to be carrying a chip on her shoulder; fact was, he couldn't tell by her actions they'd ever had cross words.

He found a cup, poured coffee into it, and handed it to her, keeping his guard up all the while. "Figured you'd be busy around headquarters. What you doin' out here?"

"Thought I'd ride out and take a look at your herd, an' "—she reached into her saddlebag—"I snitched some o' Pa's pipe tobacco. Figured you might be runnin' low by now."

Sanford figured the tobacco for what it was—a peace offering. He and Joe Bob had plenty of smokings, but he didn't let on to her he had enough for even one more pipeful. He accepted the gift and smiled. "Thanks, ma-'am. I wuz jest sittin' here wishin' I had enough to allow myself another smoke. Me an' my partner are runnin' pretty low." He looked over to the tree trunk Joe Bob sat by only to see him raise his eyes heavenward and mutter something. To Joe Bob, there was no such thing as a white lie. Jess smiled inside. His partner would give him hell later.

He and Hope spent the next couple of hours riding around the mass of longhorns. He studied her while she studied the cattle. He noticed she didn't miss a thing. "Don't see any that shouldn't make the drive in good shape. They all got plenty of meat on their bones.''

Sanford nodded. ''They're in good shape, an' they gonna need it in order to come through a Montana winter. Only a few left to slap our brand on. We should be ready to head 'em out in ten days to two weeks.''

''How long you figure to reach Montana?''

Sanford shoved his hat back and scratched his head. ''I'm countin' on bein' 'longside the Powder River in six months, gonna have to if I aim to dig out any kind o' place to burrow into during the winter. These here cows gonna have to fend for themselves, an' that's gonna take a whole lot o' fendin', 'cause them winters up yonder are pure hell. Wind, snow, ice, you get it all in that country, an' the summers can be as hot as those we have here. Too, I gotta figure on shelter for the men. Reckon we can all use the same hole 'til spring. We'll build the house, bunkhouse, stables, and sheds then.''

Hope opened her mouth to say something, but quickly clamped it shut. Sanford wondered what she was going to say, but didn't ask, figuring she might open the conversation again about making the drive. Before their talk went further, Jess heard the distant sound of Ransome beating on the triangle. Time for the nooning.

Back at the chuck wagon, Sanford introduced Hope to his and Joe Bob's crew, and didn't miss the admiring glances each man had for her. Why he should feel it he didn't know, but his chest swelled with pride, sort of like she was his woman. If he could keep things on a friendly basis, he figured to talk to her about coming back and taking her to Montana once he had the ranch livable.

After eating and having a pipe that he made sure to pack with the tobacco Hope brought him, Jess told Joe Bob he was going to ride home with Hope and then go into Fort Stockton the next day. ''Figure to check on them desiccated vegetables.'' He'd learned that word from Marcy's book at the same time he'd learned *anti-scorbutics* and had waited for a chance to use it. The book also told him they were dried, compressed, and would keep for years if not exposed to moisture. ''We either gotta have a block o' them, or cart one heck of a lot o' canned stuff with us, an' we just flat ain't got room to haul a bunch o' cans an' jars around, an' the wagons wouldn't stand the weight, 'specially tryin' to get 'em across a river.''

Joe Bob nodded. ''While you're gone I'll see can we get the rest o' them mavericks branded.'' He cast Sanford a sly grin. ''An' while you in there, being we're so low on pipe tobacco, you might get us a little more.''

Jess wanted to punch him in the ribs, but Hope wouldn't understand. Instead he tightened the cinches on Hope's saddle, threw the hull on his buckskin, and they headed for the Circle B headquarters.

''You figuring to go on in town this afternoon, Jess?''

''Yep, thought I would.''

''Stay the night with us and ride in in the morning.''

Sanford thought on the idea a few moments. ''If yore pa is there, I might do that. Him an' me need to have a little talk.''

When they rode up to the corral, Hope nodded at a big sorrel gelding. ''That's Pa's horse, reckon he's here.''

Sanford climbed from his saddle and held his hand to help Hope down. ''Go on up to the house. Tell yore pa I need to talk with 'im. I'll take care o' your mare.''

While caring for their horses, Sanford studied what he intended to do. It brought a hollow feeling to his chest and tightened his throat muscles. He might as well put his cards on the table about Hope going on the drive. She might never speak to him again.

He couldn't imagine why she was so intent on going on the cattle drive. She obviously had no idea what hardships she, as well as the men, would suffer. Yes, she was one helluva hand with cattle; yes, she could ride just about anything with hair on it; yes, she could rope with the best of them—but very little of that came into play on a two-thousand-mile trail drive. He walked to the house, reached for the back door, and sucked in a deep breath.

Bishop greeted him as soon as he entered. "Hope tells me we need to talk."

"Yes, sir, an' we need Hope here while we do it."

Bishop stared at him a moment. "Son, I never take a drink during the day, but somethin' says you an' me both better have one 'fore we set down an' start this talk."

Sanford gave him a weak grin. "Mr. Bishop, I hear tell that stuff in them bottles is jest fake guts—but right now, reckon I'll take any kind o' bravery I can git."

Bishop poured each of them about three fingers of bourbon in a water glass. They locked eyes, held their drinks out to each other, and knocked them back. Sanford gasped, choked, and sucked in a deep breath. Bishop grinned through watery eyes, wiped his mouth on his sleeve, and rasped, "Damn, that's smooth, ain't it."

"I reckon it is, sir. If I got any throat left."

"Okay, boy. What we got to talk 'bout?"

"First, get Hope, an' might's well git Mrs. Bishop in here, too."

Bishop's bellow was loud enough to call the cows up from the south pasture, but it got the desired results. Hope and her mother walked into the kitchen together.

"Mercy, Mr. Bishop, we were only in the parlor. You didn't need to yell like that."

"Ma, Sanford tells me we gotta talk. He figured y'all

needed to be in on it." He looked at Jess. "All right, son, let's hear it."

Ma Bishop busied herself setting out cups for each of them; then, when they were seated at the kitchen table, Sanford looked at Bishop. "I'd like to start the drive in ten days—two weeks at the latest. Can you be ready?"

Bishop nodded. "Easy."

"I got a few loose ends needs tyin' together, an' me an Joe Bob'll be ready, too. Now, I need to tell you about the trail boss. Joe Bob don't want the job. We talked it over an' he says he'll feel a lot better not havin' to give nobody any orders. I don't like it, but I agree with him. I'd hate to have to whip or shoot a man for hurtin' Joe Bob's feelin's, so I'll boss the drive."

Bishop nodded. "Figured it that a way all along."

Sanford tightened his stomach muscles and sighed. He might as well get on with it. "'Nother thing. We gotta talk 'bout who's goin'." He had made up his mind to keep his temper under tight rein, and when Hope broke in, he just looked at her.

"When you say you're gonna talk about who's going, you're aimin' that at me—right?"

He nodded. "Yep."

"Well, I'm here to tell you, right now—I'm goin'. Ain't no ifs, an's, or buts about it."

Sanford leaned back in his chair, took a swallow of his coffee, bit his tongue, and gave Hope a hard look. "I'm goin' to 'splain somethin' to you." She opened her mouth to butt in. Sanford raised his hand to silence her. "You keep your mouth shut 'til I'm through, then you can talk all you want—but right now you gonna listen to *me*."

Hope's mouth worked sort of like a fish out of water, then shut, her jaw muscles pushing out knots at the back of her cheek. She glared green fire at him but kept quiet.

Sanford took a swallow of his coffee. "I gotta admit, Hope, you're 'bout as good a hand with cows an' horses I ever seen, but that don't count for a helluva lot on the trail. Yeah, you can shoot, too, but again that ain't all. On the trail you won't have any time to do the things a woman needs to do alone. Some o' the things I'm gonna say ain't fit to talk about front o' people, but I figure it's got right down to the nubbin, I gotta talk 'bout them so's to be sure you understand.

"Long's they's water handy, the men in my crew gonna take a bath every day. Whether they want to or not ain't the question. They gonna do it 'cause that's the way I run a crew—clean. That'll be a little hard for either the men or for a woman to do if we have even one set of male and females on the drive.

" 'Nother thing, men as well as women got personal things they need to do ever' day. I don't need to spell out them things, you know what they are. With a woman along, the men would have to find a hidin' place—an' where we goin' they ain't many places to get outta sight—for you *or* them, an' they's other things I ain't gonna talk 'bout 'cause they ain't fittin' for a man to say to a woman, but bein' a woman, you know what them things are. So! To wrap it all up in a few words, a woman on a trail drive would be a pure hindrance. She'd make everybody's job harder, a whole helluva lot harder." He'd never taken his eyes off of Hope. "Now, if you got anything to say, say it."

Her eyes hard as glass, she said, *"I'm goin'."*

9

SANFORD LOOKED FROM Hope to Bishop. "Find yourself another trail boss. I'll get my cows off your land soon's possible." He stepped toward the door.

"Mr. Sanford," Ma Bishop said before he could get out the door. "I think you better hear what I have to say before you leave."

About to put his hat on, Jess stopped and turned around. He'd never been rude to a woman and would not start now. "Yes'm, I'm listenin'."

"Sit down. Let me get you a cup of coffee. I'm gonna tell you something, and when you leave here I want you to go sit by your fire and give it some thought."

Ma Bishop waited until he had his coffee in front of him before she began. "First off, I ain't gonna tell you why this is so important to Hope; you might not understand—but I do. At any rate, it would embarrass her. I don't want to do that, but it *is* very important, and it's just as important to you. You'll have to take my word on that." She fluttered her hands in front of her. "Oh pshaw, I'm makin' a mess of this. I'm gettin' way ahead of myself. Let me start over."

She pulled her chair from the table and sat. "If Hope went up the trail with you, it wouldn't be a first. Woman by the name of Amanda Burks went up the trail with her husband back in seventy-one. They ranched over east quite a ways, a place called Banquette, in Nueces County.'' She waved vaguely toward the east. ''Back then, good steers were sellin' for 'bout fifteen dollars a head here in Texas, an' most o' them were killed for the hides and tallow. They fed the meat to the hogs.

''Mr. Burks didn't figure to take his missus along, but when he was about a day on the trail, he sent a rider back for her. Never heard why 'cept maybe he was lonesome for his woman. She made the trip in a buggy, up an' back without misshap. I ain't sayin' it was easy on her, or the men, but she did it. When they came back, they went right on with their ranch until he up and died. She's run the ranch all by her lonesome ever since. I'm askin' you, before you say a flat-out no, to ride over and talk with her. If you don't, and if you stick with your decision, it's gonna change what the whole rest of your life could be. I've watched you, young man, and I don't think you want that.''

Sanford looked from her to Hope, who now sat wide-eyed, her face pale. She gnawed on her lower lip. She was afraid and he couldn't figure out why. He'd seen her in some pretty bad situations and never seen her show fear. He locked eyes with Ma again. ''If it's as important as you say, ma'am, I reckon I better give it some thought.'' He took a swallow of his coffee. ''But, ma'am, you gotta know, it ain't possible for me to ride over an' see Miz Burks. Banquette is a long distance from here, an' ain't no way I could go see her an' make it back in time to start the drive, but I'll give it more than a little thought, ma'am. You have my word on it.'' He stood. ''Gonna stay here tonight, sleep in the bunkhouse. I'll ride to the fort in the mornin', see if the quartermaster's got any extra 'scorbutics he'll sell.'' He tipped his hat and left.

Jess stared at the ceiling long into the night. He'd promised Ma Bishop to give a lot of thought to Hope coming on the trail drive, but he hadn't figured on thinking on it all night. When daylight came without him sleeping a wink, he was no closer to making a decision than he'd been when sitting at Ma's kitchen table.

He crawled from his blankets, washed up at the horse trough, ate breakfast with the crew, and headed for Fort Stockton.

At the fort, he headed straight for the sutler's. He didn't think the trader would have any antiscorbutics, but thought he might be able to make a deal with the quartermaster.

The sutler, a man by the name of Buford, looked questioningly at Sanford; he apparently had few civilians come in his store. "What can I do for you, mister?"

Sanford cast a glance about the store at the stacked merchandise, and as he thought, there were no bales of pressed vegetables. "Jest wonderin', you ever handle any o' those dried and pressed vegetables the folks on wagon trains like to have along?"

The sutler shook his head. "Don't have any call for them since the wagons quit passin' through. Why?"

Jess walked over and sat on a barrel of crackers. "Gonna make a trail drive an' don't want my men gettin' sick. Thought if you had any, bein's they ain't much call for 'em anymore, you might be willin' to sell 'em to me for a pretty good price."

"Nope. I haven't had a call for that sort o' thing in quite a spell. Sorry."

Jess stood, grimaced. "Well, it was worth a try. Sorry I bothered you."

"No trouble, son. Wish I could help—" He stopped, held up his hand, and frowned. "Wait a minute. If the quartermaster has any, he might be willin' to trade with me for

some of the things I carry that he can't. Stuff he needs—
or wants. He hasn't had any more call for keepin' that sort
of thing than I have. He can't do business with you, but he
can with me.'' He walked around the end of the counter.
''Sit tight. I'll see what I can do.''

He hurried out the front door, leaving Sanford in the
store alone. Mighty trusting and helpful soul, Jess thought,
leaving me with all this stuff. 'Course he might be thinking
to get pretty deep in my pockets.

While waiting, he meandered about, looking at merchandise on the shelves and stacked neatly on pads about the
store. He made a mental list of things he might not be able
to get in the general merchandise store.

About twenty minutes passed before the sutler returned,
sweating. He nodded as soon as he got in the door. ''He's
got three bales, three cubic yards. Seemed happy to make
a trade, but wanted to get rid of it all. Any chance I could
talk you into takin' what he's got.''

Sanford frowned. Three bales was twice what he figured
he'd need, and he didn't know yet what kind of deal he
might make. But if the price was right, he probably should
take it all. He'd be needing quite a bit once he got to Montana, enough to last until a garden could produce his needs.

He shook his head. ''Don't know. That's a whole lot
more'n I need. How will he trade?''

The storekeeper, not hiding a hopeful look, said, ''Son,
I got to make a profit of some kind on this, you understand
that. But I'll do you right.''

They haggled awhile, and when Jess figured he'd made
the best deal he could, and it was less than half what he
figured he'd have to pay, he told the sutler to make his
trade with the quartermaster, stash the bales in the back
room, and he'd send a wagon for his purchases. Then he
went about stocking up on smoking tobacco, coffee, canned

peaches to give his men a treat, sugar, flour, all the things he thought he could get cheaper here than in the general store. "I'll have my men pick it all up at the same time. Much obliged." He left with a feeling the sutler was satisfied, and knowing he was.

On the way back he avoided coming in sight of the ranch headquarters buildings. He still hadn't done the thinking he'd promised Ma Bishop he'd do. All the way to the herd he thought of reasons why Hope shouldn't go, and reasons why it would be all right. His list of "shouldn'ts" came out far longer than his list of "all rights." But he ended every argument with himself with Ma's words that it would be a sorrowful thing, would even change both his and Hope's lives for the worse, if he refused to take her. "Ah, hell," he muttered when the herd came in sight. He still hadn't come up with one *good* reason why he should let Hope go.

He rode to the fire, climbed from the saddle, and poured himself a cup of coffee. Joe Bob walked over and sat down. "Looked the herd over. Cain't find no cows ain't been branded. We almost ready to hit the trail."

Sanford packed his pipe and lit it. "I bought a bunch of stuff in town, got the 'scorbutics, peaches, stuff I thought might break the routine of beans, bacon, an' hardtack." He took a couple healthy pulls on his pipe. "Send one of the men with the buckboard into the sutler's in the mornin'. Buford's expectin' him."

They sat in silence, drinking their coffee. After a while Sanford felt Joe Bob's gaze on him. "What you starin' at me for, partner?"

Job Bob shrugged. "You jest mighty quiet, Jess. Ain't yourself. What's the trouble?"

Sanford studied his partner a moment, sighed, and took a swallow of coffee. He might as well tell Joe Bob about the conversation he had with Ma Bishop. Joe Bob had as much stake in the happenings on the cattle drive as he himself did. He started at the beginning and told it all. ''Joe Bob, I cain't figure what she meant when she said it'd change our lives. Been givin' me the worries somethin' awful.''

Looking smug as a cat that ate the cream out of the churn, Joe Bob leaned back against his saddle. ''I know what she meant. An' Jess, I ain't said nothin so far, 'cause it ain't none o' my business—but I know, an' I think she's right.''

''Well, for hell's sake. If it has somethin' to do with me, it's some of your business. Tell me.''

Joe Bob stood, poured them each a full cup, and again sat. ''Don't know, Jess. Oughta should maybe let you muddle round in the mud all by yourself.'' He took a swallow of coffee, then looking even more smug, grinned. ''Nope, reckon I'll tell you. Jess, Ma's been tryin' to tell you Hope's yore woman. An' Hope knows it wuz meant to be that way an' she's scared to death won't either o' you find each other agin if she lets you ride off without 'er. She figures once you get up there in that Montana country, you won't never come back.''

Sanford wiped his brow, some of the sweat not caused from the heat. ''Ah, she looks on me as sort of a good cowhand, a saddle pard she likes to work with. Why, heck, Joe Bob Brown, I ain't never said nothin' to her 'bout maybe hitchin' up together for life; don't figure she'd take kindly to me gettin' that friendly all of a sudden.''

Joe Bob's grin widened. ''Jess, you mighty smart in some ways, but I'm here to tell you, you ain't got as much sense as a danged turkey chick in a rainstorm when it comes to womenfolk.''

Sanford felt blood come to his face. He pinned his partner with a hard look. "Yeah, I admit I ain't very smart 'bout women, but I never knowed you to win any prizes for knowin' 'bout them neither."

Joe Bob shook his head. "Jess, I just ain't never seen one I figured to get in double harness with." He grinned. "But you know what? One o' Mr. Bishop's older hands's got a daughter I kind o' figure's been givin' me the eye ever' time we git around each other. Reckon she's 'bout twenty years old, shoulda been married by now, so somethin' must be wrong with 'er or somebody'd already done asked 'er."

Sanford figured it was time for him to show how much he knew about women. "Partner, you ever figure maybe *she* ain't seen nobody *she wanted* until you come along? Which one is she?"

Joe Bob studied the bottom of his cup, slanted his look to take in the chuck wagon, frowned, then gave Sanford a shy glance. "Jess, she's Bessie Adams. Her pa's old Nance Adams. Reckon old Nance has been with Mr. Bishop since slave days. He's cantankerous as a outlaw bronc. Might not take to me courtin' his daughter."

Sanford stood, went to his horse, stripped the gear from it, and proceeded to curry it. After a while he glanced at Joe Bob. "Partner, what you jest said don't make no sense at all. I figure you ain't gonna never find out how he thinks on the subject till you either ask him, or ask her. But however you look at it, sounds like me an' you got us a heap o' trouble, an' we ain't got much time to take care o' it 'fore we start pushin' them cows up the trail."

Joe Bob locked gazes with Sanford, and this time his face was solemn. "Like I done said, Jess, that word *trouble* always sits right in the middle o' any talkin' we do, an' woman trouble is some o' the very worser kind."

The next few days Sanford kept only a few men with the

cows to keep them loose-herded. He doled out money to the hands so they could go to Fort Stockton and let their hair down a bit before beginning the demanding, often boring, and always dangerous months ahead of them. Joe Bob kept the books on how much each man drew so when he and Jess got enough for a regular payday all would be straight.

Every night Sanford gave his problem thought, a lot more than he figured Ma Bishop figured he would. He stayed away from headquarters so he wouldn't have to face Hope, and she hadn't ridden out to the camp since Ma Bishop had laid it on the line about his refusal to take her with him. He figured she must be ready to pitch a fit.

Bishop rode out for talks and planning at least every other day, and finally, two days before they thought to bunch the two herds and start the drive, Bishop asked Sanford and Joe Bob to come to the house for dinner. It was then that Jess told the ranch owner of his decision about Hope coming on the drive. Bishop's face hardened, but he didn't say a word.

"I'll be in 'fore sundown. We'll let the womenfolk know then what they can plan on," Sanford yelled when Bishop rode off.

Before riding to the ranch, Sanford and Joe Bob washed in the creek and put on their finest clothes, which were new Levi's, new bib shirt, and new boots. They'd bought the clothes when they bought their weapons, but never had an occasion to wear them.

When they got to the house, Bishop invited them into the kitchen for a drink before Ma had them set up to the table. "Reckon before I set down with this whiskey, Mr. Bishop, I need to talk with Ma a bit, then you an' me need to talk some more." Jess looked at Mrs. Bishop. "Ma, could you an' me step out on the porch for a little powwow?'' Hope hadn't showed up yet, and he wanted to reach an understanding with Ma first.

On the porch, Jess held her elbow and helped her down the steps, figuring to get as far out of earshot from those in the kitchen as possible. ''Ma, don't know whether I got things figured the way you meant 'em the other day.'' He grinned, although he didn't feel much like it, then continued, ''Ma, want to tell you right off I been thinkin' 'bout Hope a mighty lot ever' since I first seen her when I come here to work. Figured if it was all right with you an' Mr. Bishop, I'd come back from Montana to court Hope—'course that'd be after I got us a house built an' ever'thing ready for a woman.'' He took a swallow of his drink and studied her over the rim of his glass to see how she was reacting.

She didn't look like she was getting her danger up, fact is she had sort of a smile crinkling the corners of her lips. He sucked in a deep breath. ''After you said what you did, I got to figurin' maybe that'd take a mighty long time, an' bein' straight-out truthful, I was scared some other waddy'd come along an' marry up with her without me havin' a chance. Was I readin' you right, Ma? You reckon I'd stand a chance with Hope, even takin' her on this drive to a mighty lot o' hard livin' for a while?''

Ma stood back from him and studied him until he squirmed. Then she smiled. ''Jess, hard living ain't gonna bother that girl none long's she's with her man, and yeah, you was readin' me right. You sayin' you'll take 'er along?''

''Yes'm, reckon that's what I'm sayin', even if I got a whole passel o' doubts 'bout doin' it, an' when we all get around the table, I got some things that's gotta be done if I agree to let 'er come. How you think this's gonna set with Mr. Bishop?''

"Son, you an' me's gonna see one of the biggest fits pitched by a grown man what ever got pitched, but you let me take care of it. 'Tween me an' Hope we'll wear 'im down.''

They turned to walk back to the kitchen when Jess stopped her. "Ma'am, I'm gonna tell you what one o' the things is that's gotta be. First off, I want Bessie Adams to come with us, so the two o' them, both bein' women, can sort o' look after each other's needs—you know what I mean, woman needs.''

Ma pinned him with a look that said she knew that wasn't the only reason. "All right, Jess, that might be part o' the reason, now let's hear the rest of it.''

Sanford felt himself flush; he felt as guilty as though Ma had caught him and Hope in the hayloft alone. "Well, ma-'am, fact is, I think Joe Bob and Bessie are sort o' taken with each other. Sorta like to give 'em a chance. It's true they ain't said nothin' yet, but they been lookin' at one another for some time now.''

Ma pursed her lips, whistled silently, then said, "Whoooeeee! If we thought Mr. Bishop was gonna raise all sorts of Hades, we ain't seen nothin' 'til we watch old Nance pitch a fit.'' She grinned. "C'mon, I wouldn't miss this whingding for nothin'. Let's see how much of a pure ring-tailed tornado we can stir up.''

Jess held back a moment. "One more thing, ma'am. You gotta make out it's yore idea for Bessie to come along. Don't want Joe Bob to think I'm meddlin' in his business.''

Ma took his elbow. "You got it, cowboy. Dang, why didn't I think o' that in the first place?''

" 'Nother thing, Ma.'' He felt his face turn red. "Don't want you to say nothin' to Hope 'bout the way I feel 'bout 'er. I figure they's some things a man's gotta say for him-self. She's gonna be right huffy for a while, until we get back to bein' partners in our daily work, then I figure she'll simmer down.''

Ma again pinned him with that look that said she knew how a man thought. ''Jess, don't you thaw 'er out too much 'fore you go see the preacher man.''

Now his face *did* feel on fire.

They headed toward the kitchen.

Sitting around the table after supper, Sanford looked straight on at Hope. ''If you an' yore ma can get yore pa to agree to a couple of things I spiked out, reckon you can pack trail gear. We leave in two days. You gonna learn to be a first-class drover, startin' at the bottom. That means ridin' drag.''

She stood, knocked her chair over, and threw her arms around his neck, thanking him. The only thing *he* was thankful for was that she didn't kiss him right there in front of her ma and pa.

10

SANFORD DIDN'T SLEEP well. He kept waking, listening, thinking. Although he'd been on cattle drives before, this one was different. *He* was the boss, he and Joe Bob were half owners of the giant herd, *and* the responsibility for the safety of his crew *and* the two women weighed heavily on him.

It didn't make a difference that one of the women was as good a puncher, as good a shot, as good a rider as any man in the crew; the fact remained, she was still a woman, and if all went well—his woman—but right now it seemed that wouldn't work out.

About midnight, a slow, steady, cold rain set in, and he gave up trying to sleep. About four o'clock, by his best guess, he rolled out of his blankets only to find Ransome already up with coffee made. Jess poured a cup without saying a word, sat, and glanced at the buckboard he'd had fixed with a canvas cover to haul the extra supplies, with space enough left for the two women to sleep out of the weather.

Hope had protested the special treatment, but Sanford's stubborn streak welled up in him. He'd locked gazes with her with no give in his. "We gonna do this my way, woman. Get used to the fact that on the trail, I'm king, boss, God, if you want to put it that strong. If I say do it, that's the way it's gonna be.''

Now, he let his look hold a moment longer on the wagon. She lay in there, probably hating him for trying to keep her off the drive, hating him for being in charge and making her do what he thought was right, hating him for God only knew what reasons, but as long as the drive and its people were his responsibility, they'd do what he thought best. She oughta be pretty happy to be in out of this weather—but he wouldn't bet on it.

He drank his first cup of coffee and started on his second before the crew stirred out of their blankets. The smell of frying bacon soon brought all of them to the fire. They ate, wrapped bedrolls in groundsheets, saddled their horses, and got the cattle up.

Sanford told the point riders to lead the herd northwestward until they came on Coyanosa Draw. They'd follow it, but leaving plenty of space between the draw's banks and the herd for swing and flank riders so they could, hopefully, turn the herd before they ran over the lip of the bank in case of a stampede. He wanted to hold close to the draw until they reached the Pecos River. There, they'd ford the river and follow it until he told them different. He figured to take the same trail Charley Goodnight and Oliver Loving used to get them as far as Cheyenne. From there he'd blaze his own trail up to the Powder River.

Wet and cold though he was, Sanford chuckled into the neckerchief he'd tied around his face. True to Ma Bishop's predictions, Mr. Bishop and Nance Adams had raised more hell than Jess had seen in many a day, but Ma had sat there quietly drinking her coffee, letting them blow off steam, then she had leaned forward, putting her elbows on the table, and softly said, "Mr. Bishop, Mr. Adams, I already said how it's gonna be. Now y'all hush up and get your things ready for the drive." They had spit and sputtered awhile, but finally they did it the way Ma said.

Bishop had sent Gant Langford as his rep, to sell his herd and to bring back the money.

Sanford reined his horse to ride alongside the strung-out cattle. The big mossy-horned steer that led his herd up from Marfa had again taken the lead. This first day, the drovers kept busy turning the bunch quitters back into the herd.

After what seemed hours, he reached the drag riders, who, in the rain, were no worse off than if they rode point. When the weather dried and the dust boiled from under thousands of hooves, and heat from the cattle engulfed them, it would be a different story.

Sanford reined in beside Hope. She was huddled down in her slicker, her hat pulled low on her forehead. "Hope, the herd's pretty well strung out now, so why don't you get on up to the buckboard and get under the canvas with Bessie? Might be a little warmer, know it'll be drier."

She stared at him a moment. "Jess Sanford, know you didn't want me along on this drive. Know you figured you might have to baby me along. Well, it ain't gonna be that way. I'll swing my weight right along with the best man you got. I'll ride back here long's any man, an' when we bed 'em down, I'll come to the fire for my chuck an' coffee. *Then* I'll get in the wagon."

Sanford's jaws tightened, his eyelids closed to slits, he nodded with a sharp jerk of his head, wheeled his horse, and headed back to the point. Stubborn hardheaded danged woman.

Today, Joe Bob scouted; tomorrow would be his turn. He tipped his head forward and let the water drain off his hat brim, thinking how much worse things could be. It rained soft enough that the runoff wouldn't raise the creeks much, and gently enough there was no lightning to scare the cows. The Comanche and cattle thieves were probably holed up out of the weather, so there was not that to worry about. He nodded to himself. Yeah, things could always be worse.

Although *his* herd was trail-broke, the Bishop cows weren't, so he ordered his men to drive the cattle hard for two, maybe three days, then slow them to the normal ten or twelve miles a day, letting them drift along, grazing as they walked. The only thing the punchers had to do then was keep them in line and strung out.

Two and a half days after leaving Bishop's ranch, Sanford, scouting well ahead of the herd, looked on the swollen waters of the Pecos. They'd have to swim the herd across.

The banks were steeper where he sat his horse than he liked. The cattle or horses might bring trouble on themselves getting to the water. He rode along the riverbank until he saw what he wanted. It wasn't ideal, but for a distance of maybe fifty yards, a gentle slope led to the river's edge. He headed back to the herd, and when within sight of the point riders, he waved his arms, signaling them which way he wanted them to lead the cattle. He reined his horse about such that he could show the way.

They were lucky, he thought, in that so far it had been a wet drive. The cattle weren't thirsty and would be easier to manage once they reached the river. On his first drive with Mr. Goodnight, they lost cattle due to thirst; of course they'd been on a different route until reaching the Pecos. His worry now was to keep from losing cattle to the river.

He frowned, thinking to bed the herd on the south side and cross the river in the morning. He thought on it a moment before deciding to cross, let the herd drink its fill, then bed them down for the night.

The cattle reached the river, everything going smooth;

the swing and flank drovers kept the cattle swimming as straight across as the sluggish flow would allow. Then, abruptly, the tranquil scene went to hell in a handbasket.

Sanford, sitting his horse on the opposite bank, saw a rider leave his drag position to enter the river farther downstream from the herd. The bank in front of the drover dropped off sharply with an undercut caused by past heavy rains.

Sanford knew the rider couldn't see the undercut. He stood in his stirrups, yelled, waved for the rider to come back upstream, but the bawling of the cattle and yells of the men made his voice as feeble a thing as a leaf hitting the ground in a windstorm.

The drover's horse planted his feet solidly to ease down the bank. The bank caved under him. He fell. The rider had no time to kick free of the stirrups and his horse pinned him underneath.

Sanford spurred his gelding into a run down the bank and into the muddy waters. A vise of fear clutched his chest. Oh, God, he prayed silently, don't let that be Hope under that horse. He swept the riders on the far bank for sight of her. He couldn't pick her out of the mass of humanity and cattle. By now, other riders headed for their fallen crew member.

Sanford, almost across the river, tried to think what horse Hope had saddled that morning. He'd not paid enough attention when she spiked out her string of ponies for the drive. In the few minutes it took for him to cross, he cursed himself soundly for a fool. The tightness in his chest and the lump in his throat were suffocating. Brassy fear flooded the back of his mouth. His horse reached the bank and climbed the slick sides on the run.

By the time Sanford reached the fallen rider, the horse had regained his feet and stood trembling at the edge of the swollen waters. Sanford left his saddle on the run. The rider lay where he'd fallen.

It was only when he knelt at the man's side that he realized the mud-covered figure was not Hope. Even though the man was hurt, Sanford breathed another silent prayer, this one of thanks, while he pushed the man he knew as Nettles to his back. "You hurtin' anywhere?"

"My leg—only my leg."

A glance showed the jeans stretched tight around the already-swollen leg pressed into the mud. By now other riders had brought their horses to a stop alongside. "You men get them cows across, let 'em drink, then bed 'em down. I'll take care o' this man," Sanford yelled while pulling his bowie. He slit the man's jeans and long johns from the bottom to above his knee. He glanced at one of his drovers, who hesitated to leave. It was Hope.

"Give me a hand, Hope. Hold him steady while I check his leg." Sanford went to the river's edge, filled his hat with water, came back, washed the mud from the dirty, swollen limb, and as best he could, pressed his fingertips to the bone and probed from above the man's knee to his ankle. He looked up to see Nettles, white-faced, jaws tight, staring at him. "It might be broke, boy, but I don't figure it's a bad break. I couldn't feel where the bone separated any. Soon's we get to Pecos, I'll take you across the river an' let the sawbones take a look—if they *is* a doc there. If they ain't, I'll fix it best I can an' keep you off'n it 'til you feel like ridin' agin. We can both be thankful the rain turned this bank to soft mud."

"You—you mean you ain't gonna leave me there? You still gonna take me with you?"

Sanford studied the leg a few moments and nodded. "Don't see no reason why not, less o' course you wanta draw yore time an' stay there in town."

Nettles shook his head. "Naw, boss, I'd as soon let you fix it. I wanta stay with this outfit. Ain't been with such a good bunch since the war."

Sanford glanced around him. He and Hope were the only ones there; the rest were just now urging the end of the herd onto the opposite bank. "We gotta git this man across the river an' lay 'im out by the fire 'fore I see what I can do toward fixin' that leg." He looked into Nettles's eyes. "Reckon you can sit a horse 'til we git you over there?"

Nettles nodded. "Yeah, I can do that, but I figure it'd be easier if you'd let me hang on to yore buckskin's tail to the other side, then you can drag me to the fire an' do what you got to. Slidin' through the water ain't gonna jounce me like tryin' to sit a horse."

Sanford thought on it a moment, nodded, and said, "Reckon you're right, Nettles. We'll get you in the water 'fore I bring my buckskin around in front o' you. Grit your teeth. This ain't gonna be fun."

With Hope helping, he dragged the waddy into the stream, mounted his horse, and edged him ahead of the injured rider.

They soon had Nettles lying by the fire on the opposite bank. Hope toweled him off with a flour sack while Sanford fetched a cup of coffee.

Sanford looked at Hope. "Want you an' Bessie to sleep on the ground tonight. We'll put Nettles in the wagon. We got about a day's drive to Pecos. He'll stay in the wagon until we get him in to see a doc. We'll bed the herd on this side o' the river, across from the town."

Sundown the next day saw them making camp. Sanford left Joe Bob in charge while he and Hope forded the river with the buckboard. While looking for a doctor, smells of chili, peppers, beans, frying meat, and coffee came to his nose. He glanced at Hope, hungry for the food he smelled, and even hungrier for a smile, or a kind word from her. "You reckon you could stand my company long enough to eat supper with me after we get Nettles taken care of?"

She looked at him straight on. "A body's got to eat, so yeah, I'll have supper with you, but only after we know this cowboy's all right."

Still looking her in the eye, he drawled, sarcasm dripping from each word, "Aw now, ma'am, I sort o' figured on lettin' him lie out here in the wagon while we eat, *then* I figured to get him taken care of. And, on second thought, if my company is so distasteful to you, reckon I'll eat alone, *after* we get 'im taken care of, of course."

She broke her gaze from his, raised her chin, and looked straight ahead.

This time of night there were few people out and around. Sanford spotted a man lounging against a post in front of the blacksmith shop.

He jumped from the boot and asked the man to direct him to the doctor's office. The man pointed across the street. "Right at the top o' them stairs yonder. If he ain't there, you can find 'im in the saloon next door."

Learning there was a doctor in town was good news, but having to maybe drag him out of a saloon sounded bad. He looked up at Hope. "Circle the wagon around and pull it up in front o' that building. I'll see if the doc is there."

At the top of the stairs, Sanford knocked and got no answer. He pushed the door open. The room stood empty. He retraced his steps to the wagon. "He ain't there. I'll see if he's in the saloon."

He pushed through the batwing doors and looked around. There were only four or five people standing at the bar. One slovenly, unshaven man sat at a table—a half-empty bottle of whiskey in front of him. Jess walked to the bar.

"Know where I could find the doc? I got a hurt rider outside."

The bartender grimaced. "Lots o' luck, friend. That lump sitting yonder is what we have that passes for a doctor. Sober, he isn't all that bad. But you see how he is right now? Well, that's the way he is most of the time."

Sanford nodded. "Thanks, mister." He walked to the table, caught the drunk under his arms, picked him up, and dragged him through the front doors. Outside, he scanned the street for a horse trough, saw one two doors down the street, and half dragging, half carrying the mumbling, stumbling, sodden excuse for a human being, he reached the water trough and dumped him in. He held the man's head underwater for a moment, lifted it clear, then pushed it back under, until he gasped and tried to fight Sanford's hands off.

The drunk, spitting and sputtering, mumbled, "Wh-wha-what the hell you doin' to me? Let me go. It took all day and a bottle o' good whiskey to get me in the shape I was in. Now you've ruined it."

"Gonna tell you how it is, doc. I got a hurt man in the wagon down yonder an' you're gonna fix 'im—you're gonna fix 'im right. You understand?"

The doctor, bleary-eyed and dripping, pulled himself into a semblance of sobriety. "Can't operate on a man, hands aren't steady enough. I'll try anything else, though, but when I get through, you'll buy me another bottle to make up for the one which you just wasted when you dumped me in that trough."

Sanford nodded. "That's yore funeral. Now let's get on with it."

An hour or so later the doctor pronounced Nettles as being fit to ride in a couple of days, no broken bones, but some deep bruises and a wrenched ankle.

"What do I owe you, doc?"

"Two dollars and another bottle of red-eye."

Sanford told Hope to see that Nettles got fed, and for her to eat, he was going to the saloon and buy doc a bottle, then he wanted to see if the general store had any books.

Listening to the bartender talk, and then the doctor, he felt shamed at the way he used the English language. His mother had taught him better, but he'd gotten lazy with words, and didn't make sure he used the right word, or if he did, he cut off its ending. He was determined to try to talk better, and if he could do it, so could Joe Bob.

In the store, he found three new books, and some that had been traded, probably fifteen or twenty times. They were dog-eared, and a few had pages torn but pasted back together. Books of any kind were scarce here on the frontier, and people treasured them. They would read the same book many times, but sooner or later someone would show up with one they hadn't seen before and they'd trade.

Books in hand, he walked out on the boardwalk, looked down the street toward the café, and saw the wagon. When he got to it, he looked in the bed to see if Nettles had eaten. The wagon stood empty. Through the window he saw Hope sitting at the table. Nettles sat across the table from her.

He went in and walked to the long family-style table. "The doc said you could ride in 'bout two days. He didn't say nothin' 'bout you gettin' around now. You gotta take it easy, boy, give them bruises a chance to heal."

"Aw, boss, long's nothin's broke, I might's well do what I can. They'll heal faster that way."

Sanford stared at him a moment, raised his eyebrows, and shook his head. "Do it your way."

Hope and Nettles drank coffee and ate a bowl of peach cobbler while Sanford ate supper. Even though the meal wasn't much different than what Ransome cooked, Sanford enjoyed it more. Just sitting up to a table instead of on the ground, leaning against his saddle, made a lot of difference.

About half through his meal, three riders, unshaven, dirty, with tied-down holsters at their side, pushed through the front door. Sanford gave them only a glance. He didn't expect hardworking men to be clean at the end of a day. He flicked another glance at them. When his look again touched on the tied-down holsters, his back muscles tightened, and even with having eaten, his stomach felt hollow. These weren't hardworking cowhands—they were riffraff.

Sanford ate slowly, trying to watch them but not make it obvious.

All three brazenly looked at Hope, their eyes hungry. Between looks, they'd say something to each other and all would laugh. Sanford stiffened, and keeping his right hand under the table, using his left to eat with, he slipped his Colt from its holster, holding it in his lap. Speaking softly from the corner of his mouth, he said, "Hope, don't waste no more time. Finish yore pie, leave the coffee set, an' you an' Nettles get outta here."

She lifted her chin, giving him a stubborn look. "I'm not finished. Don't tell me to cut my meal short."

Sanford caught himself in time not to blare back at her. His voice still soft, knowing it had steel in it, but being careful to be sure it didn't carry beyond the two of them, he locked eyes with her. "Don't argue with me. They's gonna be trouble. Get outta here."

Her face white—Sanford knew from anger, not fear—she pushed up from the bench and leaned to help Nettles. She reached the door, Nettles limping at her side, when the three gun hawks stood. Sanford brought his hand from under the table's edge, his six-shooter pointed at them. "You men figuring on goin' somewhere?"

As one, they spun to look at him. The tall thin man

closest to the door said, "What the hell business is it of yours?"

Sanford thumbed the hammer back. "Reckon this makes it my business. Didn't like the way yore eyes tried to undress my woman. Now, you done ordered yore supper, so when the man brings your food, sit down an' eat."

Their gazes traveled from Sanford's Colt to stare into his eyes. Their looks, to the last man, came from cold, steel-gray eyes. "If she's your woman, why's she leaving here without you? I don't figure you got any claim on her at all." The same man as before did the talking.

Sanford picked up his cup with his left hand and, looking at them over the rim, took a swallow. "You don't sit down, I'm gonna lay you down with a .44 in your gut." Not looking at Hope, he put his cup back on the table. "Hope, get outta here. I'll be out in a minute, soon's I finish my supper." Only an instant passed and the front door slammed, then a sound as though the back door opened and closed broke the silence that gripped the small café, that and the scraping of the benches when the three men seated themselves. Sanford thought maybe the last noise was that of the cook getting out of harm's way.

A sly grin broke the corners of a squat, heavy-muscled gunman's mouth. "Way I got it figured, cowboy, we in a Mexican standoff. You leave and we'll be on you like a duck on a june bug. So I reckon we'll just sit here 'til you get tired o' holdin' that six-shooter, then we gonna blow you to hell."

Sanford shook his head. "Ain't that way atall. Y'all gonna unbuckle yore gun belts an' let 'em fall to the floor. *I'm* gonna walk around behind you, pick 'em up, check you for knives or hideouts, then I'm leavin' here feelin' mighty safe." He stood.

"Now careful like, with yore left hand, pull them belts loose from the buckles."

The three leaned back from the table, sucked in their guts, and reached for their belt buckles. The tall, hatchet-faced waddy's hand moved ever so slowly, then flashed for his gun. As soon as he made his move, the other two reached for their weapons.

Everything moved in slow motion. Sanford didn't wait for their six-shooters to clear leather like he'd been told you were supposed to do in order for it to be self-defense. He thumbed off shots as fast as he could ear the hammer back. They had their handguns in action now. Sound exploded around him. A streak like a hot branding iron creased his side. A black-rimmed hole opened in the slim gunman's chest. Sanford's left arm went numb. Another black hole showed between the eyes of another of the gunmen, pink and gray something or other sprayed from the back of his head. The squat gunman who opened the ball fell to his side. Sanford's Colt snapped on empty. He stood there, knowing in an instant he would die without another weapon to defend himself. Silence again folded around him. The acrid stench of gun smoke burned his nostrils. Smoke clouded his vision—then it cleared enough to see.

The tall thin gunfighter lay on his back, his legs hanging over the bench, his revolver lying on the floor a couple of feet from his hand. The short, muscled one lay on his side—not dead, still trying to bring his gun up for a shot, a hole in his chest oozing blood. The third man who hadn't spoken a word during the affair lay across the table. That pink-gray stuff that had blown off the back of his head was brains. Half of his head was missing.

Sanford walked to the one still trying to fire his pistol, kicked it from his hand, dropped his Colt back in its holster, and walked to the door.

11

SANFORD LEANED AGAINST the doorjamb. He felt weak, sick to his stomach. He hadn't been in many close-up gunfights. He'd killed men, but mostly from a distance with a rifle. He sucked in a breath and looked toward the wagon. "Nettles, if you ain't banged up too much, see if you can find the law in this town."

Before Nettles could climb from the boot, people from every direction converged on Sanford. The man closest to him said, "Don't bother, I'm the law here. What happened?"

Before Jess answered, he tried to straighten himself against the door frame, but his ribs burned like fire, and his shoulder pained like it had been run through with a hot poker. The people closest to him looked as though they were made of smoke, wavering back and forth. He felt cold, but he sweated like a horse run too hard and too long. He hated himself for it but knew he was going to pass out. He grabbed for the doorjamb, missed, and vaguely saw the boardwalk coming up to meet him.

When he opened his eyes, he lay on the rough boards in front of the café, with a crowd of people standing gaping down at him. He must not have been out long. Hope knelt at his side. "Don't move, Jess. I sent someone to get the doctor. He shouldn't have had time to crawl back in that bottle you bought 'im." She stared at him, worry lines pinching her brows together. She pulled his shirt away from his shoulder, gasped, then her look traveled to his side. It was then the doctor arrived.

"Stand back, men, give me room to see how badly he's hurt." He glanced at Sanford's shoulder, turned him on his side, and looked at the back. "Hmmm, lucky. Went all the way through. Won't have to probe for it." He pushed Sanford flat and peeled his shirt from his side. "Lot of blood, but not bad, just scraped along the ribs. Not much more'n a crease." He looked at a couple of men standing gawking at the wounds. "You two, get him up to my office. Carry him gently; he's had enough rough handling for one day."

Hope pushed one of the men aside. "I'll help. He's my man, ornery as all get-out, but a good man. I'll make *sure* he's handled gently."

When they got him on his feet, Sanford tried to keep his rubbery legs under him, but they wouldn't obey. "You just lean on me, Jess Sanford. I know it hurts your pride to depend on me for anything, but if you don't do as I say, I'll hurt your other shoulder." She had that stubborn look about her, so Jess did what she said.

The marshal, a small tough-looking man of about forty, grunted, "Shape you're in, don't figure you're goin' nowhere 'til after the doc gets through with you. I'm goin' inside an' see what kind of hell you raised in there, then I'll want to hear your side of the story."

Despite his pride, Jess leaned on Hope as much as he did the stranger who supported his other side.

In the doctor's office, Hope peeled his shirt off while the doctor took a package of bandages from a shelf and reached for a bottle of alcohol. Hope stood back, her eyes shooting green sparks. "Put that stuff back on the shelf, then wash your filthy hands. You want to kill 'im with festerin'? After you wash your hands, pour some o' that alcohol over them, *then* you can start to work on him."

Putting the packages back on the shelf, the doctor growled, "No question but he's her man. Damn, I never seen a woman so protective."

Sanford, feeling much better, but ashamed of having passed out, looked up into Hope's eyes and grinned. A fiery red pushed its way through her deep tan. She lowered her lids to mask her feelings. "Well, you said to them gunmen I was your woman, didn't seem fit for me not to say my side of it now when it might make a difference in how you were treated."

Still grinning, he put his hand over hers. "You an' me, we got a lot o' talkin' to do someday."

When the doctor had taken care of Sanford's wounds, he cautioned Hope to keep him still. "He may be a rugged dude, but two bullets hitting a body comes as quite a shock. Least he needs is a good night's sleep, then no work for a few days until he gets that blood built back in his system."

Sanford looked the doctor in the eye. "Like hell, doc, I got a cattle drive to make. Ain't nothin' keepin' me still for a few days—tonight maybe, but then that's it."

Hope shook her head and, staring at Jess, said, "You can believe him, doctor. He's the stubbornest man who ever came down the trail. He'll be ridin' tomorrow."

Sanford tried to sit up, but groaned and lay back. "Thought the marshal would be back by now. He might wanta hold me on some sort o' charge. I killed three men in that café."

Hope placed her hand on his chest. "See there, you're too weak to get up, and the marshal will be here when he gets through lookin' at the havoc you raised down there.

An' about those three men; I know you had it to do or you
wouldn't have, so quit worryin'."

The marshal looked at the three men, two dead and one
still breathing, but not for long, if he knew anything about
gunshots. He checked the pockets of the two dead, and by
the time he reached the stumpy one to clean out his pockets,
he had joined the other two in hell.

The marshal turned his pockets inside out. Odd, he
thought, each of them had exactly the same amount of
money, all in gold eagles, sort of like they'd taken it from
a common fund. He collected their gun belts, went outside,
and took saddlebags, heavy saddlebags from their horses,
then told some men in the crowd to take the bodies to the
undertaker.

He glanced toward the doctor's office, saw lantern light
painting the window, grunted, and headed for his own office. "That man up there ain't goin' nowhere for a while,"
he muttered.

In his office, he trimmed the wick on his lantern and sat
it close to him on his desk. He sighed, reached in a drawer,
and pulled out a thick sheaf of wanted posters.

Thinking this would take some time, he stood, poured
himself a cup of coffee that looked more like some of that
tar he'd seen in the pits outside the small town of Los
Angeles in California country. He again sat, rolled a cigarette, and one by one leafed through the posters, studying
each for a few moments.

When he turned the last one, he shook his head, frowned,
and went through them again. He again shook his head.
"Know danged well I've seen somethin' on them three."
He had a habit of talking to himself when he was alone; it
helped him think. He reached to flip through them again,
but stopped his hand, leaned to look at other papers on his

desk. He shuffled a few of them aside and picked up a dispatch he'd gotten only three days before. "Knowed I'd seen somethin' on them."

He read the dispatch through a couple of times, dragged on his cigarette, took a swallow of coffee, and again read the dispatch. "Looks like that young fellow upstairs yonder bagged hisself a real covey o' quail—the Turnbull gang. Don't know yet if they's any money on their heads, but I'll find out." He looked at his old beat-up silver pocket watch. Almost two hours had passed since the shooting. "Better get up there an' tell that young'un I ain't gonna lock 'im up." He stood, stepped toward the door, frowned, and turned back.

He picked up the saddlebags he'd taken from the gunmen's saddles, hefted them, feeling the weight, then opened them. The bags held what he figured was the loot they'd taken in the Monahans robbery the dispatch had talked about. He stashed the bags in his desk bottom drawer and headed for the doctor's office.

Sanford looked at the Regulator clock on the wall and squirmed. "How long's it been since we seen that marshal? Know it don't take this long to look at three shot-up men."

"Just lie still, Jess. You're not goin' anywhere tonight."

"The hell I ain't. I'm goin' back to camp if the marshal don't lock me up."

"It's been a little over two hours. He'll be along soon." Hope's chin raised and seemed to harden. "And like I said, you're not goin' anywhere tonight. I'll take Nettles across the river and tell the men what happened. I know Joe Bob'll be beside himself with worry if we don't show up tonight, so I gotta go, but I'll be back in the morning." She looked at the clock again, and before she could speculate about what had happened to the marshal, he opened the door.

Sanford stared at him a moment. "You gonna lock me up, Marshal?"

The lawman walked over, pulled out a chair, turned it around, then straddled it. "Tell me what happened down there. The whole thing, don't leave nothin' out."

Jess told him the story from start to finish, then settled himself more comfortably on the bed. His shoulder hurt like ten kinds of hell all rolled into one. "Marshal, what I told you is the way it happened. Know it don't seem like much to start a shootin', but when they already ordered their dinner, then got up an' started to follow Miss Bishop out without eatin', an' my seein' the way they looked at her, I knowed they wuzn't up to no good." He frowned. "Didn't figure on shootin' 'em, just wanted to hold 'em in the café 'til Miss Hope wuz safe outside, then figured to take their guns, an' bring them guns to you to keep 'til we could get back to our crew." He looked at the coffeepot simmering on the stove. "When you make that coffee, doc?"

"Don't know, two, maybe three days ago. Want a cup?"

Sanford shook his head. "No way, I'll wait 'til I get back to camp." He looked at the marshal. "Mister, I didn't figure on no shootin', but when that stubby one started to draw, I knowed against three of 'em I better get my gun to smokin'. Tell you honest, I didn't let 'em clear leather 'fore I started firin'. If I had, I wouldn't be here."

The marshal's eyes squinted in what would pass for a smile. "I ain't holdin' you. When you're able, you can leave. Them three wuz wanted for a bank robbery up in Monahans. They pulled the job three weeks ago. Don't know if there was money on their heads, but I'll find out tomorrow an' let you know."

Jess felt blood rush to his face. "Marshal, I didn't shoot them men for no money, I wuz jest makin' sure my woman wuz safe."

"Don't make no difference, son. Any reward on 'em, it's yours. Like I said, I'll let you know." He stood, tipped his hat to Hope, and left.

A strange fire in her eyes, Hope stared at Jess. "I'm going to get Nettles back to camp and settled in for the night, then I'm coming back and sit with you 'til mornin'."

"You ain't gonna cross that river twice in the dark, an' you'll be alone comin' back." He looked to the side of his bed. "Doc, git a couple o' those men downstairs to help me get to the wagon, I don't feel up to tryin' it alone right now."

"Don't be a fool, boy. You start that hole in your shoulder to bleeding again and you'll be laid up awhile—or die. You stay right where you are."

Hope had lost her stubborn look; now concern and something else Sanford couldn't figure out showed in her face. "Oh, Jess, please do as he says. I'll have Joe Bob come over and sit with you."

He studied her a moment, then nodded. "All right, you do it like you said an' I'll stay put 'til mornin'. But when that sun cuts the edge o' them hills, I'm gettin' up."

She sighed. "Jess Sanford, you're the most hardheaded man alive." Suddenly her eyes swam with tears. "Oh, Jess, please take care of yourself. I—I couldn't stand it if anything happened to you. Why do you think I wanted to come on this cattle drive? It sure wasn't so I could spend six months in the wet, the cold, the heat. I—I wanted to take care of *you*."

He wanted—tried—to reach for her, take her in his arms, but both his shoulder and his side wouldn't let him do it. They shot pain through his whole body when he tensed his muscles.

He looked long into her eyes, then said, "Hope, didn't know you had any feelin's for me." He grimaced.

" 'Course it was plain to see you hated me most o' the time, but didn't know you had anything else inside you for me. We gotta talk 'bout this when it's the right time.''

"Jess Sanford, why not now? Talk to me now, Jess."

He smiled. "Danged woman, you wait'll you get a man helpless, maybe lyin' on his deathbed, an' you want to talk 'bout things a man needs both his arms to do some o' the talkin' with." He shook his head. "Nope, we gonna talk when I can pull you close an' tell you how miserable you make me when you get mad. We'll talk when I can tell you a few things about how *I* feel." He twisted to get more comfortable. "Nettles is sittin' down there in the buckboard. Go down, get him back to camp, an' send Joe Bob over. I'll see you tomorrow."

She stood, stepped toward the door, turned back, leaned over the bed, and kissed him soundly. Then, her face flaming, she rushed from the room.

Sanford looked long at the door until the doctor, whom he'd forgotten was in the room, broke his thoughts. "Son, if I was you, soon's I got well enough, I'd hog-tie that woman, and get her to a preacher quick as scat. Now you just lie there and rest. I'm going to the saloon and get me a drink. Don't reckon I been this long without one for ten years—not since the Comanche killed my wife. . . ." His voice broke and he hurried from the room.

Sanford scowled, ashamed of the way he'd treated the doctor. "Well," he breathed into the silence, "reckon that'll teach me not to judge a man 'fore I know why he is like he is. He must of loved *his* woman more than life."

He lay there in the dim lantern light thinking of Hope. Knowing now that Joe Bob had been right about why she wanted to come on the drive.

12

TRUE TO HER word, Hope sent Joe Bob across the river to sit with Jess through the night. The next morning, at Jess's insistence, his partner helped him down the stairs, with the doctor telling him every step of the way he'd kill himself by sundown.

Standing at the side of the wagon, Sanford looked at the sun. It stood at about ten o'clock. "Kind of late for breakfast, but let's you an' me go have us some eggs, bacon, an' biscuits 'fore we get on the trail."

Joe Bob nodded. "If'n it'll keep you from crossin' that river an' climbin' in the saddle, I'll eat every egg in town."

Jess grinned, even though he was hurting something fierce. "Aw, come on, Joe Bob, I been hurt worse'n this an' rode all day. Ain't nothin' wrong with me a good cup o' coffee won't fix. Let's go."

It was obvious to Sanford that his partner dragged his heels on finishing breakfast. After sitting there for over an hour drinking cup after cup of coffee, the marshal came in. "Thought I seen your buckboard out yonder. Been workin' all night, but I got the answer I wanted. Them three each had a thousand dollars on their heads. I got permission to pay you out of the money they took from the bank. Got it in my office, so when you finish eatin', come down an' I'll give it to you.''

"If it's all right with you, I'll let my partner here pick it up. Meet Joe Bob Brown, Marshal, he'll go with you, an' I want you to keep a third of it.''

The marshal opened his mouth to argue, but Sanford stopped him in midsentence. "Ain't gonna hear no argument outta you. It's yours." He looked at Joe Bob. "Partner, you take it all so's it'll be all legal like. Sign a receipt for it, then give the marshal back a thousand. That way cain't nobody ever say he didn't give it all to us.''

Joe Bob looked at the marshal. "Mr. Marshal, reckon you better do like the man says. You don't know it, but you been dealin' with the hardest-headed man in the state of Texas.''

The marshal grinned. "Reckon that's one thing I do know. Last night when he told that pretty lady he was gonna be on the trail this mornin', I didn't figure they wuz any way he could get outta that bed, but here he is, an' if that hard head don't get 'im killed, I'd like to see you boys again someday.''

Joe Bob pushed back from the table. "If we ever come this way again, suh, you can bet on it. Now let's go get that money." He looked at Jess. "Stay put. I'll be back soon's I get through.''

On the way to the crossing, Sanford told Joe Bob about his new goal of teaching himself to talk better. "That's a big, raw, new land up yonder, partner, an' the ones who can read, write, an' talk good are the ones what'll make it a state someday. Ain't sayin' I want to be gov'nor, or even serve in the legislature, but helpin' make whatever town we settle close to into a good town will be enough for me. So I figure talkin' good, people'll listen to me better. That means us both, Joe Bob. We gonna someday talk such that men'll listen when we open our mouths."

Joe Bob urged the horses into the muddy stream, and while keeping them headed as straight across the river as the slow-moving flow would allow, he looked at Sanford. "What in the name o' old Ned got you onto this trail? We ain't never had no trouble makin' people know what we wuz talkin' 'bout."

Sanford frowned, keeping his gaze between the ears of the horse in front of him. "Got to listenin' to the way the bartender talked; then, when sober enough, the doctor talked mighty pretty. Joe Bob, it just flat felt good listenin' to them, an' even though that doc was about half-drunk, he still talked better'n you an' me. We gotta learn, partner."

While the team pulled the wagon to the top of the bank, Sanford felt Joe Bob's gaze on him, and finally, he heard his partner say, "That what you want, Jess, reckon we'll give it a mighty hard try."

Before the wagon rolled to a stop, Hope stood, hands on hips in its path, her face pale, and somehow her eyes showing both anger and worry. "Jess Sanford, you're gonna kill yourself. And whether you care or not, these men, and two women, put their faith in you to get them where they're going safely. You owe us that, mister, and like it or not, when we pack that buckboard and head the herd out, you're gonna ride that wagon until *I* say you're fit. You understand what I'm tellin' you, cowboy?"

If his wounds hadn't hurt so bad, Sanford might have given her an argument, but then, looking at the way she stood, and the look on her face, he saw no give in her at all. Jess knew then, despite how he felt, he wouldn't give her any sass. He let a slight smile crinkle the corners of his eyes. "Yes, ma'am, reckon you're right." And he knew right then he'd had a glimpse of how it would be when and if they ever pulled in double harness. He'd give in anytime he knew her to be right about their common good—and he was thankful he had enough sense to recognize the fact.

In short order, the provisions were repacked in the buckboard, leaving space for him and Nettles, and the herd was up and moving. Sanford had told Joe Bob to keep them headed up the Pecos, that long before they were to leave the river he'd be up and about.

The jouncing of the wagon caused him pain, but it also forced him to admit to himself that he never would have been able to sit a horse all day, so he settled back and stewed about being stove up.

The second day, Nettles left his place in the wagon, and when Jess tried to accompany him, Hope got that stubborn look, not even an ounce of softness in it. He let her have her way and was glad she'd taken a hard stand. The steady throbbing pain in his shoulder let him know he wasn't fit to ride just yet.

With Pecos three days behind, they crossed the river at Horsehead crossing, and after the cattle bedded down, Joe Bob squatted in the wagon at Sanford's side. "What you figure to do now, Jess? We gonna stay on Mr. Charley's trail, or we gonna break loose from it?"

Sanford frowned and settled himself easier in the wagon bed. "Partner, if Goodnight did it right—an' I figure he did—I don't see no reason to change what worked for him." He took a swallow of the coffee Joe Bob had brought him. "Figure we'll drive 'em up this side o' the river, which Goodnight didn't, but then we'll ford agin at Popes crossing in order to cut out the big bend the river takes. From there, we'll be back on his trail up to Fort Sumner." He nodded. "Yeah, that is a little different than the way Mr. Goodnight took, an' once we're headin' right agin, I figure to stop at the Bosque Grande ranch a couple o' days an' let the crew rest up.''

Hope brought him his meals to the wagon, but the fourth day she allowed him to climb down and eat at the campfire with the crew. Sanford looked at Joe Bob. ''Partner, why don't you ask Bessie if she don't want to set here and eat with us? She must get all-fired lonely settin' in that wagon alone since Hope's seen fit to set with me.''

Joe Bob's smile would have dimmed a sunrise. ''Why, I reckon that's a right good idea, Jess. Never would a thought o' it myself.''

Sanford's look told Joe Bob he wasn't fooling him one bit, and when Joe Bob went to get Bessie, Hope pinned Jess with that straight-on look. ''Jess Sanford, you're about as subtle as a sledgehammer, but I've seen the way they look at each other, every look showing raw, unbridled need. And despite that need, I truly think we could have gone all the way to Cheyenne without them even having a cup of coffee together.'' She smiled. ''Thanks for being like you are, Jess. You're mighty exasperating at times, but I reckon I'll keep you as a saddle pard.''

Jess hid a grin. ''Well now, that's right kind o' you, ma'am. I wuz sort o' figurin' to start lookin' for somebody to side me soon's you let me outta that danged wagon. You just saved me a awful lot o' trouble.''

She stared at him a moment—long enough for Jess to think she'd taken him seriously. ''Jess, you try finding another waddy to ride with and I believe I'd shoot him—you, too.''

He grinned. ''Didn't figure I'd have much luck anyhow. Some in the crew might be able to ride, rope, shoot, or whatever, good as you, but compared with you, they'd a been right down hard to look at all day.'' He nodded. ''Yep. Reckon I'll keep you.''

She looked him straight in the eye. "Cowboy, you might not realize it, but I'd be harder'n a fast-stuck cocklebur to get rid of."

Joe Bob and Bessie walked to the fire, Bessie hanging behind a bit. Joe Bob, frowning, said, "Danged near had to threaten 'er. She said she hadn't ever figured on eatin' with the crew, said her pa would tan her bottom if he knowed she was flouncin' 'round in front o' a bunch o' men." He grinned. "I told 'er that *I'd* be the one to tan her hide if she flounced one little bit. Think she believed me."

From that time forward, Bessie spent every meal with them, except when foul weather kept her under the wagon's cover, and that was only because Joe Bob, afraid she'd catch the miseries, wouldn't let her out in the rain.

Each day dug deeper into summer, and the days grew hotter, dustier, and the terrain rougher. Five days out of Pecos, Sanford saddled up after breakfast and climbed in the saddle. Hope said never a word. She stood, hands on hips, shaking her head, pulled her horse alongside his, and toed the stirrup.

They rode silently about a mile before she broke the silence. "You know I'm not lettin' you ride all day. When we stop for a noonin', you're climbin' back in that buckboard an' gettin' some rest." Jess only smiled, and after the nooning, out ahead of the herd about a mile, Hope rode beside him, tight-lipped and hard-eyed.

Although no rain had fallen for several days the grass stood green and tender, the cattle sleek and fat, and the pace slow and leisurely. Things were too quiet.

Sanford's back muscles tightened. He gave a slow measured gaze to the land. He searched the shadows and the ridgelines, the rocks and arroyos. He saw nothing to cause alarm, but the feeling persisted. They were riding into trouble.

At the risk of seeming a fool, he looked at Hope and held his voice low, calm. "Hope, rein your horse around easy like, then put spurs to 'im. We got somebody watchin' us. Now git!"

As fast as he acted on his own words, Hope was out ahead of him, and lucky she was. Shots sounded at their back as soon as they turned. An angry whine buzzed by Sanford's ear, too close—then another. "Kill that horse if you have to, but git back to the herd." The wind swallowed his words. He looked over his shoulder and saw at least a dozen riders burning powder behind him. The ones he had feared since leving the Circle B were the Comanche and Mescalero Apache. His pursuers were neither. They rode hard saddles and their dress was Western. Outlaws.

He tried to swallow the lump in his throat. Fear for Hope consumed him. He drove his gelding hard, staying close to her back. Another glance showed the raiders closer. A glance ahead showed a rock upthrust he'd seen soon after leaving the herd. He judged the herd to be not far over the next rise. With that thought, his point riders came in sight. Closing in on them, he yelled to Hope, "Keep ridin'. Send up the swing riders." Before he reached his men, they had rifles out, firing at his pursuers. They didn't dare dismount and fire from the ground; the herd might stampede over them, right into the rifle fire.

First, he made certain Hope minded his words, then pulling his Winchester from its scabbard, he swung his horse and triggered a shot at the lead bandit. The raider threw up his hands and fell from the side of his horse, his rifle flying free. Two more bandits fell from their horses at the same time. The rest reined their ponies about, dug heels into their sides, and drew away from the cattle.

Sanford's men urged their horses to give chase. He held up his hand. "Let 'em go. If I'm right, we gonna get another chance at 'em." He looked at Twilley, who now rode at his side. "Bob, I'm gonna ride ahead a little." He smiled grimly. "Not too far from you men, though. Gonna find a place to make camp where we can defend the herd." He urged his buckskin out ahead of the point riders, Gant Langford, Joe Bob, and Twilley.

A couple of times while riding away from the herd, he looked back at them and shook his head. No way a man could figure a damned dumb cow. Gunfire directly ahead of them and they had plowed straight ahead, never a quiver, never an indication they wanted to run. Yet a simple thing like a tumbleweed blown into their midst and they'd stampede.

While looking for bedding grounds, and watching closely for places the outlaws might ambush him, he let part of his mind dwell on Hope. His chest swelled with pride. She was stubborn as an old mule, but thank God she picked the right times to bow her back. She hadn't hesitated a second when he'd told her to head back to the herd. He nodded to himself. Yep, she was a whole lot of woman.

He came to the rock upthrust at the top of a small rise, stopped behind it, and searched the land ahead. All he saw was bunchgrass, cottonwoods along the riverbank, and empty distance, but what he looked for—a good bedding that could be defended, sloped off from the bottom of the rise. He twisted in the saddle and waved his arm to come straight ahead.

A couple hours later, sentries posted and the night watch set, Sanford sat by the fire with Hope, Joe Bob and Bessie, and Langford and Twilley. Sanford felt Langford's eyes on him. "What's the matter—you been givin' me funny sort o' looks ever since we tangled with them outlaws."

At Sanford's request, Langford had made it a practice of using the quiet time after supper to teach Joe Bob and him better English, and in keeping with his teaching, he said, "Jess, it's *those* outlaws, not them outlaws, and the reason I've been casting you a strange glance or two all afternoon is, did you notice that any of those men who attacked us looked familiar?"

Sanford stared over the rim of his cup, pulled it away from his mouth, and grinned. "Langford, you might not of noticed, but I wasn't studyin' nobody to see whether we wuz old friends right then. I wuz tryin' to show them as little of my backsides as I could in order to keep *all* my sides in one piece. Why? You see somethin'?"

Langford twirled a cigarette, licked it, smoothed it with two fingers, put it between his lips, and lighted it. "Jess, think back to the first time you ever saw Mr. Bishop and me. There was one other man in the saloon then, the man you stomped a mud hole in, and then stomped it dry."

Sanford closed his eyes to slits and, triggered by the smell of Langford's cigarette, pulled out his pipe, packed, and lit it. He shook his head. "You don't reckon jest 'cause he got whipped, he'd carry grudge enough to try to get even?"

Langford stood and walked around the fire, a deep furrow between his brows. He stopped and faced Sanford across the fire. "Jess, some men are like that. Think on it. No one around those parts ever heard of Banack getting beat before, and when he did, their glee couldn't help but show. He couldn't stand the thought of not being top dog. I figure he's out to get even, along with getting one helluva fine herd of cattle."

Sanford sat quietly, picked up a stick, and idly drew marks in the dirt between his boots. If Langford was right, he'd have to take care that none of his men, or the women, exposed themselves to more danger than necessary. But that wouldn't cause much change in the way they'd been doing things. He looked up at the three men.

"Make sure we have enough guards on the horses, double the night herds, keep Ransome and the chuck wagon close ahead of the point." He turned his attention to Hope. "Above all, I don't want either o' you women off by yourselves. When you have to have privacy, I'll send four men to circle whatever area you're in. Hope, you're comin' off the drag, ride swing from now on."

Hope opened her mouth to say something, obviously going to give him an argument, then apparently changed her mind. She nodded. "We'll do it your way, Jess."

Her prompt agreement worried him. It wasn't like her. He'd started her out to learn trailing cattle from the ground up, and riding drag was where he'd told her she'd be assigned. He figured any change from that, she'd look on as an indication he didn't think she could carry her load. He shrugged. It didn't look as though they would ever have more than a day or so not filled with anger—but let her think what she would as long as she was safe.

He crawled between his blankets and lay staring at the stars hanging close enough to touch. He cursed himself soundly for giving in and letting her come. The Mescalero Apache and the Comanche were worry enough; now renegade whites entered the picture, and in his mind, they were worse than Indians.

13

DESPITE HIS WORRIES, Sanford slept soundly until he heard Ransome stirring around, rattling pans and tossing wood on the fire. Tiredly, he sat, put his hat on, dressed, shook out his boots and put them on, strapped on his belt and holster, rolled his blankets, tied them behind his saddle, and went to the river, stopping on the way to relieve himself. The fact that the bandits hadn't attacked during the night worried him, but he knew it wasn't cause to let his guard down—they would pick their time and place.

At the river he reversed the things he'd done when he left his blankets, piled his clothes and gun belt on the bank, and waded into the waters, still icy from the mountain snows that spawned them.

He'd brought a bar of lye soap with him, and even though the soap was strong enough to take the bark off a tree, Sanford, shivering, scrubbed himself hard, making sure he removed all the dirt. Satisfied he'd cleaned his hair as well as his body, he dunked himself two or three times to rinse, then ran as fast as the shallow water would allow to the bank.

Almost to his pile of clothes, he stopped short, sliding on the slippery bank. The dim outline of a person showed

in the murky predawn light—right where his clothes should
be. He strained to see who it was. "Who's there?"

A deep-throated laugh came through the chill air. "Come
on to your clothes, Jess. I want to see if you're as rough
and tough without your clothes and gun as you are with
them."

"Hope! What the hell you think you're doin'? Git on
back to the fire."

"Oh no, Jess. I have you right where I want you. I'll
leave when you promise to treat me like the other hands.
You've gotten to treatin' me like a woman again. I ain't
gonna have it that way. Wasn't gonna cause you any trouble on this drive when we left home and not gonna start
now. So you better promise or I'll sit here 'til the crew
wakes up."

At her first words, Sanford felt anger rise to his throat.
He swallowed hard, then grinned into the darkness. This
was as good a time as any to test her certainty she was all
man. "Go ahead, Hope. Sit there long's you want. I'll come
up an' sit with you 'til the air dries me nuff to get dressed.
Ought to be right nice sittin' there with no clothes on. Why
don't you take yours off, too. I'd like that, both o' us sittin'
there like that. The boys'd probably get a real kick outta
it, too. Jest keep sittin' there, gotta wipe the mud offa my
feet first, then I'll be right up."

Knowing she couldn't see anything but his shadowy
form in the dark, he made a great show of wiping his feet
in the grass, then stepped toward her.

"Jess Sanford, don't you dare come up here like that."

He took another step.

"Oh, damn you, Jess, stay right where you are."

He took another step. "Aw, Hope, figure to let you see
right close up how rough an' tough I am. That's what you
said you wanted, wasn't it?" Another step and all he heard

was "Oh, dammit. Jess Sanford, you have to win every time, don't you?" He heard the words, but they grew fainter while she ran toward the fire. Now it was his turn to chuckle deep in his throat.

He wouldn't have gone through with his threat, but she didn't know that. He chuckled again, let himself finish drying in the still air, then put his clothes on and headed back to the fire.

Hope sat by her saddle drinking coffee. She slanted him a glance, then stared into the fire, her face a beautiful rosy shade in the flickering light from the flames. Knowing the fire wasn't responsible for all of the reddish tint, Sanford chuckled again, and the look she threw his way would've wilted a prickly-pear cactus.

While Jess drank his first cup of coffee Ransome yelled to come and get it or he'd throw it away.

The crew ate while some relieved the morning watch at the herd. None of the night watch reported anything to cause alarm. As soon as they'd eaten, they got the cattle up and started another day.

Three days later, to rest the crew and the cattle, they bedded the herd on the Goodnight Bosque Grande ranch. Sanford again wondered why they'd not been attacked, then figured Banack must be waiting for a better place—if it had been Banack leading the attack.

Sitting at the fire that night with the usual ones gathered around, Sanford puffed his pipe a couple of times and looked at Joe Bob. "When we get to Fort Sumner, I want to hold the herd outside o' town long enough to ride in an' restock on coffee and such—anything we might be runnin' short on. Have Ransome make a list. I'll take the buckboard. Too, I want to ask around an' see if Banack an' his bunch been hangin' 'round."

"You going in alone, Jess?"

He looked at Hope. "Yep. Figured on it."

She locked gazes with him, then lowered her lashes to stare into the fire. "This herd and all of us are still under your care, Jess. Maybe you oughta take some of the boys with you."

He shook his head. "Reckon I'll be more sure you're all safe by leavin' you here. Either Joe Bob, Twilley, or Langford can get this herd where it's going without me." He grinned. "Besides that, I'm a right careful gent. I don't figure on gettin' in no—uh, gettin' in *any* trouble."

She didn't answer, but a worried frown creased her brow.

After breakfast the next morning, Sanford, soap and towel in hand, stopped by where Hope sat mending a shirt. He allowed a slight smile to crinkle the corners of his eyes. "Goin' down to the river for a bath, Hope, figured you might want to go with me."

Her face colored, her green eyes sparked, but she smiled. "One of these days, Jess, I'm gonna take you up on that and see if you really mean it." It was his turn to blush now. He hurried away. She won that round.

Hope watched him until he disappeared over the riverbank. She wondered if one day she might not really stand, take his hand, and walk with him wherever he led. She wondered if one day he would want it that way. She wondered, in the dark of night, huddled in his blankets, if he ever thought of her, if he ever wanted her like she now admitted she wanted him. She sighed. Maybe, if that day ever came, it would take away the cause of their squabbles with each other. Her mind turned to his idea of going into Sumner alone. That was cause for real worry.

She stood, stuffed the shirt she was mending back into her gear, and walked to where Twilley sat with a cup of coffee. "Bob, when we leave here, find four or five of the men you figure as the best fighting men we have, and when we get to Fort Sumner, follow Jess into town. Don't let him know. Stay out of sight, but if he braces Banack, and Banack has men with 'im, make sure it's a fair fight. I'll go with you."

Twilley stared at her a moment. "No, ma'am, you ain't goin' in. Sanford would scalp me if I let you do that."

"I'm goin'. Don't want to hear another word about it."

Twilley leaned back against his saddle. "If you go, ma-'am, you go alone."

She gave him a hard look, knowing he had her beat. She stared at him another moment then lowered her eyes to look at the ground. "If that's what it'll take to keep him safe, reckon that's the way it'll be—get good men, but don't take Joe Bob or Langford."

"Yes'm. Wouldn't have it any other way. We'll cover his back. Don't you worry none." He stood and, not wasting any time, went to Ben Quaid, talked awhile, and went to four others. He had left the last puncher and reclaimed his cup of coffee when Bessie came and sat by Hope.

"Miss Hope, wanta ask you somethin'."

Hope, again mending the shirt she'd been working on, took one more stitch. "Bessie, I'm gonna quit talkin' to you at all if you don't quit callin' me 'miss.' But go on, ask."

"Oh, miss—uh, Hope, old habits are hard to break, but what I want to talk to you 'bout is Joe Bob Brown."

Hope frowned. "Now, don't tell me that man's been botherin' you. He's such a gentleman I don't think I could believe such."

Bessie threw up her hands in obvious horror. "Oh no, Hope. It's just the opposite. That man ain't been botherin' me at all. Don't seem like he even knows I'm a hurtin' woman, hurtin' for wantin' him so bad. Why I get him his food, his coffee, even offered to wash his clothes, but he jest real polite like thanks me but don't let me do nothin' for him.''

Hope pushed the needle through the material again, studied her handiwork a moment, and wondered if she should tell Bessie what she had wheedled out of her mother as to why it had to be Bessie that would go along with her on the drive. Then she decided to heck with it, there was no reason why she shouldn't tell her.

She looked into Bessie's eyes. ''Gonna tell you something, and if you ever let on I told you, we won't be friends anymore. Understand?''

Bessie, wide-eyed, stared at Hope. Using her fingers, she twisted them in front of her lips as though locking them. ''Oh, Miss Hope, I won't say a word. Sho don't want to lose you as my friend. You the onliest one I got.''

Hope smiled at Bessie's lapse back to calling her ''miss.'' ''Bessie, have you tried to figure out why you're on this cattle drive with me?''

''No, ma'am. Jest thought as how yo mama an' daddy wanted 'nother woman along to keep you company.''

Hope nodded. ''That's only part of it. The main reason they picked you was because Jess Sanford asked for you and nobody else.'' She leaned close to her friend. ''Now, I don't know this for a fact, but what I suspicion happened is that Joe Bob had said something to Jess about not bein' able to make any time with you, bein's your pa was always around, so Jess just took the cow by the horns and asked Ma for you to come along.''

Bessie stood and poured them each a cup of coffee. ''Miss Hope, what you say might make some sense if Joe Bob showed he liked me, even a little. But Pa ain't around now and he still ain't done nothin'. . . .'' Her sentence strung out into a small wail.

Hope hugged her. "Now don't you worry your head about all this. I figure Joe Bob's an awful shy man. Our first step was gettin' him to sit and eat with you. One of these days he'll let you know how he feels."

Bessie's shoulders slumped. "Yes'm, maybe he will, an' in the meantime, reckon I jest go on a-hurtin'." She straightened and smiled. "Less'n, o' course, *I* take the bull by the horns myself, an' throw and hog-tie 'im."

Hope looked long into Bessie's smiling face. "Tell you something else, Bessie. You an' me got the same sort o' problem. My man ain't said a word to me neither." Then she smiled. "And I guarantee you before this drive ends, I have no doubt but what *I'm* gonna throw and hog-tie *him*." She stood. "Now, I reckon we better get to doin' or we won't get nothin' done all day."

The two day rest had been good for the crew *and* the cattle, and now, a week later, they drew alongside a town. Sanford called the men around him. "Men, we won't be usin' this time here to get any drinkin' or womanizin' done. I'm figurin' we gonna have a bit o' trouble 'fore we leave here, an' I want the herd protected at all times. I promise you, though, when we get to Las Vegas, farther up in the New Mexico Territory, we'll take a break and you men can go in town. Okay?"

They all nodded, and Langford said, "You're the boss, Jess."

Sanford had a couple men unload the buckboard, leaving the team in the traces. He climbed to the boot and reined the horses toward town. It took less than an hour for him to draw rein behind the sutler's store. He knocked the dust from his hat and clothes, then opened the back door and went in. He breathed deeply of the mixed aroma he always found soul satisfying. The mixed scents of ground-roast coffee, peppers, leather goods, tobacco, new clothing—they reminded him of his infrequent trips to town when he was a small boy.

He walked about, spotting the things he knew were on Ransome's list, then he walked to the counter. "Howdy, got a list o' things I'll want to pick up 'fore I leave town. Can you have them ready for me?"

"You payin' cash?"

Sanford smiled. "That's the only way I do business. You have them ready." He stepped toward the front door, hesitated, and turned back. "I'm lookin' for a man—big, bigger'n me, probably travelin' with a pretty rough bunch. You see anybody fit that description?"

The sutler grimaced. "Except for size, there's probably ten men every day comes in here like that. Cain't say I have or I haven't seen your man."

Sanford nodded. "All right. I'll be back in a hour or so and load my supplies."

He walked out onto the dusty street, looked in both directions, saw a saloon catty-corner across from him, and headed for it. He thumbed the thong off the hammer of his Colt on the way.

When he pushed through the batwing doors, he slipped to the side and studied the men in the room. It being after sundown, he didn't have to wait for his eyes to adjust to the lantern light. There were ten men; six of them played poker at a back table, and four stood at the bar. He went to where the bar curved into the wall, stood there a few moments studying those who stood at the long polished surface, decided he'd never seen any of them before, and ordered a beer.

He'd taken only a couple of swallows when one of the

poker players cursed, stood, and yelled at the bartender, "Cain't git a drink in this damned place? Ain't nobody been to the table with drinks since I come in here."

The bartender said in an even voice. "You want a drink, come get it. We got nobody to serve tables."

The big man looked back at those at the table. "Deal me out this hand, boys. I'll git a jug." He stomped to the bar, scowling, cursing. It was only when he walked under the lantern and the light shone full on his face that Sanford recognized him. His stomach muscles tightened. The leaders in his neck pulled at his head. The man he looked at? Banack.

The gunman ordered a bottle, picked it up, and glanced along the bar. He froze, then slowly put the bottle back on the bar. "Well, well, well, if it ain't the nigger lover from down Fort Stockton way. Where's yore nigger friend?"

Holding his beer with his left hand, Sanford lowered his right hand to his gun belt. "Banack, I got no *nigger friends*, but my best friend and partner is a *Nigra*. You call him a nigger agin an' I figure to blow your damned head off. No point in fightin' you with fists. I done kicked hell out o' you that way one time."

Banack said over his shoulder, "Hey, boys, you wanta meet a pure-dee damn fool? Look over yonder at the end o' the bar, that's Jess Sanford. He figures to take me with handguns. Ain't no problem there, I can beat 'im—but just in case I cain't, don't none o' you let 'im walk outta here."

One of the men at the bar, a tall thin youth, looked at Banack, then toward Sanford. "Looks like these here men figure to box you, mister. Don't seem like that's fair." He slid down the bar toward Jess. A slight motion of his hand and he held a gun in it—the fastest draw Sanford had seen—and the gun pointed at the table at which Banack's friends sat.

''Don't none o' you gents move a finger. These two gonna have a fair chance at each other, an' when it's over, if that big man at the end of the bar's the one still standin', him an' me'll take on the rest o' you. Now jest sit still.'' He said to Jess over his shoulder, ''Get on with yore talk.''

Sanford, despite the cold lump in his stomach, couldn't hold back the smile that threatened to crinkle the corners of his lips. Amazing how fast the tables turned on a man. He looked at Banack; the curve of the bar stood between them. It would cause them to have to raise their guns above it in order to get off a good shot. He took a couple of quick steps to remove that obstacle and stood in the clear.

About to call Banack's bluff, the batwing doors in front swung inward and the back door opened to let in a couple of men. Sanford didn't dare take his gaze off Banack—but hoped his tall thin friend would keep things even. It was then his new friend spoke again. ''Don't none o' you new arrivals take a hand in this. These two gents done decided to have a shoot-out, an' I'm here to see that big man at the end o' the bar gets a fair chance.''

''We come in here for the same reason, mister, so point yore gun at them at the table.'' Sanford recognized Twilley's voice. He gave Banack his full attention.

With a swing of the pendulum, the odds were now in Sanford's favor. He saw dismay, then fear, flicker in Banack's eyes. The gunman, still poised for a draw, glanced at the thin youth, then at Sanford's men. ''Aw now, Sanford, don't seem like jest 'cause we had a fistfight down yonder in Texas we should take it to a gunfight now.'' He forced a weak smile. ''Hell, we could even be friends.''

Sanford stared a moment. ''Banack, you an' me, ain't no way we could be friends. I don't make friends with gutless slime like you. You tried to kill me only a few days ago— so whenever you're ready.'' His hands hung loosely at his sides, his muscles relaxed, his eyes never leaving those of Banack.

Somehow he knew the youth who had befriended him had holstered his side gun. Now it could turn into a wholesale shoot-out. The odds again being even, Banack's men would surely get into the act.

Banack's eyes squinted slightly at the corners. Sanford's hand stabbed for his gun, but he knew Banack had beaten him to the draw. Banack's handgun blossomed a streak of flame a shade before Sanford squeezed the trigger. Banack's shot tore splinters from the puncheon floor at Sanford's feet. Sanford's shot went where he looked. A small, black hole appeared just inside Banack's left shirt pocket, knocking him back a step. He brought his revolver up again. Fire again streaked from its muzzle—at the same time Sanford's second shot caught him in the brisket. Banack caught his balance and tried to raise his six-gun. It came level with Sanford's chest, but the gunman bent at the waist, triggered his shot into the floor, and fell on his face, dead before he fell. Hate had fired his last shot.

The room reverberated with the shocking blast of gunfire. The acrid stench of gun smoke clouding any chance to see what happened, Sanford turned his six-shooter toward the table where Banack's men had sat and triggered off his last four shots.

Through the smoke, the tall, thin youth stood, leaning casually against the bar, his side gun still holstered. He looked at Sanford and grinned. ''Didn't see no point in me gettin' in on the fight. Y'all did right well without me.''

The smoke thinned, Sanford could see to the table where Banack's men had sat. One lay on the floor, his legs draped over the rungs of his chair. Two others sprawled facedown beside the table. The fourth lay on his back against the wall, and the fifth, on hands and knees tried to climb to his feet.

Twilley raised his pistol and thumbed back the hammer. ''Let 'im be—unless he decides to do somethin' with that six-shooter on the floor in front of him.'' Sanford's words came out flat, hard.

He looked at the young man who'd backed him. ''Thanks.''

A slight smile breaking the corners of his lips, the youth said, ''*De nada;* jest wanted to keep things even.'' Before he could say more, the batwings crashed inward. The man who came through them in such a hurry stared around, then his look took in the sprawled bodies.

His gaze swung to the bar and centered on the tall, thin man. ''Told you, son, any more hell-raisin' by you an' I'd lock you up 'til you rotted.''

The youth shook his head. ''Ain't fired a shot, Marshal. Come pull my Colt from its holster yourself. Take a look, an' a smell. It ain't been fired since I cleaned it last night.'' He grinned, rolled a cigarette, lit it, and glanced around. ''I wuz gonna take a hand in this shindig until Mr. Sanford's friends showed up, then I seen the fight wuz gonna be even, so I just stood an' watched. You shoulda been here, Marshal. These here is some bunch o' fightin' men.''

The marshal swung his gaze around the room, then centered on Sanford. ''Tell me about it.''

Sanford told him the whole story. ''They brought it to me, Marshal. Ain't sayin' I wouldn'ta forced it if they hadn't. They attacked me an' my men out by our trail herd.'' He glanced at the young man now standing at his side. ''Ain't no question they'da killed me if this gentleman hadn't kept 'em honest.''

The marshal gave the youth a sour look. ''Don't get the big head, Billy. This man called you a gentleman only 'cause he don't know you.'' He raked the men in the room with a glance. ''Men, I want you to meet Billy Bonney, some call 'im Billy the Kid.''

14

BEN QUAID, STANDING behind Twilley, said, "Holy hell! That's Billy the Kid? Heck, he ain't much older'n me. Reckon I got a chance yet o' gettin to be a known man."

The marshal gave Quaid a stone-hard look. "Youngster, if'n yore boss even sees you practicin' a fast draw, he oughta tan yore britches for you."

"You can take that idea to the bank, Marshal," Sanford said. "I'm only just now makin' a fair-to-middlin' drover outta him. 'Sides that, we got 'bout a dozen different kinds o' Injuns we can burn powder at without lookin' for the likes of these to brighten up a day."

The marshal gave the bodies on the floor another glance. "Billy's done a lot of things, but lying ain't one of them. He says the way you told it is the way it happened. I believe 'im. I got no reason to hold you."

Sanford nodded, but all the time he'd been watching the man struggling to get to his feet. Blood ran down the man's face from a scalp wound. His eyes wild, he looked at the marshal, then at Sanford. His hand swept his holster, and finding it empty, his eyes looked to the floor. His revolver lay almost at his feet. As though in a daze, he stooped to pick it up.

Sanford, thinking to fire into the floor in front of the man, drew, thumbed the hammer back, and slipped his thumb to fire. An empty, metallic click sounded loud in the room. It was then he remembered emptying his gun during the fight.

The gunman blindly groped for his gun. Without thinking, Jess holstered his six-shooter, took three quick steps across the room, and brought a right fist to the side of the man's head. The gunman staggered sideways, crashed into the wall, and fell in a heap. Sanford pulled his Colt, opened the loading gate, dropped the empties into his palm, put them in his pocket, slowly fed fresh loads into the cylinder, then dropped his revolver gently into its holster. He walked to the marshal, tipped his hat, and said, "Marshal, you not gonna charge me with nothin', I figure to be gettin' my stuff from the sutler's across the street an' gettin' on back to my cows."

"Ain't holdin' you, boy. Good luck on your drive."

Sanford reached in his pocket, pulled five cartwheels from it, and handed them to the lawman. "Here's enough to pay for buryin' that scum." He walked toward the batwings and called over his shoulder, "See you next trip, Marshal."

The old lawman growled, "Do me a favor, son, an' don't stop in my town next time you come this way."

Sanford laughed, but somehow he didn't think the marshal was making a joke. Outside, he told his men he'd rather they wait until they got to Las Vegas or Trinidad to visit a saloon, that he was going back to the herd and would like them to ride with him.

On the way back, there was little talk, and no laughter. The only sounds were the rattle of trace chains and the creak of saddle leather. Sanford knew the lack of talk was because this was the first time some of his men had been blooded. A killing isn't a thing to be taken lightly.

When he drove the buckboard alongside the chuck wagon, he saw none of the crew had turned in, even though it was far past time to be in their blankets. Sanford turned the care of the horses over to one of the men who hadn't been in town with him and walked to stand in front of Hope. She sat by her saddle staring up at him. "You all right, Jess?"

He nodded. "Might not a been but for you." He went to his bedroll and picked up his cup. Late though it was, almost ten o'clock, he figured to have a cup of coffee and unwind. He poured his coffee and sat by Hope's side. Tiredly he looked at her. "Thanks."

She nodded and scooted a little closer.

Sitting there, drinking his coffee, with Hope close enough, he could feel her warmth, his world set itself right again. He pushed the gunfight to the back of his mind.

It was hard at any time to think of things other than the woman sitting next to him, but with her this close, with her woman scent in his nostrils, it was all he could do to keep from pulling her even closer and telling her how much he wanted her, despite the men still sitting around. But if he did that, and she felt the way he did, she would ride right on to the Powder River with him. He wouldn't subject her to the hardships the first year or two of putting a ranch together would bring. He finished his coffee, told the men they better turn in, and went to his blankets, but long after pulling his covers up to his chin, he heard the kid, Ben Quaid, telling those who'd stayed behind about the gunfight and meeting Billy the Kid.

His thoughts turned to the route he should take. If he drove straight for Raton, he might save a day or two, but chances were the creeks would be dry. Or he could stay alongside the Pecos to Las Vegas and probably have water much of the way. Too, he might avoid the Comanche by driving up the Pecos, but if he did that, he'd have Apache to worry about. He shrugged. His and Joe Bob's thinking that if they didn't have trouble to talk about they'd have *nothing* to talk about—now he extended that idea to *thinking* about trouble. He turned on his side and went to sleep.

The next morning he headed the herd toward Las Vegas. In the distance on his right—he judged it to be about ten miles—an escarpment stood about seventy-five feet high. He studied it awhile, knowing it would cause no problem, but could be an ally in case of stampede. The landscape looked slightly rolling, with bunchgrass growing heavy. In any direction he saw no trees, even Spanish dagger and other varieties of cactus were sparse, and although none was visible, the land was broken by dry washes, deep ravines, and buffalo wallows that could hide Indians. Sanford hoped all he would see was the distance that stretched on forever.

He ranged out ahead of the herd a couple of miles. For his nooning he chewed on a strip of jerky and drank warm water from his canteen. Wind kicked up a light powdering of dust, caking his face with a muddy mixture of sweat. He wiped the sweat with his bandanna and studied the far northwest horizon.

For more than an hour he'd noticed a purplish-blue haze. Since they were not close enough to be sighting the deceptive purple of mountains, the colors had to mean weather, and as if to confirm his belief, the colors deepened faster than they would if he had been approaching the Sangre de Cristo range. He reined his buckskin about and headed for the herd.

He came on Langford and Twilley at the point. "Pass the word back. We got weather blowin' in. Tell the drovers to ride tight to the cows. If they stampede, let's try to keep 'em runnin' together, but if they start spreadin', tell the boys to get the hell away from 'em. Don't want nobody hurt. We'll just have to spend a week gatherin' 'em again. Another thing: if they's large hail in them clouds, or if they's lightning, get off their horses, protect themselves—to hell with the cows.''

They nodded and one on each side of the herd headed toward the drag. Before they could get out of range, Sanford yelled, ''Tell Hope to get to the buckboard. She's a better driver than Bessie.'' Again they nodded.

Soon the wind picked up, blowing in gusts. High, thin clouds blew over the sun, but brought little cooling. Although gusty, the air became increasingly muggy, and even through the dust, Sanford smelled rain.

Heavy, greenish-black clouds moved toward the herd, and lightning threw the roiling storm mass into bold relief. Then sharp, jagged bolts reached the ground at the leading edge of the frightening, moving darkness.

Sanford continued to eye the approaching storm, thinking, then said into the teeth of the dust-laden wind, ''Hail, tornado, floods. Ain't none o' it good—an' we might get it all.''

Abruptly, the wind blowing out of the center of the storm ceased. An eerie quiet shrouded the land, as though the inside of the storm sucked up all sound, all energy.

Small hail, about marble size, fell for a few seconds—then stopped, as though getting its wind for a much larger effort. The next shower of hail grew increasingly larger. At first, it was the size of a two-bit piece, then the size of a knotted rope, then the size of a large fist. A bolt of lightning burst over the top of the cattle. They lurched into a quickening run, then into an all-out stampede.

Sanford urged his gelding into a run away from the side of the crazed cattle, brought him to a halt, and peered into the sheets of rain, looking for the buckboard. It didn't take long to find it—careening out of the death-dealing ice balls and rain, coming directly toward him. Hope, standing in the boot, pulled on the reins, trying to stop the scared horses. She glanced toward Sanford when the wagon drew abreast, her eyes wide with fright, then back to the team.

Sanford dug his spurs into the gelding, pulled alongside, first of the wagon, then of the horses. He grabbed for the reins, missed, then grabbed again. He caught only one, and fearful he'd cause the team to make a sharp turn and flip the buckboard on its side, he turned loose. As soon as he released the one rein, he launched himself for the back of the near horse and landed far forward on the horse's shoulders. A swing of his hands and he had the straps for both horses in his clutch.

A little at a time he turned them from the path of the cattle and slowed them to a stop. "You an' Bessie get under the wagon." The crash of hailstones swallowed his words. He crawled back along the wagon tongue and lifted Hope from the seat. Holding her close, he jumped to the ground and pushed her under the protection of the bed, then went after Bessie.

When he had both women under the wagon, he told them to stay there until the storm passed. Hail now fell only sporadically, and in ever-decreasing size, but rain still came as though thrown from a bucket. Sanford cocked his head to look skyward. The bottoms of the clouds hung low to the ground, rolling and twisting, but he didn't see that which he feared—a funnel cloud.

Before going to his gelding, he ducked his head under the wagon bed again. "Soon's this lets up, Hope, see if you cain't catch up with the strays. I'm gonna see how far the cows run, an' how far they done spread out. Gonna start pushin' 'em back on the trail."

He went to his horse, climbed aboard, and headed north.

By the time the rain quit, Sanford came onto a few stragglers, and figured they had run themselves out of steam before the rest of the herd. He cast back and forth across the muddy trail, looking for fallen or crippled horses or cattle, but his greatest fear was of finding one of his riders, or worse, a boot, or hat, or bits of muddy, bloody clothing.

He came onto the chuck wagon and saw Ransome sitting in the boot, cursing the team and popping his whip above their backs. "Gotta git this wagon where I can start supper. These men gonna be starved time they git back from chasin' them danged crazy cows."

"Pull up anytime, Ransome. I'll tell the boys you're back here. We'll probably be a couple a days findin' all our cows, so start supper anytime you want." He kneed his horse to a lope and left Ransome behind.

Only a couple hundred yards ahead of the chuck wagon, he came on what he most feared. He stopped, ground-reined his horse, and walked to the sodden body, now only pulpy, bloody flesh ground into the mud, along with shreds of clothing. There wasn't enough left to tell who the rider had been. He stared at the flattened mass that less than an hour ago had been a human being. His throat muscles swelled around a lump that grew larger while he looked. Then the blood and clothing dimmed through his tears.

Ransome drew the wagon to a halt beside him. "What's the mat . . ." His words trailed off.

Unashamedly, Sanford turned his tear-streaked face to the cook. "Helluva way to die." His voice came out choked, broken, strained. "His horse ain't here—cain't tell who he was, probably won't know 'til the crew comes in for supper." He sucked in a deep, shuddering breath. "Take the wagon ahead at least a quarter of a mile 'fore you stop to fix supper. Don't reckon the men'll be too hungry after this, but gotta be ready. I'll git a couple o' hands to help dig a grave. Hope they ain't no more o' this up ahead.''

Sanford rode slowly along the muddy trail, searching each inch of it for sign of another body. He had one scare, but it turned out to be a cow. He found two other head with broken legs and shot them, figuring to butcher them. The crew had had their fill of venison and antelope.

When he rode to where the men circled the herd, his eyes searched out Joe Bob, Langford, Twilley, the kid, and of course he knew Hope, Bessie, and Ransome were far back with the wagons. He heaved a great sigh of relief, and at the same time a pang of guilt shot through him for finding solace that the victim hadn't been one of them. When the crew saw him ride up, they rode up to him. Langford pushed his hat off his forehead. ''Getting worried about you, Jess. I've accounted for all but one rider, the two women, and Ransome. You seen them?''

Sanford frowned. ''All safe except the rider. We gotta bury 'im. You know who he was by now, so get a couple men with strong stomachs an' his blankets. I'll take the men back and fix him for burial. I'll want the men to gather around while I read from the book.'' He kept his face devoid of expression, afraid he'd show too much feeling. ''Langford, if the waddy wuz one of your men, figure you'd want to read over 'im.''

Langford nodded. ''I appreciate the thought, Jess. Yes, he was a Circle B rider, and I'd like to say a few words over him.''

Later, the burial over and the watch set on the herd, the crew sat by the fire. There wasn't much talk; they sat staring into the flames, drinking coffee, and one by one tossed the grounds from their cups and drifted off to their blankets.

Sanford lay in his blankets staring at the star-studded sky, hurting for the lost Circle B rider, yet thankful they had lost only one man on the trail—so far.

He lay there long into the night, listening to the wind whisper its way southward, hearing an occasional snore from the men, smelling the fresh-washed air, and feeling the hurt gradually go away. Despite the danger, the hardships, every man here was free, perhaps more free than other men at other jobs. He knew of no cattlemen anywhere who would trade places with those others. His drover would not be forgotten, but for the rest of the crew, they were alive and life would go on. He closed his eyes and let sleep take him.

Simon Bauman hadn't been doing much sleeping since he'd left home. When he wasn't spending money his father sent him, he sat stewing, in a dark funk. Finding Jess Sanford and killing him had become an obsession. Each day, he grew more deeply convinced that Sanford had taken unfair advantage of him. The facts became so twisted he believed Sanford had beaten *him* with the posthole digger. He convinced himself he'd been attacked from behind, never given a chance to defend himself.

At the moment he sat at a poker table in Fort Worth, a small stack of chips in front of him. He'd been losing steadily, and was in an even worse mood than usual, but at least, he'd gotten his first clue as to Sanford's whereabouts. Long-haired Jim Courtright told him Sanford had headed for the Big Ben when he left town, but advised Bauman to leave the big, salty man alone, he was not a man to push.

Bauman squeezed his cards out, hardly thinking about poker. Salty or not, he thought, Sanford hadn't seen the day he could take him with guns. Hell, he'd already killed three men in stand-up gunfights. He wouldn't admit to himself

that the three men he'd killed were little more than kids
having a Saturday-night drunk.

He looked at his hand again and bet the rest of his stack
of chips. A man across the table called—and beat his three
tens with three aces. Bauman threw his cards to the table,
opened his mouth to accuse the man of cheating, and
looked into the palest, bluest eyes he'd ever seen. Luke
Short, perhaps the fastest gunfighter known, smiled. "Go
ahead, greenhorn. I haven't had the pleasure of shooting
the likes of you in some time now. Besides, this country
out here has too many of your kind. I'll shorten that count
a little."

Simon Bauman pushed away from the table, stood, and
left the White Elephant Saloon. He had to get on his way.
He had a man to find—and kill.

The fourth day out of Fort Sumner, Sanford figured they
were about halfway to Las Vegas, one of the oldest towns
in the New Mexico Territory, and *wild* was the word that
fit it.

After supper that night, he drank his coffee, tossed the
dregs from his cup, stood, and went to the chuck wagon,
checked the wheel bolts and axles, went to the buckboard
and did the same, walked back to the fire and picked up
his cup, put it down, and circled the group of men.

Joe Bob looked up. "For hell's sake, Jess, what's the
matter with you? You're as restless as a soiled dove in
church. Set an' have another cup o' coffee."

"Don't wanta set. Gonna take a walk."

A swell of ground took the camp out of his sight before
Hope caught up with him. "Mind if I tag along, Jess?"

He frowned and faced her. "Yep, I do mind, Hope.
Don't want to cause talk 'bout you. You're a mighty beautiful woman, and the men might talk, us bein' out here

alone like this. I'd hate to have to shoot one of 'em for loose talk. Go back.''

She stopped, stood back, and pinned him with those green eyes that looked right through a man. "Jess, that's the third time you said I was beautiful. Know I ain't, but long's you think so, that's what counts." She frowned. "Why ain't you never *showed* how pretty you think I am?"

Sanford sputtered, glad for the dark so she couldn't see how red his face must be. "Wh-wh-what you mean, show you?" Even in the dark, he could see her cheeks color a bit.

"You know what I mean. The way a man shows a woman who he thinks is pretty. You ain't never put your arms around me. You ain't never kissed me. Fact is, when I get undressed for bed, I gotta look to make sure I'm a female. Another fact is, you ain't never done *nothin'* to *make* me know I'm a woman."

He took her hand in his and continued their walk. "Girl, it ain't like I ain't wanted to. Lord knows I've thought about you, an' dreamed about you most ever' night since I first laid eyes on you, but your pa runs more cows, over more country, than I ever hope to have. Even if you agreed, I couldn't take you away from all that an' put you up in a soddy—at first, while I try to make a go of it."

She stopped and turned toward him. "Jess, don't you know that just being with you would outweigh anything I got with Pa? Ma helped him build their ranch, and if she can do it, I can." She stepped toward him and again looked at him head-on. "Or maybe you don't think I'm as much woman as my ma."

"My Lord, girl, I have never in my born days seen any woman to match you in pure spunk, beauty, nothin'." He pulled her another step toward him. She came the rest of the way—and was in his arms. He looked into her eyes, then gently brushed her lips with his own. She reached up and pulled his head closer, crushing her lips to his.

After a long, long moment he stepped back, letting his arms drop to his side. "Hope, I shouldn'ta done that."

"Why? Didn't you want to?"

He stared at her. "Woman, I wanted that kiss more than anything in this world, wanted it for a long time, but didn't know how you'd take it—or how your ma and pa would take to the idea."

"Well, now we both know 'bout me, an' I don't know how my folks'll feel, Pa 'specially. I figure Ma had this figured out soon after you came to work for Pa. Fact is, she kind of warned me you was a wanderin' man. I figured all along if that was the case, then I'd just wander *with* you."

Sanford laughed. "You did, did you? Figured it all along. How long you been thinkin' 'bout us this way?"

Still close enough that he could see her frown, then grin, she said, "Jess, that first day when I was gonna show you around the ranch? Well, I sorta got the idea when we come back with you all cut up, and I been gettin' to know it right strong through the months since."

She moved close to him again, close enough that her woman scent in his nostrils and the feel of her breasts pressed to his chest caused him to want to forget the *right* thing to do.

Hope continued as though unaware of the turmoil she caused. "Jess, I was 'bout ready to give up 'bout you an' me til, I heard you an' Pa plannin' the trail drive, an' you about to go off down yonder to gather some mavericks. I decided right then to take the bull by the horns. Come hell or high water, I wasn't gonna let you get away without a fight."

Sanford pulled her to him, lightly brushed her lips with

his, then crushed her strong, yielding body to him and kissed her until he felt her melt closer to him. After a while, afraid neither of them would stop, he pushed her away. "Sounds like the only fight we got might be with your pa. How we gonna tell 'im 'bout us. I ain't lettin' you go back to Texas without me, an' I cain't go for quite a while yet. Gotta get our ranch started."

She looked at him straight on. "Jess Sanford, don't reckon you're gonna say it, so I *am*. I love you, Jess, have ever since I first saw you—always will. I'll live in a soddy or anywhere else with you."

"Hope, I ain't much with words, but I love you, too. Soon's your folks say it's all right, I want to marry you."

She chuckled. "Whether they say we can or not, we're gonna do it, an' we ain't waitin' for a letter to get there and an answer to come back. I figure we better do it right sudden, if you want me to stay an honest woman."

15

SANFORD TOOK HER by her shoulders and gently turned her toward camp. "Go, Hope. Go back to the fire before I lose any control I still got."

She resisted the pressure of his hands. "Jess"—her voice came out husky, full of desire—"Jess, keep me out here with you tonight. I don't want to go back, I don't want to ever go anywhere without you."

His grip tightened on her shoulders. "Hope, now we know the hunger, the love we share, it's gonna be hard, real hard to not give in to it. It's gonna be worse on us than not knowin' how we feel—but we cain't give in to it, girl. Much as we think right now it would be all right, it would just flat be doin' you wrong. I ain't gonna do that. When we lay with each other, it's gonna be the right thing to do, an' right now it ain't. You know it an' I know it." He stepped back, fumbled for his pipe, packed and lit it. "Now, let's get on back before the crew starts talkin'."

They had another cup of coffee when they got back, and Hope sat as close to Sanford as she dared without shouting to all around them that she was his woman. She noticed Bessie looking at her with a strange but winsome smile. When they finished their coffee, they went to their blankets.

Hope lay there, staring into the darkness, her mind and body yearning for the touch of Jess to be upon her; then, long after she thought Bessie asleep, her friend whispered, "You done got yo man. I knowed it soon's you came back to the fire. Looked to me like you coulda lit up the whole camp without havin' no fire nor nothin' to help you."

"Oh, Bessie, you reckon the men noticed?"

Bessie chuckled. "Lordy, missy, a man ain't got the kind o' eyes a woman's got. They blind when it comes to seein' a woman's feelin's. You, me, an' Mr. Jess is the onliest ones who knows, an' I bet even Mr. Jess is a layin' yonder in his blankets wonderin' what hit 'im." She chuckled, then broke out into a deep-chested laugh.

Hope pushed the covers down and hugged her friend to her. "Oh, Bessie, you're priceless. How'd we go so long without makin' friends?"

"Might not a never done it without this cattle drive. Now I got to git the same thing done with my man as you done with yores. How'd you do it, Miss Hope?

Very unlike her, Hope giggled. "Bessie, I just flat out turned to him, looked 'im in the eye, an' asked him what was wrong with me." She went on to tell Bessie every detail of the walk she'd taken with Jess. When she finished, she thought a long time as to whether she should tell her friend why she had been asked to come on the drive. Then she decided she would, and see what the consequences turned out to be.

"Bessie, gonna tell you somethin', don't know it for fact, but puttin' two an' two together, I figure it makes sense. First off, Ma told my pa an' your pa she wanted you to come along an' keep me company. *But,* before that, Jess asked Ma to make sure you came along. I figure Joe Bob told Jess he wanted you for his woman an' Jess figured he had to get you away from your pa to make it happen. Makes sense, don't it?''

''Oh Lordy, Miss Hope, it makes sense when you say it. You reckon there really is a chance Joe Bob wants me?''

Hope lay back and pulled her blankets around her. ''Bessie, if he don't, he's a bigger damn fool than I think he is. Now we better get some sleep. Tomorrow's another long day.''

''Yes'm, but for you it'll be a mighty happy time livin' it, now you know what yore man thinks.''

Not far from where Hope and Bessie talked, Sanford lay on his back awhile, then turned to his side and his back again. Finally, knowing he wouldn't sleep until he solved his problem, he crawled from his bedding, dressed, and walked out away from the camp.

As far as he knew, wanted posters on him hung in every post office in the South—and West.

For a long time after he'd run from home, he checked the post office walls in every town to see if his picture might be plastered there. He'd never seen even one wanted notice and thought it strange. The Baumans were a mighty prominent family in Tennessee. He'd never dared hope he wasn't a wanted man.

Now Simon Bauman came back to haunt him. Without knowing whether his past stood in his way of his happiness with Hope, he wouldn't, couldn't ask her to marry him. He chewed on the problem of finding out whether they were still looking for him—or if they had ever looked for him. For the first time he let himself hope he hadn't killed Bauman. Maybe Simon had been alive, and in his own beat-up, exhausted state, he'd failed to detect signs of life in the man. Maybe—maybe—maybe.

He returned to his blankets only to continue gnawing at his problem.

The next morning, tired from lack of sleep, Sanford drank his morning coffee before the crew awakened, saddled a big bay he'd cut out as one of his string, and rode from the bedding grounds. Less than a mile from the herd he reined his horse in and sat thinking. He'd long ago told Joe Bob why he'd left home. Why not tell him his present problem? He nodded and headed back to the herd. His stomach growled, reminding him he hadn't eaten breakfast.

All that day Sanford waited for a chance to corner Joe Bob for a talk. It wasn't until late that afternoon they rode alone, out ahead of the cattle. He slanted a look across his shoulder. "Joe Bob, I got troubles. Last night, just like you thought would happen 'fore we left the Circle B, Hope let me know how she felt." He felt his face heat up. "I sorta told her how it was with me, too."

Joe Bob gave him a sour look. "Wish I had them sorta troubles. Bessie ain't give me no hint whatsoever she'd give a plugged nickel for *me*."

Sanford turned his gaze to stare between his horse's ears. "Gotta talk to you 'bout Bessie, but right now reckon I ain't got a hint 'bout what to do. Partner, I can't ask Hope to marry me without knowing if the law is lookin' for me. Just wouldn't be right."

"You ever tell her 'bout that fight you an' that man had back yonder?"

Sanford shook his head. "Never said nothin' bout it to nobody but you. Ain't nothin' a man talks 'bout."

Joe Bob snorted. "This's somethin' you gotta talk about with her, Jess. You jest don't say nothin' 'bout marryin' up with 'er, you gonna hurt her somethin' awful. My idea is, ain't nothin' you could tell 'er 'bout yoreself would cause 'er to not want to get on with yo love." He twirled a cigarette and offered his tobacco to Jess. "Tell you what, I'm gonna give some thought to how to find out if you're a wanted man. If I come up with somethin', I'll try it on you. Till then, you figure out how I can get Bessie to tell me what she thinks o' me."

Sanford grunted. "Hell, Joe Bob, I can tell you that right now, you gotta get 'er alone an' jest flat out tell 'er, no ifs, an's, or buts 'bout it."

"S'pose she don't want me? S'pose she laughs at me?"

Jess shook his head, amazed at how little his partner knew about women. Since the night before, he'd begun to think of himself as knowing quite a bit about the gentle sex. "Tell you what, Joe Bob, if she says she don't want you, an' even if she laughs, which she ain't gonna do, you ain't gonna be one damn bit worse off than you are now. All you gotta do is stand up to your problem, look it in the eye, brace yourself for the worst, an' tell 'er."

"Be more like me to fall flat on mah face, then I'd sho nuff be in trouble."

Sanford glanced to the west. The sun, a large, fiery red ball, brushed the thin line of the horizon. "We better get on back to camp. They done bedded the cows by now."

That night by the fire, Joe Bob noticed Bessie looking his way more often than usual. He figured Hope had told her about her feelings for Jess, and now she was all braced to have him try to make time with her. Probably ready to tell him how the cow ate the cabbage, tell him he was a no-good man, tell him she wasn't in no way interested in him, tell him she figured he tricked her onto this cattle drive.

After stealing a glance at her, he stood to get himself a cup of coffee, changed his mind, tossed the dregs from his cup, and went to his blankets.

He continued to think about her. She was smart, was

always at his side to help when he needed her, seemed to read his mind when he had a problem—and to top it all off, she was some kind of woman.

He and Jess had never spent time with the soiled doves of the cow towns they'd been in. He'd not seen a woman he wanted for nothing other than her body, and he'd heard and seen enough of the diseases spread by those women to figure it was best to do without.

But Bessie was different. He noticed every time Hope went to the river for a bath, Bessie went with her, and they both came back smelling clean and fresh. And back at the ranch she kept every man from coming sniffing around. Yeah, she was his woman, but how was he to let her know it? He went to sleep with her in his thoughts.

His dreams were of Bessie taunting him, pushing him from her when he got too close, looking at him like he was one of the dogs on the ranch, laughing when he tried to tell her how he felt.

He woke, sweat streaming from his body even though the night had a chill to it. He looked for the Big Dipper, saw it was about three o'clock, pushed his blankets from him, and got up.

At the fire, he pulled the coffeepot from the ashes, poured a full cup of the thick night-old liquid, took a swallow, and wondered it hadn't dissolved his granite cup. "This ain't gonna do," he growled. "She's my woman an' I gotta find a way to make her look at me like I'm her man." He drank the rest of his coffee, stood to get another cup, grimaced, picked up the pot, and headed for the river.

Joe Bob bathed, then scubbed the pot out and brought it to the fire. Ransome was up and readying the fire to cook breakfast.

"Water for fresh coffee." Joe Bob handed the pot to the cook. "Gonna ride out an' let one of the boys come in for coffee.'' He saddled and left, thinking his sleepless night hadn't accomplished anything. He hadn't even given thought to Jess's problem. He pushed Bessie from his mind and thought of his friend, a man he'd do anything for, even give his life if he had to.

Still in his blankets, Jess watched Joe Bob ride out. He ain't slept much neither, he thought. Well, we got a long way to go yet 'fore we get these cows to Montana, an' both o' us gotta get our women off our minds if we gonna get there at all. He finally came up with the conviction that he would have to stay away from Hope, not lead her on when he couldn't marry her, not knowing if a lawman would pull a gun on him in any one of the towns they had yet to put behind them.

The days passed; they reached Las Vegas, and Jess held the herd there for two days, splitting the crew and letting half go into town at a time to cut the dust from their throats. When they left Las Vegas, headed for Raton, Jess put Gant Langford in charge of the drive. He headed for Raton or Trinidad, whichever town he might find Uncle Dick Wootton in.

In Raton, he found Wootton had left the day before to go back to his hotel at the foot of the pass on the Trinidad side. About to toe the stirrup, he looked across his saddle into the eyes of a man he knew, and not much of what he knew was good. Black Jack Slade, the bandit leader from the other side of Cimarron Canyon, over in the town of Red River.

''Howdy, Slade. Didn't know you got this far from your nest.''

Slade nodded. ''Howdy, Sanford.'' He smiled, but no humor showed in his eyes. ''I might say the same for you, but then you've always been a wandering man, from what I hear. What you doing up this way?''

Sanford wondered how much to tell the handsome out-law, then decided it didn't make any difference. Slade prob-ably already knew about the herd coming up the trail. He grinned. "Got six thousand longhorns, an' thirty-two Winchesters not far behind me."

Slade's eyes widened in mock horror. "Uh, now. That's a pretty good bunch of rifles. You trying to scare me off, Sanford?"

Jess shook his head slowly. "Nope. Jest want you to take a good, hard look at your hole card an' figure what it'll cost you to try for my herd."

Slade smiled. "Now that's right kind of you, Sanford. Might save you and me some misery."

Jess nodded. "Way I figured it." He climbed into the saddle, nodded, and headed toward the pass.

The trail across the pass wound around the sides of the mountains, cutting from view the town that lay below. When Wootton's hotel came into sight, so did Trinidad. Sanford reined in at the hotel and looped his reins over the hitch rail in front. Wootton sat in a rocker on the porch.

"Howdy, Jess. Heered tell you was headin' my way. Got my pencil all sharpened up so's I can crawl deep into yore poke."

"Why, you old hoss thief, I bet you been sittin' here figurin' how to get ahold o' my whole herd." He reached for Wootton's hand and gripped it tightly. "How you been doin', Uncle Dick?" Even though Wootton wasn't his un-cle, Jess had called him that from their first meeting—everyone did.

"Hell, boy. Been doin' good, 'cept the years keep on passin' by. Seems like only yestcrday I took them nine thousand sheep across the desert to Californy, an' that's been a considerable while ago."

Jess nodded. "Yeah, it has, old-timer; 1852, if I recollect right."

Wootton nodded. "You got it right, son."

Jess pushed his hat off his forehead and wiped sweat. "What you gonna charge me a head to bring my herd across yore pass."

Wootton looked at him through narrowed lids. "You said 'your' herd. They for a fact yore cows?"

Jess nodded and smiled. "Half o' them are. All set to go ranchin' up Montana way. The other half b'longs to a rancher, Thaddeus Bishop, down in the Big Bend. Hell, he even sent his daughter along. He don't know it yet, but I ain't sendin' her back. When he finds out I done married her—that is, if I can solve a problem I got ridin' my shoulders—he's gonna pitch a ring-tailed fit."

Wootton slapped his leg and laughed. "Well, hot ding it, boy, git the problem solved." He sobered. " 'Bout them prices you askin' 'bout." He pulled a pad from his shirt pocket, licked the lead on his pencil, and figured a moment. "Tell you what, Jess. You bring yore cows across, an' if you promise to accept it as a weddin' present, I'll charge you a nickel a head, ten cents fer them other cows you got with you."

Sanford studied the old man a moment. "Old-timer, reckon you know it'll be right easy to find use for that money. Shore now, I'll accept it, an' if I cain't find some way to solve my problem so's I can get married, I'll send it back to you."

Wootton was shaking his head before Sanford finished his sentence. "Naw, young feller, you ain't sendin' nothin' back." He rocked a couple of times, fast. " 'Sides that, you gonna find a way to get yore marryin' done." He straightened in his chair. "Now tell me when you figger to git yore herd to the New Mexico side. Gotta hold up traffic on this side 'till you git yore last cow down.'' He rocked a couple more times, pulled out his pipe, packed and lit it. "You an' Joe Bob still partnered up?"

Jess nodded. "Yeah, Uncle Dick, figger me an' Joe Bob's gonna go all the way together. Leastways *I* ain't never gonna split from *him*." The sight of Wootton smoking made him want to also. He soon blew a great cloud of smoke into the sharp mountain air. "Uncle Dick, allow four days 'fore you shut down the traffic here''—he hesitated— "no, make it five. Gonna rest the herd overnight on the other side, then drive 'em straight through without stoppin'. Figger it'll take twelve, maybe fourteen hours." He'd been leaning against one of the support posts of the porch roof. He straightened, stepped toward the hitch rail, and stopped.

"Met Slade over yonder outside o' Raton. If he gives me any trouble that'll make me late in crossin' the pass, I'll send a rider over to let you know."

Wootton took a great drag on his pipe and squinted up toward the peaks. "Tell you somethin', Jess, I don't figger Slade to give you no trouble. I reckon you got somewhere 'tween twenty-five and forty men with you." He shook his head. "Slade might mess with you if you had somethin' short o' half the men you got, but he ain't no damned fool. He'll leave you alone. Yore trouble's gonna happen ten, maybe fifteen miles north o' here."

"How you figger?"

"They's a man out yonder a ways, name o' Rafe Burns; ain't got no ranch, no cows, no nothin' but a bunch o' no-goods ridin' with 'im. Dollar to a dime he'll try to cut yore herd. He'll claim you're crossin' his grass. He'll either try to cut yore herd, or charge you a dollar a head for cros-sin'."

Blood surged to Sanford's head. The hairs on the back

of his neck felt like they stood straight out. "He own that grass, Wootton?"

"Nope. Don't figger he owns more'n the shirt on his back, an' he probably stole that."

Sanford nodded. "He won't cause me no trouble, Uncle Dick." He strode to his horse and toed the stirrup. "See you in five or six days." He tipped his hat and kneed his horse southward.

He camped that night on the flats east of Raton, not even tempted to go into the small settlement for a drink. Two days later, tired, dirty, unshaven, he rode into the light of his own campfire in time to hear Ransome call the crew to supper and see Hope, standing, staring into the darkness toward him. A pang of guilt speared his chest for the way he'd been avoiding her.

16

Hope came to him as soon as he dismounted. He shied from her. "Girl, I wouldn't git much closer. Figger I smell right down gamey; worse'n that even, figger I'm overripe. Ain't been close to water in 'bout three days."

So quiet the men couldn't hear, she said, "Jess, I don't care about that, I just want to be close to you. Seems like you've been gone a month, and you didn't spend any time with me before you left. What's wrong, Jess? Everything seemed so perfect for a day or two, then you acted like you didn't want any part of me."

He stared into her eyes a long moment. "Hope, I want all the same things you do, but, girl, I got some troubles you don't know 'bout, troubles that'll only bring you heartbreak. Won't do me no good neither. Figgered it best to let things rest awhile."

"You makin' all the decisions about us, Jess? Don't I have anything to say about it?"

Like a hammer it hit him how selfish he'd been in not allowing her any input into what their actions should be. "Aw, Hope, I'm right sorry 'bout the way I been treatin' you. We need to talk, then you need to think about it awhile, an' if you send me packin', I'll understand—but, girl, ain't no way I'm gitten no closer to you than I am right now until after I have a bath an' shave.'' He smiled. ''Figger the way I smell; you'd send me down the trail anyway.''

She studied him a moment. ''All right, Jess, I'll wait, but I'll tell you right now, there's nothin' you could tell me, nothin' you could have done—oh—oh well, just plain nothin' that would steer me away from you. Get some supper and sit as close to me as you wish.''

When he went to the stew pot, Ransome yelled to the crew. ''Hey, men, Sanford ain't doin' like he said. Said he'd never ask us to do anything he wouldn't do. Well, boys, the boss ain't been nowhere what might look like it helped him shave or bathe; fact is, he ain't fit company for a polecat.''

Sanford gave his cook a sour glance and looked at the grinning men. ''Tell you how it is, men. It's twenty miles to the Canadian and they ain't no guarantee water's in it, so reckon you jest gonna have to put up with me like this for a while. Still goes for all o' us: when they's water, we all take a bath—cold or hot.''

The kid grinned. ''Reckon we'll be careful to stay upwind of you, boss.''

They joshed while Jess ate, then he called them around. ''Tell you how we gonna pull off driving' this bunch o' dumb critters across the pass. Even though some o' you've been up the trail before, ain't none o' you ever took a herd over Raton Pass. The trail's narrow, winding, with sheer drops sometimes of a thousand feet or more, so we gonna be ready as we can.'' He stood, went to the fire, and filled his coffee cup.

When again seated among the men, he continued, ''The day before we get there, we gonna drive 'em hard, an' drive 'em long. We'll start a couple hours 'fore daylight—get 'em tired by a hour or two after sundown.

"Next mornin' I want 'em up an' movin' by sunup. We gonna get to the bottom o' that pass on the other side by soon after sundown. Lord help us if we get caught after dark on the side o' that mountain. That means drive 'em hard again. Don't want none o' you 'tween the edge of the cliff an' them cows. We'll be lucky if we don't lose animals over the side, don't want to lose none o' you." He took a swallow of his coffee. "I'm gonna be just ahead o' that old brindle steer. I'll be the only point rider. All o' you will ride drag, an' if for any reason them cows decide to turn and stampede back the way they come—ride like hell. I'll do the same if they come at me."

Sanford took a fistful of dirt and scrubbed out his bowl. "All right, men, let's get some sleep."

When he stood to put his bowl and spoon away, Hope said, "Didn't even shy away from you—dirt, sweat, or nothin'."

Jess grinned down at her. "Now, ma'am, reckon you could say that's pure-dee true love."

Sanford slept well that night. He realized the thing that bothered him most was not talking his problem over with Hope, and now that he'd made up his mind to share his secret with her, the tension left him.

The next morning at breakfast, he told the men about Black Jack Slade and about Rafe Burns. "From right this minute, I want your weapons clean, fully loaded, an' close to hand—an', men, don't shy away from using them if we get in trouble."

Riding out ahead of the herd, about fifteen miles south of Raton, Sanford watched a cloud of dust draw ever closer. Finally, men—he guessed about a dozen of them—led the cloud toward him. He soon made out the handsome figure of Slade riding a few yards ahead of his men. Jess slipped the thong from the hammer of his .44 and eased it in its holster to make sure it wouldn't stick.

Still out of six-shooter range, Slade held his hand up, palm outward, in the universal sign of peace. Sanford had heard enough about the man to know he didn't lie. He relaxed.

When Slade rode to within earshot, Sanford yelled, "Howdy. Know this ain't no friendly visit. What brings you to see me?"

First, Slade glanced at the approaching cattle, then nodded with a satisfied smile. "Come to see if you'll sell me fifty, maybe a hundred head of your critters—if the price is right. Eagle's Nest and Red River are running shy of beef, an' we're getting tired of venison and elk. Figured with you in charge, your cows'd be in good shape, no tallow run off them." He again glanced at the approaching longhorns, nodded, and said, "I was right."

Sanford studied Slade a moment, wondering why the outlaw chief hadn't simply brought enough men to take what he wanted. Too, Sanford could use the money the cattle would bring. His own men would need a few cartwheels in their jeans when they came upon towns where they could buy a drink, or time with a woman. Bishop had given him money for *his* men. He nodded.

"All right, Slade. I'll sell you anything up to a hundred head."

Slade hooked a leg around his saddle horn. Now the dickering would begin.

"Give you twenty bucks a head, and I'll take a hundred head."

Sanford allowed a slight smile to crease his lips. "I figured on twenty-eight. Sorry, Slade, cain't let 'em go for that."

"Twenty-two fifty," Slade countered.

Sanford could see the big bandit was enjoying the game. "Tell you what, Slade, bein's you want a hundred head, I'll let 'em go for twenty-five." He grinned. "Only reason for that is the 'rithmetic is easy. Twenty-five hundred dollars."

Slade frowned and shook his head. "Hell, and they call me a bandit." He pulled a sack of Bull Durham from his shirt pocket, twirled a cigarette, put fire to it, and smoked it down to about half before he looked at Sanford through slitted lids. "Sanford, we coulda rode in here and took what cows we needed, but we played it honest with you. Why're you tryin' to rob me like this?"

Sanford let go of the laugh he'd been holding back. "Jack, you and I both know you could of took 'em, but you sat back there in your den an' figgered how many men it'd cost you, so you reckoned it'd be cheaper to pay some o' your ill-gotten *dinero* for them." He sobered. "Twenty-five a head is my final offer."

Slade's eyes crinkled at the corners, a smile threatening. "Sanford, I oughta only buy fifty head and see if you could cipher the total amount." He shook his head. "But I'm not as mean as you've probably heard. All right, a hundred head it is, at twenty-five a head."

Sanford glanced at the sun. It showed about four o'clock. "Gonna have to make sure the hundred head are all my cows. Probably take 'til 'bout dark to cut 'em out, then I'd just as soon y'all bed 'em down out a ways an' you an' your men stay for supper—stay the night, for that matter, so's we can watch you."

Slade grinned. "Hell, Jess—don't you trust us?"

"Jack, I figger I got a choice. Sorta like what would I do if I had a pack o' lobo wolves in my midst. Would I want 'em out yonder in the dark, surroundin' me where I couldn't see 'em, or would it be better to have 'em in here where I could keep my eyes on 'em?'' He raised his eyebrows. "Figger I like yore company so much I'd like you right in the middle o' my camp."

Slade pulled his leg from around his saddle horn and nodded. "We'll accept your invite, Jess." He slanted a sardonic grin. "Bet I sleep better'n you do."

When the deal was closed with a handshake and the money exchanged hands, Slade's men helped cut out a hundred head and drove them about a mile before circling them. They left two men with the small herd.

The atmosphere around the fire that night was relaxed, the men joshing each other, some playing poker, a few gathered around a waddy with a guitar, singing songs, and others sit quietly talking. Hope, sitting close to Jess, said, her voice soft, "Jess, that man, Slade, it's hard to believe he's an outlaw. He's such a gentleman, he has a sense of humor, and he's one of the most handsome men I've met."

"Hey now, girl, you gonna make me jealous." Sanford laughed. "Jest jokin', Hope. Yeah, he's all you say, but you could have added one more word—dangerous. I'd hate to cross 'im."

"Where'd you know him, Jess?"

"Met 'im when Mr. Charley Goodnight sold 'im some cows last time I was up this way. That's why I wasn't too worried 'bout 'im." He laughed. "My opinion, he's a right likable *hombre*."

Soon everyone turned into their blankets, and the next morning before leaving, Slade gave Sanford his second warning about Rafe Burns. "You get a chance to cut 'im down, Sanford, do it. Give 'im a chance and he'll backshoot you."

Sanford nodded. "I'll watch 'im, Jack. Thanks for the business, *and* the warning."

"*De nada*. 'Tis nothing, amigo." He tipped his hat and he and his men rode to their small herd.

Sanford looked at Twilley. "This's the day. Drive 'em hard. I want these cows tireder'n a brushpopper after a month in the chaparral."

Twilley nodded. "You got it, boss."

The Canadian River, only a mile or two to their west, gave them trouble. The herd tried to veer toward the water, especially when they grew tired and thirsty. The drovers stayed busy pushing bunch quitters back into line. Every rider changed horses twice that day, and before it was done, Sanford wished he could change riders. His men wore themselves to a nubbin by the time he motioned Joe Bob to circle them up and start them milling. They made a dry camp.

For each of the past few days, Sanford had spent fourteen or more hours in the saddle. When he filled his plate that night with beans, bacon, and a couple of hardtack biscuits, he shuffled to Hope's side and lowered himself to the ground with a groan. Hope slanted him a look. A frown creased her forehead. "Jess, you're wearing yourself to a frazzle. Your cheeks're gaunt. You've lost weight, and I'm downright worried about you."

He sighed. "Ma'am, you figger some way to do my job easier, let me know." He gave her a tired smile, knowing there was no sparkle to it. "Once we get these cows the other side o' Trinidad, things'll get easier."

Still looking worried, she stood and poured him a cup of coffee. "If you don't ease up, you'll make yourself sick."

"Hope, I ain't doin' nothin' no other trail boss ain't done. A bath, a good night's sleep, an' a chance to hold you close to me'll make me a new man."

Hope smiled, a bit whimsically to Jess's thinking. "Sure

would like to see that 'new man' show up pretty soon, cowboy. I'm just downright hurtin' to be held close to him.'' She twisted to look right at him. "When you gonna tell me what trouble you got ridin' your shoulders?"

"Soon's we put a Mr. Rafe Burns on our back trail."

She nodded. "That's all the time you got. If you don't tell me by then, I'm gonna tell the crew you walked me out in the dark an' took advantage o' me."

Sanford had just taken a swallow of coffee. He jerked forward and spewed it out past his boots, then coughed. "Y-you wouldn't do that . . . would you?"

Hope laughed, deep in her chest. "You know I wouldn't, but I'll think of something about as bad." He believed her.

The next morning, Jess had the men up at three o'clock and the herd moving by four. He figured by first light they could be onto the narrowed trail winding up the side of the mountain. Tired as he'd been the night before, he'd lain awake and thought of ways to make the drive safer. He'd never heard of it being done before, but he decided to throw a loop around the old brindle steer's horns and lead it at the pace he wanted the herd to move, figuring he could keep the steer solidly on the trail and the rest of the herd would follow. And if he could get them on fairly level ground while daylight held—he might not lose any cattle.

As soon as the cows moved well, still on relatively flat ground, Jess tossed a loop around the brindle's wide horns, then took a dally around his saddle horn. He'd thought to tie hard and fast to the horn, but decided against it. If the cantankerous old steer decided to bolt, Sanford wanted to make sure he could turn the home end of his rope loose and get the hell away. When his rope settled around the horns and Sanford took up the slack, the big mossyhorn shook his head a couple of times, looked like he'd contest who was in charge, but then settled in to follow. He didn't even object to the fast pace Sanford set.

Leading the brindle steer, Sanford kept eyeing the slopes above. A lot of rock sat clinging to the sides of the mountain by a most precarious hold, but they'd been there for centuries. He hoped some tiny root hadn't grown in between any of them and the more solid cliff, or that water hadn't seeped between some of them and the cliff wall during the winter and frozen, thus loosening them. A rockfall in the middle of the already-skittish herd might set them to running.

Along with the climb, the vegetation changed every hundred or so feet. The cedar brakes gave way to pine, the air thinned, and by the time he topped out at over seven thousand feet, he'd pulled his sheepskin from his bedroll and slipped it on.

Uncle Dick, true to his word, had stopped all traffic from the Trinidad side, and Jess had the whole trail for his cattle. To make sure, he'd sent Langford ahead a day and a half earlier to warn Wootton.

Climbing the steep uphill grade had been hard, the cattle had tried to slow and take their time, but Sanford's drovers had kept pushing them, yelling, slapping the hindmost on their rumps, riding their horses close. And in the lead, Sanford had almost had to drag the big brindle steer. Now, over the top, with a downhill grade, the opposite became true—and he was the only rider there to hold them back.

Jess spent much of his time holding back on the lead rope he had around the steer's horns; then, what he feared most happened. About a hundred yards ahead, a boulder about the size of his horse broke loose and roared down the mountainside. It hit the trail and bounded over the cliff to fall several hundred feet to the canyon.

Old Brindle's eyes widened, his nostrils flared, and he

pulled back, fighting the rope, trying to turn in the middle of the trail.

Sanford held the bitter end of the rope, making sure his fingers, or thumb, didn't get between the taut lariat and his saddle horn. There had been many a cowboy who lost fingers or thumb that way. The dally tightened around the horn. The rope pulled back across his thigh, tight, pinning his leg to the saddle. Sanford urged his buckskin ahead. The downhill grade was the only thing that made it possible to overpower the two-thousand-pound steer. He literally dragged the steer for fifty or more feet, then the big brute calmed, seemed to accept there was nothing to fear, and again followed docilely. The mountain air, cold as it was, didn't stop rivulets of nervous sweat from running down Sanford's neck to be soaked up by his shirt collar and neckerchief.

They made better time coming down the Trinidad side than he'd figured. He had the brindle approaching a run when he bottomed out, and when he passed Wootton standing on the porch of his hotel, Sanford yelled, "Be back an' settle up with you, Wootton."

The sun had long ago slipped behind the peaks to the west, but daylight still held. He led the cattle out onto the flats north of town, loosened his rope from Old Brindle, rode to the drag, and told Joe Bob to circle them up and bed them down. Then he headed back to see Uncle Billy. When he came on the wagon, Hope driving, he told her to bring Bessie and spend the night in the hotel; they could bathe and sleep in a feather bed. He didn't have to say it twice. Hope reined the team around and followed.

Back at the hotel, Sanford settled up with Wootton, and added the price of Uncle Dick's best room to the amount, despite Wootton's protests that he add it to his wedding present.

Sanford decided to eat supper at the hotel. Uncle Dick ate with them. Their meal finished, he looked at Jess. "Got somethin' to tell ya, when yore ladies go to bed, boy." He squinted at Hope and Bessie. "Seen Burns this mornin' down in town."

Sanford swept the two women with a glance and again looked at the old trapper. "Spit it out, Wootton, these ladies done shared ever'thing else on this drive."

Wootton looked a little doubtful, pulled his pipe out, packed and lit it, then nodded. "Reckon they have. All right, I'll tell ya right here an' now. Burns wuz sayin' as how he wuz gonna make a whole bunch o' money off'n the big trail herd gonna cross his land—gonna either get money or cows."

Sanford felt his stomach muscles tighten and his neck hair tingle. He gave Wootton a cold smile. "What'd you tell 'im, Uncle Dick?"

The old mountain man laughed. "Told 'im to bring his supper in a paper sack, an' a lantern, 'cause he'd done cut hisself out a sizable job. Told 'im he'd be there all day an' most o' the night an' still wouldn't get the job done.

"He got real ugly lookin'—ain't as though he ain't uglier than hell anytime, but he looked mean, said as how he figgered he wuz fast as any o' you Texas pistoleros. Said he'd handle you." Wootton settled back in his chair. "Told 'im you wasn't no gunslinger, but I heard you never missed what you shot at."

Sanford stared at the table a moment. "Gotta tell ya, I got a right salty crew, Wootton. They don't look for trouble, but ain't none o' 'em takes a step back for nobody. Reckon that's why most o' 'em was down along the Texas border; the Rangers didn't bother 'em long's they kept their hell-raisin' over in Mexico, an' wasn't one o' them scared

of the *federales*.'' He nodded and took a swallow of coffee.
''Let Burns turn his dogs loose.''

Wootton grinned. ''Figgered as much.''

Jess looked at the women. ''Y'all get a good night's rest.
I'm headin' back to the men. Wanta be there case anythin'
happens.''

''We'll go back with you. Two more rifles would help.''

Jess looked at Wootton, grinning. ''What I didn't tell ya,
Uncle Dick, was that my two women were salty as the
men.'' He turned his attention to Hope. ''Naw, y'all get
some rest. Ain't nothin' gonna happen this close to town.''

Hope opened her mouth as though to argue the point,
Jess cut her off. ''That's the way it's gonna be, ladies.''
He stood, tipped his hat, and headed for the door. ''See
y'all in the mornin'.''

As soon as he came within sight of his camp, Sanford
knew something was wrong. The fire blazed brightly when
he figured it would have burned down to glowing embers.
The men all stood, and there were more men there by the
fire than he had on his payroll.

Jess pulled his horse in, still a distance from camp,
slipped his Winchester from its scabbard, stepped from the
saddle, and ground-reined the gelding. The ride from town
allowed his eyes to adjust to the dark. Even though there
was no moon, he could see enough to define dark or moving shapes against the landscape.

He stood, not moving, and searched his surroundings.
When reasonably certain the strangers in camp hadn't left
anyone outside the ring of light, he eased toward the fire.
About fifty yards out he dropped to his belly, then slithered
toward the rear of the chuck wagon. He soon came within
earshot. The visitors had apparently arrived some time ago.

A big, burly, red-haired man was talking. He looked as
though he'd never trimmed the bushy beard flowing onto

his chest, and from the looks of him, he hadn't had a bath in a month. Sanford sniffed, thinking he could smell the man from where he stood behind the chuck wagon.

Red asked, ''Where's your boss? You said he'd be back soon after sundown.''

Joe Bob answered, ''He mighta stayed in town for supper. On this drive he don't answer to us, an' ain't none o' us asked him.''

Red turned his attention to Joe Bob. ''Well, I see we got us a smartmouthed nigger here. When I want anything outta you, I'll kick it out.''

Langford stepped forward. ''I'm going to tell you something, an' I'm only going to say it once. We have no 'niggers' in our crew. Every man here is a *man*. We draw no other distinction between them, and if you want to continue doing so, I reckon I'll have to teach you how the cow ate the cabbage.''

Red—Sanford now figured him to be Rafe Burns— looked Langford up and down, then pinned him with a look that Sanford, even from where he stood, could tell dripped poison. He guessed the man outweighed Langford by at least fifty pounds. Burns gripped his fists into a ball. ''You'd fight me? Man, I eat boys like you for a snack.''

Langford grinned—and unleashed a right that whistled before reaching the point of Red's chin. The big man lifted off the ground an inch or two and landed flat of his butt. He shook his head, tried to roll to his knees, and Langford drove his boot toe into the side of the huge man's head. Burns dropped like a sack of meal. His men reached for their weapons, but found themselves staring into the maw of twenty-nine six-shooters.

Sanford eased his finger off the trigger of his Winchester and again watched and listened to what went on. Joe Bob looked at Langford. '' 'Preciate you steppin' in foah me,

Mr. Langford.'' He looked at Burns's men. ''Jest so's you'll know, this herd belongs one fourth to me. So when that bag o' cow pies there wakes up, tell 'im foah me, I'm a rich 'nigger.' Got more'n he'll ever have from honest work. Now pick up yoah boss, get 'im outta here, an' if you come back, he'll be dealin' with Mr. Sanford, Mr. Langford, or me; most likely all three. But first, bein' a careful sort man, reckon y'all better drop yoah gun belts.'' Without looking at any of the men, Joe Bob added, ''Six or seven o' you pull their long guns off their horses an' stack 'em here by the fire. We'll take our pick after they gone.''

Sanford watched until Burns's men rode off with him across his saddle, then he stepped from behind the wagon. ''Nice work, men. I shoulda stayed over at Wootton's place, would have if I'da knowed you had ever' thing at the end of a six-shooter. Did Burns say what he had in mind?''

Langford shook his head. ''Wouldn't say 'less you were here.''

Jess lowered the hammer on his rifle and rested the stock on his boot toe. ''Reckon we know what he wanted. He wanted to make it appear legal—like he owned the grass we gonna cross.'' He walked to the fire, poured himself a cup of coffee, and swept his men with a glance. ''Men, we not givin' him even one cow, or one dollar. He'll be back. Maybe not in the mornin', or even the next day, but he'll be back. We'll be ready.''

17

SANFORD HAD THE men get the herd up and moving by daylight with orders to shoot anything that even looked like it wasn't friendly. "I'm going in and bring Hope and Bessie back. Keep 'em movin', we'll catch up with you."

He collected the ladies and was a mile out of town when a lean, lanky man rode from the side of the trail and held up his hand. Sanford thumbed the thong off the hammer of his Colt. "Howdy, stranger. What can I do for you?"

The lanky man sat his horse for a moment in silence. "You cain't do nothin' for me, mister. But you can do something for yourself. Turn that wagon around and head back to town. Mr. Burns is gonna cut your herd, or collect a dollar a head. Either one, you're gonna be better off if you ain't around. Your crew made him some sort o' mad last night and he ain't of a mind to put up with no nonsense."

"Move outta the trail, stranger, an' you won't get hurt." Sanford said the words quietly, calmly, but his guts churned and the blood pushed at his brain. He'd had about all of this sort of thing he was of a mind to put up with.

"Don't figure I'm gonna let you ride on out there. If you don't want your womenfolk in danger, turn around."

Sanford had enough, and he wasn't going to jeopardize Hope and Bessie. His right side was toward the rider. Without further words, his hand flicked to his .44, drew, and sent flame spitting toward the lanky rider.

The skinny one, at the last minute apparently, saw that Sanford was going to kill him. He went for his gun, but was too late. Sanford's slug knocked him from the saddle.

Jess, knowing his eyes were hard as agates, looked at Hope. "Take the wagon toward the herd. I'm gonna find out who this ranny is. He'll live another few minutes, then I'll be along."

Hope's face was white, her lips trembling. "You didn't give him a chance, Jess—no warning. Aren't you even gonna bury him?"

Jess stared at her a moment, white-hot anger still burning his gut, a red haze clouded his vision. "Tell you somethin', woman. I ain't buryin' 'im. I ain't doin nothin with 'im. He's jest one we won't have to kill out at the herd. Now ride."

Watching her drive the wagon off, and then look back at him, Sanford felt his anger cool, bit by bit. He'd not been this angry since he whipped Simon Bauman.

It was now he came to know himself a little better. No one thing ever carried him to the point of killing. Small, related things built resentment in him until finally one caused him to explode. That waddy lying there in the trail had been the trigger. Sanford checked the man's pockets, pulled a letter from his coat, found a few dollars in loose change in the man's trousers, and unbuckled the gun belt from around the waddy's waist. He then kicked his buckskin into a lope.

Back at the herd, he told his men to ride with hammers on full chambers. "We're not gonna palaver with Burns. I'll let him ride in an' tell me what kind o' deal he wants to make, but that's the end of it. If any of his men so much as lets a hand hang close to a handgun, kill 'im.''

Joe Bob studied his friend a long moment. ''Jess, we cain't just kill men without they go for their guns.''

''The hell we cain't. They got more men than we do. Our men gonna be spread out along the flanks of our cows. Burns's men'll have the advantage. We need an edge, an' gettin' our hardware unlimbered 'fore they do will give us some of the edge we need. *Savvy, amigo*?''

Two days passed without any trouble, then midmorning of the third day, a cloud of dust approached. Sanford twisted in his saddle to find Langford. ''Take four men with rifles and get in the chuck wagon. Don't fire 'til I do, then make every shot count. Joe Bob, take another four men and get in the wagon with Hope an' Bessie. Make 'em lie down in the bed an' don't let nobody get close to that wagon. Twilley, bring eight or ten men up here to side me. Leave the rest with the herd.''

He felt rather than saw his men carry out his orders, then from the corners of his eyes he saw he had been joined by several of his drovers.

Burns rode to within twenty or so feet of Sanford. ''That's close enough, Burns. What're you here for?''

Burns squinted at Sanford. ''Who the hell are you?''

''I'm the man you was lookin' for last night when my *segundo* damn near tore your head off. I'm Jess Sanford, an' I ask again, what you want?''

''You're on my grass, Sanford. I charge a dollar a head for cows crossing my range, or I cut your herd for enough to pay the toll. Today, I'm paying fifteen dollars a head so's you can afford the toll.''

Dust from the horses ridden by Burns and his crew rolled over them, enveloping them in a cloud, but not enough that

Sanford lost sight of Burns's men and the hands they had hanging by their side.

Sanford felt like his head was being squeezed in a vise, and he would swear later the hair on the back of his neck stood straight out. Blood rushed to his neck. "Burns, you own this here land we ridin' across? If you do, I want to see proof of ownership. You show me that an' you can cut my herd. Otherwise turn your horses and get the hell outta here."

Burns's men reined their horses farther apart. "You men pull your horses close again, or I'm gonna make one helluva lot o' empty saddles 'tween you." They closed ranks. "Now, Burns, let's see your deed or title to this land."

Burns's eyes got mean, showing red where the whites should be. "I don't carry no title around with me, but this's my land." He looked at his men. "Cut out two hundred head."

"You make a move to cut *one* cow outta that herd an' we'll empty every saddle you got. You don't own this land, you don't run no cows on it. You ain't got a claim to bein' no kind o' rancher. Now get the hell outta my way. We're comin' through."

Burns's face turned a deep red to match his eyeballs. Veins stood out in his neck. "I'll be damn . . . ." His hand flashed to his side.

Jess had his thumb hooked in his gun belt. When Burns broke his sentence off, Sanford's hand made the short move to his holster. His first shot crossed Burns's hurried shot. A beelike buzz sounded in his ear, along with a sting on his earlobe. His shot punched a black hole in the center of Burns's chest, knocking him backward in the saddle. By the time Sanford saw the hole, he'd already thumbed off his second shot. It caught Burns over his right eye.

All around Sanford, guns fired. He picked a rider drawing a bead on the kid. Sanford's third shot hit the herd cutter at the same time the kid's did. Two holes showed in the rider's shirt. He slid off the side of his saddle, his foot caught in the stirrup. His horse dragged him a few feet and stopped.

Silence, only the creak of saddle leather breaking it, fell on the group, then the click of fresh shells being fed into cylinders, and a soft curse. The smell of cordite hung heavy in the still air. Horses, wall-eyed with fear, reins still wrapped around their downed riders' hands, milled about with empty saddles. Not one member of Burns's crew still sat his horse.

Sanford swept his men with a glance. "Any our men down?"

Ben Quaid twirled a cigarette, swung his head from side to side, then looked at Sanford. "Nope, but a couple o' them are lookin' mighty faint."

Sanford next looked for Joe Bob, and Langford, then remembered he'd had them assigned to the wagons, and they'd not been in the gunfight. His gaze fell on Twilley. "You hurt?"

Twilley shook his head. "Ain't hurt, jest scared spitless. What you need?"

"Check the men. See how many needs doctorin'. Cain't believe we come outta that without gettin' men killed."

Twilley shook his head. "Hard to believe, boss, but reckon the difference wuz, we wuz ready for 'em. Any herds been up this way before musta give in to them. They didn't 'spect us to fight." Twilley neck-reined his horse to leave, then stopped. "Boss, you ain't gonna be so purty no more. Burns pierced yore ear. Reckon so's you could wear a earring should you take a notion." He squinted at the side of Sanford's head for a closer look. "Nope, boss, he didn't pierce it, he notched it. Maybe figured on claimin'

you b'longed in his herd.'' He grinned. ''Any rate, it's bleedin' right smart.'' He rode away chuckling.

Sanford had two wounded men. One with a rib crease,
and another with a slug through his thigh. Hope wanted to
tend to Sanford's ear first, but he wouldn't hear of it. ''Take
care o' them hurt worse'n me.'' When she got around to
him, if he hadn't known better, he would have thought he'd
been shot straight through the brisket the way she cooed
and clucked over him, sort of like a mother hen with her
chicks.

When Hope and Bessie finished bandaging the wounded,
they went to the water barrel to wash their hands. Bessie
slung the water from her hands and looked at Hope. ''Why
foah you reckon Jess sent Joe Bob back here with us 'stead
o' keepin' him at his side?''

Hope dried her hands, wondering the same thing. When
she thought she had it figured out, she said, ''Tell you the
truth, Bessie, I think Jess believes Joe Bob's got a soft spot
in him that mighta got him killed. Your man doesn't like
to hurt anybody.'' She nodded. ''Yeah, he'll kill a Injun
quick as scat, but he knows they're gonna try to kill him.
But in a case like today, I think Jess figured Joe Bob might
wait to see if they meant him harm. That woulda give them
the first shot, an' that might a been enough.''

Bessie wiped the rest of the water from her hands on her
skirt. ''Well, I tell you, girl, that Jess ain't never gonna be
accused of waitin' on nobody. Why, the way he shot that
rider two days ago, an' then not even buryin' 'im—I'm
tellin' you, child, yore man is downright *hard*.''

Hope smiled, knowing the tenderness showed through.
She nodded. ''He is that, Bessie. He's hard where it counts.
He says we're going to a hard land, and if we're gonna
survive, we gotta be tough. I'm gonna be right there with
'im when he needs me.''

Bessie moaned deep in her throat. "Umm, umm, shore do wisht Joe Bob would give me the chance to be his kind o' woman, but, girl, he still ain't said nothin' 'bout wantin' me. You reckon he still does?"

Hope stopped and faced Bessie. "I think more than ever he wants you for his woman, Bessie. Despite what Jess told him about gettin' us safe in the wagon, he would of sided Jess if he hadn't wanted you safe more'n he wanted to side his partner."

"Lordy, Hope, you do make it sound so good to me."

Hope decided right then she was going to do something about Bessie's problem. Joe Bob sure wasn't moving very fast.

They drove the herd hard the rest of the day to get away from the earlier killings. They had collected the guns and valuables of Burns's crew, buried the dead, thrown the herd cutters' horses in with their cavvy, and again headed northward.

That night by the fire, Hope bided her time. Finally, when Joe Bob threw the grounds from his cup and stood to go to his blankets, she cornered him. " 'Fore you head for bed, Joe Bob, I gotta talk to you." She looked at the men close by and pointed away from camp. "This's gotta be said kinda private."

Joe Bob cast Sanford a worried glance, like he figured Jess would come to his rescue, but he followed Hope.

Out away from the firelight, and beyond earshot, Hope turned squarely to face him. "Joe Bob, gonna lay it on the line with you. We got some things need gettin' cleared up."

"Yes'm. Don't know what they could be, but if you say we gotta clear 'em up, reckon we gonna do it."

"You got that right, cowboy. Now, gonna get right down to the bone. Why do you dislike Bessie so much?"

"Lordy, ma'am, whatever give you that idee. My, my,

she means more to me than anybody. B'lieve I love her even more'n I do you an' Jess. Fact is I know I do, an' that's a whole bunch o' lovin'.''

"Then why haven't you said anything to 'er 'bout it?''

Joe Bob pushed his hat off his forehead, shuffled his feet a couple of times, pushed his hat back on straight, and stammered, "Why, Miss Hope, reckon I'm jest pure-dee scared she'll tell me she don't like me at all. Don't reckon I could stand that. Long's I don't say nothin', an' she don't say nothin', then I can wish for what I want. But once I tell 'er, an' she tells me she don't like me none at all, that'll end it. I won't be able to go 'round 'er, sit by 'er, won't be able to do nothin' after that.''

Hope didn't let up. "Joe Bob, she ain't gonna tell you nothin' but that she feels the same way you do. She told me so. Now, I'm gonna give you till after we eat supper tomorrow night to say something to 'er, an' if you don't, I got somethin' in mind pretty bad for you.''

Hope had no idea what she could do if Joe Bob didn't do as she asked, but he didn't know that, and he'd worry about it, and with the worry, he'd work up enough courage to talk to Bessie.

Joe Bob looked toward the fire. "Reckon we better be gettin' back, Miss Hope. Please don't do whatever it is you gonna do to me. I promise to talk with Bessie soon's I can get away from y'all after supper tomorrow. Yes, ma'am, I shore do promise.''

Hope struggled to choke off a laugh. "All right, Joe Bob. You know how it is—tomorrow night.''

"Yes'm.''

The next day during their nooning, they crossed the Cucheras River and took a break for the cows to drink and for all the crew to take a bath. After their nooning, they put Walsenburg behind, now heading just to the east of

Pueblo. Sanford figured it to be about a four-day drive, much of it dry.

That night, soon after supper, Joe Bob took Bessie's plate and cleaned it and her eating utensils. When he handed them back, he stood in front of her, wadding the brim of his hat into a tight curl. She looked up at him. "What is it, Joe Bob? If you don't give that hat a rest, you're gonna ruin it."

He glanced from Bessie to Hope, who was carefully studying the bottom of her cup. He again looked at Bessie. "Ma'am, you an' me's gotta have a talk. Gotta talk sort o' private like, so if'n you'll jest git up an' walk with me, I'd be mighty beholden."

Bessie looked at Hope, shrugged, stood, and placed her hand on Joe Bob's arm. "All right, big man, let's go talk."

They walked well beyond the perimeter of firelight, and farther, until the voices from camp dwindled to a muted hum. Bessie turned to face him. "All right. No one can hear us here. What you got to talk 'bout?"

Joe Bob swallowed, trying to rid himself of the lump in his throat. If Hope was wrong, he didn't know what he'd do. Maybe pack his possibles bag, roll his blanket, and ride out. He didn't think he could be around Bessie knowing she didn't want him. "Well, it's like this, ma'am. Ever since me an' Jess wuz down yonder at the Circle B an' I first seen you, with you stayin' clear o' them other cowboys sniffin' 'round you, I got a terrible hankerin' to . . ." He choked, wondering what to say next.

"Yes, Joe Bob, you got a terrible hankerin' to do what— an' it better not be what all them others had a hankerin' for."

"Oh Lordy, Miss Bessie, ain't nothin' like that. Why, I done whupped up on one o' them riders what said what he wanted to do with you." He looked at the ground, shuffled his feet, and decided whatever she said couldn't be worse than standing here stammering and stuttering like an idiot. "Well, ma'am, reckon what *I* hanker for is to spend the rest o' my life with you." There, he'd said it. Now it was up to her.

Bessie pinned him with a look that could have punched a hole in a cast-iron stove. "An', Joe Bob Brown, just how you 'spectin' to do that? You figgerin' to git me in yo bed without a parson saying somethin' to tie us together?"

Joe Bob swallowed again. It didn't help. "Lordy, Miss Bessie, I ain't never had no thoughts that wuzn't right down Christian 'bout you." He shook his head. "No, ma'am. I figgered if you'd say you'd have me, I'd hunt us up a preacher man when we get to Cheyenne an' have him do whatever he had to do to keep yore paw from huntin' me down. Ain't too sure he won't no way."

Bessie clapped her hands to her hips. "What you want, somebody to do yore washin', iron yo clothes, cook for you, clean yore house—or is there somethin' more you want to tell me?"

Joe Bob rolled his eyes to the heavens, wishing for help. What was he supposed to say? He thought he'd said it all. "No, ma'am, that ain't all I want. Ever since I got to lovin' you so much, it jest don't seem like I can live without you."

Abruptly, Bessie melted into a softer, sort of caring woman. Joe Bob wondered what he'd said to change her. She put her hand on his arm. "What'd you say, big man, you say you got to lovin' me?"

"Why, yes, ma'am. That's the reason I want you so bad, 'cause I love you."

So soft he barely heard her, she said, "I love you, too, Joe Bob Brown. Jest didn't think you was ever gonna get around to tellin me' what I wanted to hear." She stepped closer to him, and not waiting for him to pull her to him, she stepped into his arms.

When they walked into the firelight, Hope slanted them a sidewise glance. They walked arm in arm, close, and didn't seem to know anyone else was in the world. Hope smiled. That was one more problem taken care of. Now she wondered what horrible thing it was that rode Jess's shoulders.

Long after the rest of the hands were in their blankets, Joe Bob sat by the fire. He had a pad of paper, would write awhile, lick the tip of his pencil, and again write. Hope wondered what he was doing, then passed it off as being part of the studying Jess and Joe Bob had vowed to do.

But Joe Bob wasn't studying. The letter he wrote was hard because he didn't know how to keep from giving Jess's whereabouts away. He decided to tell the truth—to a point.

18

THEY PUT PUEBLO, Colorado Springs, and Denver behind. Summer had taken a hard hold on the land, creek beds dry, grass browned, the cattle thinner. If his herd had not been longhorns, Jess would have worried.

Sanford slowed the drive even more. He wanted Bishop's cattle to sell at peak weight, and his own to get to Montana with enough tallow on their bones to pull them through the winter.

Scouting ahead, he found water in the Little Thompson River, about three days south of Fort Collins. He tested the wind. It blew from the south, and as long as it stayed that way, the cattle wouldn't smell water and stampede toward it. He kneed the buckskin back toward the herd.

He cautioned the men to keep the cows strung out, but to let them run when they smelled water. "Don't try to head 'em. They gonna run til they're belly-deep in that water." He urged his horse toward the drag to tell Hope and Bessie to stay behind.

Before he again headed for the point, Hope gave him that straight-on look. "Jess, it's 'bout time you tell me what kind o' trouble you got."

He frowned, rumpled the gelding's mane, and looked her

in the eye. "Reckon tonight after supper'll be good a time as any. That way, when you figger you don't want nothin' to do with me, you can head back to Texas with Langford."

Hope didn't break their gaze. "Cowboy, anything short of woman beatin' you ain't gonna get rid o' me."

Sanford gasped. "Aw no, ma'am, ain't nothing near bad as that, but it's almighty bad." He nodded and tipped his hat. "Tell you 'bout it tonight." He rode toward the point.

That night, with the cows full of water and every member of the crew shaved—those that had whiskers, that is—and bathed, a sense of well-being settled over the camp. Jess marveled at the difference being clean made in one's attitude. The crew joshed, kidded, laughed, and sang. He swallowed the last of his coffee and looked at Hope. "You ready?"

She threw out what remained of her coffee and stood. "Let's go."

When they left the camp, Sanford felt every eye on them, knowing all were wondering what he had to do with Bishop's daughter. Well, after tonight, they wouldn't have reason to wonder. She'd probably shy as clear of him as she would a rattler.

They walked slowly. Jess thought how perfect this could be under different circumstances. Rolling miles of prairie on one side, distant mountains, some still snowcapped, to their west, wind whispering across the plains, bringing with it the smell of grass cured on the stem, the soft lowing of cattle breaking the stillness, and walking close enough to touch the woman he wanted to spend the rest of his life with. But . . . it was not to be.

He slowed, almost dragging his boots through the tough clumps of grass. He stopped, took Hope's elbow, and turned her to face him. Before he could say anything, she was in his arms, pressing her hungry body to his, holding

her lips to be kissed. He looked into her face only a moment
before letting all his hunger, all his feelings make him do
what he figured he had no right to do.

Roughly, he pulled her closer, smothered her eyes, her
face, her lips, her neck with hungry, yearning, burning
kisses. She pushed her body closer to him, as though wanting him to melt within her. Another moment and he
wouldn't be able to control himself. With every ounce of
moral strength in him, Jess grasped her shoulders and
pushed her away. Every breath, every move, every moan
had told him she was ready for him—but he had no right.

Breathless, he stepped back. "Hope, we got no right to
do this. *I* got no right to ask you." She stepped toward him
again.

"No, woman, you got to hear 'bout me, then if you still
want me, when we get to Cheyenne, we'll hunt us up a
preacher man an' get married. *Then,* ma'am, we'll have a
right to do what we wuz awful damned close to doin' jest
now."

Hope's breath came in short irregular gasps. "Jess, I
don't care what you got on your back trail. I want you
now—right now. We can get married in Cheyenne like you
say, but let's belong to each other *now*."

He held her shoulders in an iron grip. "Hope, you're
lettin' yore body tell you what to do, an' in the mornin'
you'd feel shame—an' probably begin to hate me. Neither
of us wants that."

She stopped straining to get closer to him. He felt her
relax and step away. "All right, Jess, let's hear what you've
done that's so terrible."

He started at the beginning and told her, blow by blow,
about the whipping he'd given Simon Bauman. "I run,
Hope. I ain't sure I killed 'im, but figger I did, so I ran.
But I don't care 'bout that, he needed that beatin' more'n

anybody I ever knowed. It's the law I worry 'bout. Wouldn't want you to ever be shamed by what I done. Joe Bob an' me checked ever' post office from Tennessee to here for wanted notices, an' that's what makes me wonder. I ain't never seen a single poster on me. Makes me think—pray, maybe—I didn't beat 'im to death. Maybe he wuz close to checkin' out but didn't.''

He shook his head. "I don't know how to find out. But at any rate, I ain't askin' you to marry up with me, maybe with me wanted by the law.''

Hope stood there, staring at him, then shook her head. "Jess, you ever hear of GTT? It stands for Gone to Texas. After the war, a whole bunch of Southerners came to Texas about two jumps ahead of the law; some of them are now our most prominent citizens. I ain't lettin' nothin' like that keep us apart.''

Sanford looked at her through slitted lids. "Girl, that yore head or yore body talkin' now?''

She shook her head. "Can't rightly say, Jess. Where you're concerned, I gotta say I never been able to separate the two, but it's one thing for sure, my head *and* my body want the same thing.'' She took another step back from him. "Gonna ask you a question an' I want a flat-out-truthful answer.''

"I ain't never gonna lie to you, woman. Ask away.''

She nodded. "All right. Did you mean what you said a while ago? You know, if I still wanted you we'd get married in Cheyenne?''

Still staring at her, he nodded slowly. "Never meant nothing in my life more'n I meant them words. Jest wanted you to know what kind a man you wuz marryin'.''

"I've known what kind o' man you are from the first day I met you, Jess Sanford.'' She again stepped into his arms. This time Jess stopped it before either of them let things get out of hand.

When they walked into camp, Sanford noticed a quiet smile pass between the two women, followed by a nod from Hope. He reckoned he'd put himself through a lot of unnecessary agony.

In his blankets, Jess thought about the rest of the drive to Montana. He'd lose Langford and the Circle B crew, along with half the cattle in Cheyenne. From there it bid to be a long, dry drive if you didn't know where the water holes were. He figured he remembered enough about the country to keep them out of trouble. From Cheyenne they'd cross several streams—the Crow, the Lodgepole, the Chugwater, and others—then out of Douglas, after they left the Lightning River, he hoped for enough sumps to get them to the Belle Fourche, and from there to the Powder River.

Tired, and emotionally wrung out, Jess pushed Hope and the cattle out of mind. Joe Bob had already told him he and Bessie figured on traveling in double harness from Cheyenne on, and the last thing Jess thought on before going to sleep was they'd make it a double wedding. But Cheyenne was still a seven-day drive from where he slept this night.

The eighth day out of Fort Collins, Sanford had the men start the herd milling outside of Cheyenne. He looked at Langford. ''Separatin' the brands oughta be easy. You gather yores over yonder close to that old lightnin'-struck cottonwood. I'll take mine north o' here a quarter mile or so. We'll break out five or ten at a time an' the boys can separate 'em.''

Langford nodded. ''Jess, what you think I should tell Mr. Bishop about Hope?''

Jess shrugged. ''Damned if I know, Langford. He ain't gonna likc it any way you put it to 'im.'' He frowned, staring between his horse's ears. ''Tell you what might work. Ma Bishop backed Hope's play from the very beginnin'. Why don't you tell her, an' let her handle your boss?''

Langford smiled, no humor in it. He shook his head. "No, Sanford. I ride my own broncs. I'll not saddle Mrs. Bishop with a job I oughta do. I'm the one leaving her up here." His smile turned grim. "I'll admit, though, I'd hate like hell to try and stop 'er—you know, take 'er back against her will."

"Wouldn't be just her will, Langford, you'd be fightin' both o' us. You're a good man, but you ain't that good." He slapped Bishop's *segundo* on the shoulder. "C'mon, let's get them cows split up so's you can get yours sold."

Sanford sat his horse off to the side watching the men work the cattle. His look took stock of the shape of the herd. They were nice and sleek, which was somewhat of a wonder considering they'd been driven hard a few days, but slacking off on the pace, letting them graze more than usual had put tallow back on them. He edged his horse over to Langford's again.

"This man you're deliverin' them cows to, you still gotta dicker with him 'bout price?"

"Reckon so. Why?"

Sanford pulled his pipe out and tamped it. "Just thinkin'. Yore cows're in mighty fine shape. He don't give you at least thirty dollars a head, they's buyers here from the East, an' the Union Pacific sittin' yonder, willin' to haul 'em to market. Don't give in too easy on a price."

Langford grinned. "Jess, Mr. Bishop didn't send me up here just to mind his daughter. I've always gotten from one to two dollars a head more for his cows than he'da let 'em go for." He turned his attention to the cattle, then back to Sanford. "While you an' Joe Bob get married, I'd be pleased if you'd let my men watch your cows so all your men can attend the wedding."

Sanford thought about the offer a moment. "Tell you what. You get yore cows sold an' the money sent to Mr. Bishop, then if yore men don't mind, I'll take you up on it. You got any men what're gonna stay up here?"

"Yeah, I got three riders, young fellers with itchy feet. They want to see what's the other side of the hill."

"Think back, Langford. They wuz a time you an' me liked to wander, too. Fact is, Joe Bob an' me don't have to think back too far to remember them times. When we stumbled onto the Circle B, neither one o' us figured that wuz the end of our wanderin' days."

"You'll never be sorry, Jess. Me and my missus have seen some hard times, and a lot of good ones. I wouldn't trade anything to be single again."

"You an' yore men ridin' the rails home?"

Langford nodded. "Yep. Take too long to get there horseback. Riding the big iron horse'll cut into Bishop's profits a little, but not near so bad as payin' us wages while we came home pushin' a horse."

The wedding was a double one, like Sanford figured, and the two couples each got a suite in the hotel. Even if it hadn't been their first night together, Jess and Hope still would have gotten little or no sleep. The crew gave them a charivari, sang songs, beat on pans, fired their six-shooters, and in general raised hell.

Jess rolled to his side, pushed up on an elbow, and looked down into his wife's face, grinning. "Honey, if them waddies only knew it, they're the ones losing sleep. We'da not got much anyway." His face heated up. "I meant sleep—we'da not got much sleep."

Hope chuckled deep in her throat. "I surely hope you meant sleep. I was 'bout to reach for you again."

Jess studied her face. "Lady, I'm here to tell you—reach

for me anytime. But what I wuz 'bout to say, I'll bet I have to bail a few of our men outta the hoosegow in the mornin'.''

Hope chuckled again. "It's mornin' already, Jess. Look at the window. Day's lighting the sky." She smiled. "Wonder where the night went? I'm starved. How's breakfast sound?"

Three hours later, true to his thinking, Jess had to bail five of his punchers out of jail. Hope went with him. "I wish we could take time to spend four or five nights here. It was nice having a warm bath, eating something besides Ransome's cooking, not to mention having you so greedy for me. You didn't push me away once."

"Don't hold your breath until I do, ever again, young lady." Jess paid the marshal to let his men go, then frowned. "I'd hoped to be able to spend more time here, too, but it's pushing into August an' we gotta get these cows to the Powder, build some sort o' shelter for the winter, or we gonna sleep mighty cold, an' no matter how close you snuggle to me, you ain't got enough heat in you to keep us warm in a Montana winter."

The marshal ushered the five bedraggled punchers from their cell and turned them over to Sanford. "Be mighty happy, young man, if you and your crew would not stay much longer in my town. You wasn't the only folks they kept awake last night. I doubt if anybody got a wink inside o' a fifty-mile circle of this town."

Jess led his men outside to the hitching rack. "You men gonna suffer today, but by nightfall most o' that poison you drank last night'll be sweated outta ya. Head for the herd, relieve Langford's men, get them cows up an' headed out. We got a long way to go."

The days passed. The heat didn't let up. And no rain fell. Sanford found enough water in sump holes along creek and riverbeds to water the cows between Cheyenne and Douglas. Then he found what hell must be like.

The Lightning River bed showed only a cracked, caked surface. No water. The cattle, used to drinking every day, slowed. By the end of the third day, their sides had sunk in to show their ribs. Their flanks shrank until their hipbones looked like they'd poke through the hide. They trudged ahead, heads hanging almost to the dusty trail, dust choking them; the riders were in no better shape.

The water barrels ran dry. There wasn't a canteen among them that had over a swallow or two in it. Parched lips cracked. Dust caked them. Alkali dust coated Joe Bob's face. Only his eyes showed color through the gray cake. He quit licking his lips. The bitter alkaline taste made his thirst more unbearable.

"Gettin' worried, Jess. Them cows ain't only thirsty, they gettin' mean, try to hang a horn into anythin' gets within reach. You reckon it'd be better to drive 'em at night? Might even be better for the men."

Jess frowned. "Yore worries ain't gonna get lonesome, partner. Mine's sittin' right there with 'em." He squinted toward the bony cattle. "No, a night drive'd be easier on the men, but the next day them cows'd only mill an' walk in circles. We'd never get 'em bedded down. Let's keep 'em headed north til a hour or two after sunset. I'm gonna ride out an' see what lies ahead. We oughta be comin' on the Belle Fourche soon, an' we better all pray they's water in it or we ain't gonna get to Montana Territory with no cows at all. Maybe *we* won't get there ourselves."

Joe Bob closed his eyes tight, as though to try to bring tears to wash them out. "You notice them cows walk right close to the horses, Jess? I don't figger they jus' gettin' mean, I figger they goin' blind. Thirst'll bring on blindness in cows, you know, an' it's gettin' harder to keep 'em from turnin' back. They remember the last water wuz behind 'em, an' want to head back for it.''

Jess nodded. ''I know, partner, but we gotta keep 'em headed the way we're goin' or we'll lose 'em all.'' He reined the bay gelding he rode this day ahead, stopped, pulled his canteen from the saddle, and handed it to Joe Bob. ''Still a few swallows left in there. My spare one's empty. I'll take it with me. Tell Hope an' Bessie to split what's left in that one. I'm gonna find more if I have to dig a hole for it.'' He pulled his hat brim down to shade his parched eyeballs and headed into the blistering heat, mumbling to himself, ''Freezin' cold, snow, ice, wind, dust, hail, drought. This is damned sure what I figgered—it's a hard land. It's gonna take some right tough folks to handle the troubles this land can heap on 'em.''

Several hours later the sun, well on its way to the western horizon, continued to burn everything under its rays. Sanford didn't consider heading back to the herd—he was going to, had to, find water. His bay plodded on, head hanging, ears drooping. Several times when he caught himself napping, he'd jerk awake, scan the terrain, see nothing changed, and sink into a confused, half dreamworld again.

Coming out of one of those dream states, he saw the sun, only half of the huge red orb showing above the horizon. Gonna sleep out here, he thought. Ain't gonna make it back to Hope tonight. First time away from her.

His head swung back to look between the bay's ears— they stood up, pointing straight ahead. Sanford shed his stupor like a rattler sheds its skin. One of two things was out ahead of him—Sioux or water. If it wasn't the latter, he was dead anyway. He rode in the direction of his horse's point.

The bay quickened his pace, then in a stumbling jog went down a slight incline and stopped. Sanford sat there staring past the gelding's neck, hearing but not believing the sucking sound his horse made. He was drinking! Drinking!

Holding tight to the reins, Sanford fell from the saddle, feeling the tepid, but welcome wetness engulf him. He splashed water onto his face and, lying in it to his neck, drank until he couldn't hold more. He lay there a few moments . . . or was it hours? Feeling wet from the inside out and the outside in, he then stood. The gelding had finished drinking.

Jess looked into the darkness to the south. In two, maybe three hours the herd would be bedding down, if Joe Bob did what they planned. He filled his spare canteen, thinking now a night drive wouldn't hurt anything. Once the cattle got here and drank their fill, they'd quiet down. He climbed aboard his horse and headed back.

When he was a hundred yards or so from camp, he yelled, "Hello the camp."

"Come on in, Sanford. We ain't gonna shoot you."

Jess handed the reins to the kid and walked to stare at his crew, dust-laden and tired to the bone, lying scattered about the camp. "You men saddle up. We're makin' a night drive—to water. That is if y'all feel like it."

He didn't have to say it twice.

19

THE MEN WERE throwing hulls on horses before he got the words out. Just the thought of water brought new life into them.

The cattle, too thirsty, too tired to protest being driven farther, formed their usual long column. Jess studied them, glad the weaker ones fell to the rear, because anything in the way when the herd smelled water would get stomped.

Sanford had ridden from point to drag, and drag to point, so many times he'd lost count. He'd passed the canteen around to the men. It didn't do much more than moisten their mouths, but for now it was enough.

About two hours into the night drive, Old Brindle's head came up. He quickened his pace. "Get outta the way, men. They gonna run," Sanford yelled. He hadn't finished his warning before the herd was in an all-out stampede. This time they knew where they were going.

Sanford dug heels into the gelding and caught up with Twilley. "Take a couple men an' see if can you find a gentle slope to the river. Some o' them banks might be ten, twelve feet high. Try to turn the herd 'fore a bunch o' them kill themselves." He reined his horse and raced for Hope's wagon at the rear. Before getting there, he came on tired, weaker cattle in a shuffling heads-down run. Some of them would never get to water. They'd use up all the life they had trying to get there.

He pulled in at the wagon. "Watch where cows fall. In the morning I'll see can we get 'em up an' walk 'em to the river." He hadn't much hope the effort would work, but he had to try.

An hour later Ransome, soaking wet but grinning, sat beside the huge coffeepot, urging the fire he'd heaped around it to burn. Surrounded by cattle, the hands, along with Hope and Bessie, splashed and played in the muddy water like a group of children.

Sanford walked to Ransome's side. "Don't take much to bring happiness to God's creatures, does it, Ransome?"

The cook glanced at him. "Jess, you don't call *that* much, you done lost yore brains. What we're looking at is *life*. Without it, we wouldn't have any herd—an' maybe not many men left. Figure when they git through playin' an' soakin' up nuff o' that water through their skin, they gonna want a good cup o' coffee an' a whole bunch o' sleep. All's I can give 'em is the coffee. Figure that trail behind us gonna give 'em the urge to sleep."

Ransome was right, and Jess let every man sleep as long as he could the next morning. Some didn't crawl from their blankets until sunup.

Sanford backtrailed until he counted seven head down. He only got three of them up and to the river. He counted himself lucky. He'd thought to lose maybe twenty or twenty-five.

Joe Bob and Jess figured to let the cattle graze on the good stand of grass here for maybe four or five days, drink their fill each day, and get some strength back. The second day, one of the heifers dropped a calf.

Historically, calves didn't survive a drive, so they were

left alongside the trail or slaughtered to make a delicacy the men enjoyed—sonuvabitch stew. Jess didn't know where the name came from, but that was the only name it'd gone by on the drives he'd made. Every part of the calf was used except the hide, horns, which they didn't have, and hooves.

The fourth night, long after supper, Jess, who had spread his and Hope's blankets out of sight and hearing of the crew, turned to her. "Hope, you ever get tired o' me wantin' you, you gotta tell me, 'cause it seems like ever' time I get clean, an' put on fresh-washed long johns, I jest naturally reach for you."

Hope chuckled. "Well, I gotta tell ya, cowboy, the days gonna come in 'bout six or seven months we're gonna have to put aside havin' each other for a while. Yeah, we're gonna still want, but we're just flat gonna have to quit for a couple of months. Other than that, I can't see me ever gettin' tired of you wantin' me." She chuckled again. "On account of, if you quit reachin' for me, I'd be reachin' for you."

Jess stared down into her face, puzzling over what she meant. "Honey, you don't mean what I think you mean, do you?"

She stared right back. "That depends on what you think I'm sayin', Jess."

"You sayin' we gonna have a baby?"

Hope laughed outright. "Don't know 'bout *we* gonna have one. I sorta figured on having it by myself. 'Course, you mighta had a *little* somethin' to do with it." She giggled and pulled him to her. "We better see can we store up some of this fun while we still got time."

Sanford allowed them one more night by the Belle Fourche. The morning of the sixth day, he called the crew around. "We leave the river here, gonna track straight north to the Little Powder. That might be another dry drive—I don't remember any creeks ahead o' us 'til then. Let's hope they is.'' He toed the stirrup of his buckskin. ''All right, let's head 'em out.''

The second day after leaving the Belle Fourche, a slow steady rain set in, unusual for this time of year. Sanford would have figured on a gully washer, along with hail and lightning. He stared into the dark, gray mass above with thanks, both for the rain and for the fact that it wasn't severe. The fifth day they reached the Little Powder River. It would lead them to the Powder River in another five or six days.

When five days had passed, they joined up with the Powder and stayed close to its banks heading north. Another three days and they drove about a half mile east of Powderville, a one-building town.

Sanford, seeing the small log structure on the bluff above the river, rode to it. Sitting on the front stoop was a man of forty or so years. ''Howdy, stranger, step down an' rest your saddle. Name's Homan, Leopold Homan. Welcome to Powderville.''

Jess introduced himself and shook hands. ''Where's the rest of the people in this here big town?''

Homan chuckled. ''I'm them. Sometimes I have two or three second cavalrymen to help guard me, and to repair the telegraph lines, but they don't come around much. This's the telegraph station connecting Fort Keogh and Fort Meade.

''I rode under Custer in the Fifth Infantry during his Powder River Campaign. He assigned me as operator-in-charge of this station. In charge of what, I don't know, but I been here ever since.'' He chuckled again.

''You get lonesome out here alone?''

Homan glanced at him, then stared across the river.

"Naw, I ride into Keogh 'bout once a month, see a lot o' people, an' bring out a wagon pulled by a six-mule team. That wagon's always loaded with supplies, so I don't want for nothin', and all them people I see in Keogh and Miles Town makes me mighty damn glad to be lonesome again. Can't stand a town too long a time."

Jess looked around. "Then you don't have nothin' in the way of supplies to sell?"

Homan shook his head. "Nope, you'll have to go to Miles Town for stuff you need. Town's just this side o' the Tongue from Keogh."

He had a chew about the size of a plumb pooching his jaw out. He spit, hitting a grasshopper dead center. "Now, if you folks're hurtin' for somethin', an' I got it, I'll let you have it if'n you replace it when you go to town. Wouldn't ask that, but the Army's pretty strict on what I use."

Sanford shook his head. "Thanks, but we're doin' all right for now."

Homan pointed over his shoulder with his thumb. "Where you takin' them cows? Gonna set up to ranch hereabouts?"

Jess nodded. "Figger on it. Thought I'd get here first. They's talk down El Paso way, the N-Bar brand of the Niobrara Cattle Company's gonna come up here with a big herd. The XIT's thinkin' 'bout comin' up here, too. If I'm here when they get here, they gonna play hell pushin' me off where I got my cows. The N-Bar's a big outfit, owned by the Newman Brothers, an' the XIT may be even bigger. I figger they'll be another couple of years gettin' here. I oughta be pretty well dug in by then." He pulled his pipe out, tamped and lit it. "You have any trouble with the Sioux?"

Homan nodded. "Some. But watchin' you ride in, figure

I counted about thirty hands in your outfit. You oughta be able to handle anything they bring to you.''

Jess stood. ''Well, Mr. Homan, looks like we gonna be neighbors of sorts. I ain't taking them cows much farther, an' I'm gonna stake a claim facin' onto the Powder. Won't worry 'bout water thataway.'' He toed the stirrup and looked down at Homan. ''Anybody layin' claim to land here on the east side o' the river for maybe the next twenty miles?''

Homan shook his head. ''Not that I've heered about. So far, the homesteaders have stayed farther east. They still got a fear of the Sioux.'' He threw Sanford a sloppy salute. ''Good luck, youngster. Hope to see you every once in a while.''

Sanford tipped his hat. ''Count on it. Good meetin' you, Mr. Homan.'' He reined his horse toward the herd.

There, he told Joe Bob and Twilley they'd drift the cows north until sundown, then on the morrow they'd do the same, figuring they'd be maybe fifteen miles north of Powderville by then, and there they'd turn them loose—they would be on what he thought to be their home range, the S-Bar-B. Then the work no cowhand liked would begin— pick-and-shovel work.

Sanford ranged ahead of the drive, scouting the river-banks, the knolls, any high bluff bordering the stream. Ransome followed close to Jess with the chuck wagon, wanting to have supper ready when the crew turned the cattle loose. Finally, about midday of the second day, with the cattle behind him about five miles, he found what he wanted: a slab-sided hill about a hundred yards east of the riverbank. The river had cut through a lower hill to create a high bluff with steep banks to the water. The chopped-off side of the hill faced south.

He nodded to himself. This was what he wanted. He

couldn't imagine floodwaters rising this far, and the south exposure would keep the winter winds out of the dugout. All day, he'd ridden past cottonwoods. He'd not cut any close to where he, the crew, and the two women would winter, but they could snake in logs to shore up the walls of the dugout, and have plenty to lay atop the semicave. He squatted at the top of the hill, looking southward for the cattle to spread out on *home range*.

While sitting there, he scanned the surrounding country. Bunchgrass, broken by cedar brakes, a few clumps of Russian olive, and in the lower, moister places, cottonwoods spread across the rolling plain. He thought he'd never seen a more beautiful sight.

Riding ahead of the herd, Joe Bob was the first to reach him. He ground reined his horse and squatted beside his partner. "This it, Jess?"

Sanford slanted him a grin. "Yep, less'n you got a better idea."

Joe Bob swept the area with a long look. "Jess, I figure we done talked enough so's you know 'zacktly what I think. This looks like what you an' me spent a lot o' talk 'bout over many a campfire. Where we gonna build the dugout?"

Jess grinned. "Walk over yonder to where the hill breaks off kinda sharp an' look down. You'll be standin' dang near on top o' our home for the next few months."

"What we gonna do when we want to be alone with our women folks?"

Sanford squinted into the setting sun across the river. "Been givin' that some thought, Joe Bob. Figure on making one big, half soddie an' half dugout for the men an' Ransome with his cookin' stuff. Been thinkin' another smaller one next to it for us. We can hang blankets up 'tween us for privacy. They's plenty o' room in that hillside for what I'm talkin' 'bout.''

Joe Bob shoved his hat back and wiped his forehead. ''Don't see as how we got much choice. Winter's gonna be blowin' in on us mighty soon. You reckon we can do all that 'fore first snow?''

''Well, Joe Bob, you an' me's always said if it had to be done, we could do it. We'll start the crew in the mornin'.''

The next morning, Jess measured off the two dugouts on the hillside, and put Twilley in charge of digging out the dirt. He took another crew with axes and went to the riverbank downstream about a quarter of a mile. Joe Bob took others and went hunting. Game was plentiful; deer, antelope, bear, and fowl.

When Sanford and his crew came in for their nooning, they were all dragging. Jess had grown up swinging an ax and pulling a crosscut saw, but that had been years ago, and all morning he'd been using muscles long out of use. He flopped on the ground by Hope. ''Lordy, woman, now I know why I wanted to be a cowboy. Them woodcuttin' tools jest flat don't fit my hands no more. Cuttin' stove wood is one thing, but cuttin' a whole danged tree an' then sawin' it to length is a whole different bucket o' worms.''

Hope laughed. ''You want I should go out this afternoon and cut awhile?''

Jess stared at her a moment, trying to decide if she was serious, then decided she was. ''Woman, if I see you, or Bessie, with a pick, shovel, ax, or saw in your hands, I'll do somethin' I promised myself I'd never do. I'll turn you over my knee an' give you a paddling.''

Hope's eyes got big, her mouth formed a perfect O, and she made like she trembled. ''Oh, my goodness, but you're a big bad man.'' Then she laughed. ''Jess, you can't just make me sit for the whole nine months. Exercise is some-thin' I gotta have to keep the baby an' me healthy.'' She sobered. "I was just kidding about the work you men are doin', but Bessie an' I've both gotta have somethin' to do.''

Jess thought a moment. "Cain't think o' nothin 'cept you might ask Ransome how you could help him. Too, start makin' a list o' stuff you need, stuff he needs, an' stuff Bessie needs. We gonna have to take a trip to Miles Town for supplies right soon, 'fore snow flies.''

"Jess Sanford, it must be nigh onto a hundred degrees right now. Snow's a long way off.''

He shook his head. "No, girl, it isn't. It's mid-September, an' when them cold winds begin to blow, we're gonna be ready.''

Two men walked to where Sanford and Hope sat. They shuffled their feet a moment, twisted their hats in their hands, and finally the one standing closest to him, one of his punchers by the name of Johnson, spoke, "Boss, the two of us're asking for our time. Me an' Cutter here ain't fit for this kind of work. A half day of it is 'bout a week more'n we ever want.''

Jess studied the two men a moment, thought of trying to talk them into staying, then realized it was best this way. He was going to have to lay off several of the hands now that the drive was over, and he hated the thought of it with cold weather not far off. Winter was the season most wad-dies dreaded unless they were part of a permanent crew. These men would probably ride the grub line.

Jess stood. Most of the men were lying about, resting until their meal settled in, then they'd get back to work. "Men, we gotta talk.'' They turned dusty, sweat-streaked faces toward him. "Johnson an' Cutter say they ain't cut out for this kind o' work. None of us is. But what I wanta say is, if any more o' you feels that way, they ain't gonna be no hard feelin's.'' He studied the ground at his feet a moment, then looked at them straight on.

"Ain't gonna lie to you, I wuz gonna have to lay 'bout half o' you off anyway when the dugouts were finished.'' He frowned. "You can save yourself a lot o' backbreakin' work if you want to draw yore time now.''

Fess Taylor stood. "Shore glad you made it easy, Jess. I been hearin' that Big Bend country callin' louder ever' day since that dry drive we made. Reckon I'm gonna answer that call.''

Two more men stood. Fen Morrison spoke for him and his saddle partner. "We'll be makin' tracks for Texas, too, boss, but we'll stay 'til we got you and the crew a warm place to stay in outta the weather.'' Two others voiced the same sentiments.

Sanford knew they were staying out of loyalty. "Men, much as we need your help, I don't want you caught up here with cold weather about to set in. I'll give you your time.''

Morrison looked at the four who volunteered to see the job done. "Hear that, men? He's gonna run us off 'fore we're ready to leave. We gonna take that? Hell no. Grab them axes and shovels, or whatever you was usin'. We gonna help 'im finish his livin' places 'fore we let 'im run us anywhere.''

Jess swallowed a couple of times, trying to rid himself of the lump in his throat. "Men, you cain't imagine how much I'm obliged to you, but cold weather's comin'. Y'all better git.''

Morrison looked him in the eye. "We done spoke, Jess. You're stuck with us till the job's finished.'' Each of them hefted the tools they were using and went to work.

20

THE CREW'S QUARTERS and winter cooking area measured thirty feet into the hill and twenty feet across, and the ladies figured they'd have plenty of space with a room twenty feet into the hill and fifteen feet wide.

When the work progressed far enough so Sanford felt comfortable they could finish before cold weather, he sent half the crew to Miles for three days to satisfy whatever personal needs and hungers they might have. "When this bunch gets back, the rest of us'll go in." Jess looked at Twilley. "You go in with these men. Take Ransome with you, the women'll cook for them what's left here. Ransome needs to buy a cookstove, an' I want you to buy a couple o' them big potbellied woodburners what'll heat the dugouts."

While Twilley was gone, Jess, Joe Bob, and the remainder of the crew laid logs from side to side on top of the ones they'd placed upright along each wall, then laid heavy sod on top of the logs lining the roof. When Twilley got back, they still had to close in the front of each dwelling. Then they had to build a shelter for the horses.

Jess stood admiring their work. "Let the cold come. Figger we gonna be comfortable 'cept when it rains. I hear them sod roofs leak somethin' awful.'' He looked into Hope's eyes. "See what I got you into, honey? You left a comfortable home with wood floors an' a roof what didn't leak for a place with dirt floors an' leaks.''

Hope hugged his arm to her breast. "Jess, any place with you in it will be my mansion.'' She squeezed a bit harder. "And guess what—Bessie's gonna have a baby only a couple months after me.''

Jess pushed his hat back and grinned at her. "Don't surprise me none. Them two cain't get two feet from each other without lookin' around to see where the other is.'' He shook his head. "My, my, two babies an' a brand-new ranch.''

With all his happiness, Jess still worried about what might be waiting for him with some law officer. He'd about decided he couldn't spend the rest of his life looking over his shoulder—but what could he do about it? He now had a wife, and soon a baby to worry about. He and Joe Bob saddled up and rode out to check the cows.

The bunches of cattle they passed had put on all the weight they'd lost on the trail. "Lookin' good, huh, partner?''

Joe Bob smiled tiredly. "Yep, and from what I remember o' these winters, they gonna need ever' bit o' tallow they done put on.''

Jess frowned, his gaze sweeping the horizon, dry washes, cedar brakes, and lips of ravines. "Kind of surprised, Joe Bob, we ain't seen hide nor hair o' any Sioux. Figgered we might have trouble with 'em 'fore now.''

"Been a puzzle to me, too, Jess. We gonna have to ride a circle 'round our cows, see is they any pony tracks. We mighta been losin' a few head now an' agin.''

Sanford shifted in his saddle. "Twilley oughta be back by late today. We'll have him send out a couple o' men.''

He grinned. "You an' me's gonna take our ladies to town."

Joe Bob shook his head. "Don't reckon none o' our hands're as good at readin' sign as we are. We out here anyway, reckon you an' me can get the job done now."

Sanford nodded. "Let's do it then. You search over yonder, I'll ride a circle back to you."

Sanford had ridden only about a mile when he picked up the tracks of two unshod ponies and a couple of cattle. He didn't bother to fetch Joe Bob. He figured he could handle two warriors by himself. Besides, the tracks were fresh and he didn't want to lose them.

He rode low in the saddle, scanning every bush, every shadow. The riders didn't seem to be worried about being followed. The sign didn't show his quarry had stopped to search their back trail. They must have scouted Sanford's outfit and noticed many of them gone, with the rest busy building shelter.

The tracks led down a steep embankment to the bottom of a ravine. One pony continued driving the cows down the middle of the arroyo while the other split off to climb the opposite side. Sanford decided to follow the Indian with the two cows. He'd not broken clear of the ravine when he knew he'd made a mistake. A hard, painful knot formed between his shoulder blades, and before he found time to worry about it, a shadow crossed the ground in front of him.

He ducked. The warrior sailed over his back and landed on his feet on the opposite side of Jess's gelding. Sanford launched himself from the saddle, pulling his bowie at the same time. He landed facing the warrior, who stood with only a short-bladed kitchen knife in hand—no handgun, no rifle, only the knife.

The warrior must have seen seventy summers. He had few if any teeth, and his skin broke into a myriad of wrinkles when he grimaced. He stood facing Sanford, showing no fear. "You catch me, white man; now kill me—if you can."

Sanford relaxed barely a tad. "You speak pretty good English, Grandfather. Why do you steal my cattle?"

"Woman hungry, grandchildren hungry. Me"—he tapped his bony chest—"me, I can do without."

Still on his guard, Sanford frowned. "Why didn't you come to me, Grandfather? I would have given you a couple of cows. Ain't gonna see nobody go hungry."

"Me come to you? Ask for cows? Lone Coyote not beg." He grinned, unbelievably breaking his wrinkles into more wrinkles. "Besides, steal cows more fun."

While talking to the old warrior, Sanford stayed aware of all around him. "Who rides with you?"

"Grandson, Little Snake. Soon be big snake. Him twelve summers."

Sanford sighed. "Put your knife away, Grandfather. You can have the cows, but come to me when you're again hungry. My riders'll shoot you if you don't. Let's find your grandson."

A couple of hours later Jess rode to Joe Bob, waiting for him in the shade of a cottonwood. "Where you been, Jess? Figured you'd be here a hour ago."

Jess grinned, knowing his face showed shame. "I just give a couple head o' our cows away."

"What'd you do that for?"

Sanford told Joe Bob about the old Indian and his handsome young grandson, then shrugged. "Reckon I cain't see nobody go hungry. An', Joe Bob, if you'da seen that old man standin' there gonna fight me with no more'n a small paring knife, it'd broke yore heart."

Joe Bob grimaced. "An' you're the man what's gonna be hard enough to whip this here land in shape." He shook his head, then smiled. "Ain't you nor me hard as we make believe, an' you know what? I'm right glad we ain't."

Jess slapped his partner on the shoulder. "Let's go home."

When they got back to headquarters, Twilley was there with the rest of the crew. Sanford looked at the tired, dirty men who stayed with him while Twilley went in town, then turned his attention to the women. "In the mornin', it's our turn."

While waiting for supper, Sanford and Joe Bob took stock of the supplies Twilley brought back. He looked at his ramrod. "Don't see no smokin' or chewin' tobacco here."

"Well, boss, me an' the crew talked it over an' wasn't sure, what with all the money you're havin' to spend, you could afford it." He shrugged. "So we just figgered to do without."

Jess cleared his throat, but the lump stayed where it formed. He looked at the ground. "Reckon I'll stock up on it, then. Ain't seein' a man go without, 'specially in the cold, locked-in months ahead." He looked at his men, his pride in them showing through. "Thanks anyway, men. You gotta be the best bunch I ever rode with." He quickly turned away before he made a bigger fool of himself than he already had.

Daylight saw them on the trail to Miles Town. They all wore trail garb, but had brought along their Sunday-go-to-meeting clothes. Twilley had told them the trip in was a solid two-day ride. He'd also told them the town was full of hard cases. That knowledge brought a frown to Jess's face, but he shrugged it off. Most Western men would not harm women, and Jess figured he would do almost anything to steer clear of trouble. He had cautioned his men to do the same.

That night, they stowed their work clothes, and the next morning donned town clothes. Hope looked, and acted, like a fish out of water in her dress. Jess eyed her from head to toe. "I'll bet you've had that dress since yore ma and pa sent you off to school in Fort Stockton." He grinned, saw storm clouds gathering on her brow, and hurriedly added, "But you shore do look mighty pretty in 'em."

The next afternoon from the top of a long hill, they had their first sight of Miles Town. Joe Bob, riding on the opposite side of the wagon from Sanford, reined his horse closer to the wagon and yelled across. "Looks like a right lively little town, Jess, 'specially if all them buildin's down yonder's stores."

Jess grinned. "Now, Joe Bob, you don't want 'em all to be stores, do you? Where would the boys have fun?"

His partner returned his grin. "Reckon you're right. I forget that sort o' thing sometimes."

Entering town, they rode the dusty trail between a mixture of mostly log buildings and a few frame structures. Not a single building sported paint of any kind, except for signs on their fronts. Jess read them carefully, looking for a hotel or rooming house. The signs read BROADWATER, HUBBEL AND COMPANY, A.R. NININGER AND COMPANY, LEIGHTON AND JORDON AND COMPANY, all general merchandise. The *Yellowstone Journal,* apparently a newcomer to town, was housed in a building of raw wood not yet grayed by rain, wind, and snow. He counted three blacksmith shops, two livery stables, and thirty-two saloons. Men ain't gonna go thirsty, he thought.

Then there were the buildings that didn't name their stock-in-trade: Annie Turner's Coon Row, Mag Burns, The .44, Connie Hoffman, Fannie French, Frankie Blair's, and Cowboy Annie's, all obviously brothels. Ain't much else the boys're gonna go without either. He grinned to himself at the thought.

He and Joe Bob settled their womenfolk in rooms at a boardinghouse. Miles not yet having a hotel they wanted to leave their wives in. While Hope and Bessie waited for bathwater, Jess and Joe Bob said they would walk about the town until their turn at the tub came.

"Jess, I'm gonna go by the post office, take a look at the notices." At Joe Bob's words, Jess's face hardened. He nodded. "Think I'll go by the marshal's office—get acquainted with 'im."

Joe Bob frowned. "Think that's smart, Jess? He might have something on you."

Sanford shrugged. "Might's well find out." He pointed up the street. "Meet you in Leighton's store after a while."

When he stepped toward the boardwalk on the opposite side of the street, he barely heard Joe Bob's "I hope."

The door to the marshal's office stood open. Sanford went in. Sitting at a scarred old desk, feet propped on an open bottom drawer, was a weathered, slim, tough-as-rawhide-looking man. Crow's-feet ran from the corners of his eyes to his sideburns. Jess hoped some of them were caused from laughter, although the lawman didn't look given to much humor. "What can I do for you, young man?"

Jess shook his head. "Not a thing, Marshal. Just wanted to make your acquaintance. I just started a ranch over on the Powder southeast o' here. Name's Sanford, Jess Sanford, an' I got a partner name of Joe Bob Brown."

The marshal dropped his feet off the drawer and leaned across his desk, holding out his hand. "Howdy. Name's Bruns. That you an' your partner I seen ride by here a bit ago with your wives an' some of your crew?"

Jess grinned. "That was us. The other half o' my crew was in a couple days ago."

Jess found out Bruns could smile. The crow's-feet deepened and his lips quirked at the corners. "Met a couple of 'em. They were my guests overnight. Too much o' that poison they sell in these saloons. They tried to tree the one they were in."

"They wreck anything? I owe you any fine or somethin'?"

Bruns shook his head. "Nope. Just let 'em sleep it off. Didn't even have to feed 'em a meal." He chuckled. "Don't b'lieve either of 'em coulda kept anything thicker'n coffee down anyway." He nodded toward the stove. "Want a cup?"

Jess shook his head. "Don't think so, Marshal. I bet it's been sittin' there boilin' since before breakfast."

"You're wrong there, Sanford, but I did add some more grounds an' a bit o' water to yesterday's pot about sunup this mornin'."

"Well, win some, lose some. I figgcr I jest won one. I might stop by on the way outta town, though, an' take what you got left to plant a fence post in."

Bruns laughed. "Ain't that bad, son." He stood. "Sure good meetin' you, boy. Come by anytime." Jess shook his hand and left.

Out on the street, he looked both ways, wondering if Joe Bob had gotten over to Leighton's yet. Not seeing him, he crossed the street to meet the storekeeper.

Meanwhile Joe Bob found the post office in a small cage in the back of a feed-and-grain store. He'd had the postmaster go through the stack of letters in the cubbyholes twice. The white-haired, spindly old man looked at Joe Bob and shook his head. "That's every slip of paper I have in here, mister. There's no letter for you."

Joe Bob nodded. "Yes, suh. Much obliged for your trouble. Next time I come to town, I'll check again, maybe it'll be here then." He walked to the door, frowning. The letter he'd written to Sanford's folks might not have had time to reach them. Too, even if it had, and they'd answered, the railroad had bogged down and not gotten any closer than Bismarck since 1873. Everything coming into Miles Town was by steamboat, freight wagons, or stagecoach.

Joe Bob worried that he'd told them too much in case his letter fell into the wrong hands. In his letter, he'd been careful to make them think he knew where Jess was, and would, if he wasn't in trouble, get in touch with him by mail and have him write home. He'd assured them Jess was healthy, and doing well in a business sense.

He stood in the doorway of the post office a few moments, not seeing anything except the thoughts running 'round and 'round in his head. Coming out of his mental fog, he looked up, swept the street with a glance, and saw Sanford crossing toward Leighton's farther down the street.

When Joe Bob came through the door, Jess had already introduced himself. He looked around and saw his partner, introduced Leighton to him, and told the storekeeper he and Joe Bob were partners. Leighton nodded. "Met your ramrod a couple days ago."

They had talked awhile when Jess asked if anyone out their way was selling hay. Leighton scratched his head, frowned, and looked at Jess straight on. "Sanford, there's only one other rancher anywhere close enough for you to haul hay from his place, and he wouldn't have any. Man, Texan like yourselves, his wife and two children are north of you 'bout twenty miles. Case Gentry's his name. Had a rough time of it til just recently. Now I think he's on his way to makin' it."

Leighton waited on a customer and came back to talk.

"Way I see it, if we don't have heavy snow, those long-horns you drove up here'll make it. They're used to scratchin' for a living." He shook his head. "Much snow, though, you and Joe Bob here're gonna have a rough time of it. You do, and you need help, come see me. We'll work somethin' out."

Joe Bob studied the tall man behind the counter. "Mr. Leighton, that offer is mighty neighborly. You hardly know us."

Leighton pinned Joe Bob with a sharp blue-eyed gaze. "Mr. Brown, there are few of us hereabouts who'd still be here if along the way folks hadn't kicked in to help when we needed it." He nodded. "Yeah, we'd help you, but we'd figure you to do the same when we needed it."

The partners glanced at each other, then looked at Leighton. Jess, his eyes oddly moist, said, "Mr. Leighton, you know what? I don't feel near so far from home since I met you."

Leighton smiled. "Son, from the way you been talkin', this *is* home." He sobered. "Men, don't get the idea everybody out here is friendly. We've got some mighty salty drifters come through here. Some stayed, thinking of us as easy pickings. Be careful."

Jess smiled, knowing his smile was a wintry one. "Mr. Leighton, we don't know how to be much else."

21

HOPE, BESSIE, JOE Bob, and Jess, walked about the town, going in stores, getting acquainted, and last, Jess took them to meet Leighton and do what shopping Twilley hadn't done when he brought the boys in.

Leighton told Jess and Joe Bob about a shot-in-the-dark business venture they might want to look into. "You got any spare money right now, I believe George Miles and Captain Frank Baldwin might sell you a few hundred head." He laughed. "If you're interested in running a few hundred head of sheep, they might save your bacon if we have a winter like I hear they have in this territory every few years. Don't pay 'em over seventy-five cents a head. They got 'em from John Burgess. He was headed for the hills when he stopped at Fort Keogh, where they were building winter quarters for the soldiers. Colonel Miles let him winter his sheep on government land, and in the spring he sold his flock to the two gentlemen I mentioned. They paid him fifty cents a head."

The idea of a cattleman running sheep at first left a bad taste in Jess's mouth. He looked at Joe Bob, who had a thoughtful frown creasing his usually smooth forehead. "Jess, these winters being what they are up here, them woollies might live where cows'd die. Might be we oughta think about hedging our bet.''

In the years they'd ridden together they'd seldom disagreed on each other's ideas. Jess closed his eyes to slits and stared at a bale of Levi's sitting in the middle of the floor. He tumbled Joe Bob's words around in his thoughts a moment, then grinned. "Tell you what, partner, sounds good, but let's think 'bout it awhile. We'll make up our mind 'fore we head for home." He noticed their wives exchange glances, but couldn't read anything into it.

He looked at Leighton. " 'Preciate what you told us. We gotta think on it a little." He scratched his head. "If we decide to buy 'em, where'll I find Baldwin or Miles?''

Leighton thought a few seconds. "Tell you what. Tomorrow's Saturday, and they usually bring their families to town. I'll tell 'em you're looking for them.''

Jess nodded and told Leighton where they were staying, then added, "I ain't givin' 'im no more'n sixty cents a head.''

Leighton laughed. "You might get them for that. They bought a little over a thousand head in seventy-five; now I hear tell they have between three and four thousand." He nodded. "Yep, you just might get 'em for that.''

Jess and Joe Bob talked about the sheep deal with their wives during supper that night. Hope thought the idea might be a good one, but hesitated. She pinned them with that no-nonsense look of hers. "You gotta consider cattle are thought by many to be the future of this country. You know there're a bunch o' Texans gonna make drives up here. They ain't gonna take kindly to sheep.''

Jess clamped his jaws tight, feeling the muscles in the back knot. "Gonna tell you somethin', girl. Them people, for the most part, ain't Texans. They're mostly Britishers an' Yankees gonna get started on Texas cows just like we're doin', an' they got big Eastern money behind 'em. I don't give a damn whether they like sheep or not. It's our money an' our time we got invested here. I'll fight 'em down to a nubbin 'fore I let 'em tell me what to do. If they want a fight, then bring it to me.''

Hope looked at him, quietly shaking her head. ''Jess, here you are, ready to fight, and nobody's said nothin' to you yet.'' She nodded. ''But yeah, if they bring it to us— we'll fight.''

They talked until they'd finished a third cup of coffee, and while talking they had Joe Bob go over their finances, figure what wages for their hands would cost until they could market cows, what provisions might cost, and when certain they could handle it, they agreed they should get into the sheep business if Miles and Baldwin agreed to sell.

Jess and Joe Bob exchanged glances. Jess knew Joe Bob was thinking about the cows they'd sold to Slade down below Raton. That money made them mighty independent.

The next morning, Jess sat with Hope, his partner, and his partner's wife, finishing breakfast, when two men walked to their table. ''Leighton said you folks had somethin' you wanted to talk to us about?''

Jess figured Leighton had probably told them about the whole conversation, so they knew what he wanted with them. And the fact they'd looked him and Joe Bob up told him they were more than interested in getting rid of some of their sheep. He decided to make his first offer fifty cents a head. He could always raise the ante if he had to.

While they talked Sanford noticed three men at a corner table showing interest in the meeting. He knew they couldn't hear what was being said, so it had to be interest in anyone meeting with sheepmen. He wondered if their interest signaled trouble.

After haggling at length about price and numbers of

sheep, Miles and Baldwin agreed to sell Jess and Joe Bob a thousand head at the sixty cents Jess had first made up his mind to. In the bargain, Jess talked them into throwing one of their sheepdogs into the deal. Now Jess only had to worry about convincing his cowboys that they were also sheepherders.

When he and Joe Bob broke the news to their men later in the morning, one man quit, and the kid, Ben Quaid, thought awhile and decided to stay with the brand. Another looked Jess in the eye and said, "Boss, they's only one thing dumber'n a cow, an' that's a cowboy. Count me in. I'll stick." The others said, "Hell, cows or sheep, it's a job." They stayed.

The next day, sitting their horses behind the bleating, smelly flock, watching the dog keep them closely herded, Jess again looked to the rear. Dust, hardly discernible, not enough for a large group of horsemen, had been hanging in the distance, but tracking right along with their course since they'd started the drive. "Men, keep yore weapons loose in the holsters. We maybe got us a little trouble. I'm gonna scout out ahead an' see what kind a land we gotta cross 'fore sundown."

Other than a deep ravine, Jess found nothing that might cause them trouble in their drive.

Toward sundown, the dust hadn't gotten closer. Jess wondered why. If they meant harm, they would probably have closed the distance. He chewed on the problem. There were no ranches on the route they took, and no reason he could think of, other than the sheep, why anyone would track them. Recalling the three men in the café who seemed too interested in the sheepmen's visit, he decided if he had trouble, he'd be ready.

Around their campfire, Jess laid out his plan. "Men, re-member what we done down yonder in Texas when Tetlow's bunch wuz gonna hit us. Do the same. Make yore blankets look like you're in 'em." He glanced at Hope. "You an' Bessie stay in the wagon. Put yore bedroll 'tween you an' where the firin' is."

He swept the men with a glance. "Every one o' us is gonna stay out yonder with them sheep. Keep rifles fully loaded. Shoot anybody what comes a-whoopin' toward you. Quaid, if they try to stampede them sheep, it's yore job to turn 'em. They's a deep ravine ahead; if they get run over the lip of it, we gonna have us a bunch o' dead woollies." He stood. "I'm gonna be sure ain't nobody takin' a look at us. Y'all get ready."

Before walking from the firelight, Jess picked up a handful of pigging string and tucked it in his belt. Why he took it with him, he didn't know, then he left the camp, afoot. He'd not be apt to skyline himself against the bright starlit sky.

He walked in ever-widening half circles between their camp and where he'd seen the dust cloud.

About the same time he saw a pinpoint of light in the distance, a shadow loomed out of the dark, showing plainly against the sky. Jess went to his belly and edged toward the form that soon became the outline of a man walking as though taking a stroll in the dark. Jess wormed his way so as to cross where the man's route carried him.

His cheek resting against the dry grass, Jess watched the slim stroller pass within five feet of him. As soon as he passed, Jess stood, pulled his bowie from its sheath, and ghosted toward his quarr's back.

The man, apparently feeling someone approach from behind, took a short turn—in time for Jess to circle his neck with his left arm and hold the bowie to his throat. "You make one peep, I'll open a hole in yore throat wide enough to feed you through."

"All right—all right. Ain't makin' no noise."

Jess kept his hold on the man's neck. "What you doin' sneakin' 'round in the dark?"

"Nothin', nothin', jest gettin' away from the fire for a few minutes, jest stretchin' my legs."

Jess jerked his arm tighter. "You lie. What you figure on doin' to us?"

The slim man, standing tense against Jess's hold, abruptly relaxed. "Ain't sayin' nothin'. Do what you gotta do."

Sanford felt a twinge of admiration for the man. He thought to kill him, but rebelled at the idea.

Now he knew what he'd do with the pigging strings. "Lie flat on your stomach an' put yore hands behind your back."

He tied the man's hands, pulled his feet up in back of him, and tied them to his hands.

Squirming, the slim cowboy asked, "What you gonna do with me?"

"Gonna leave you here 'till we get through with yore friends. You're the three we saw in town today, ain't ya?"

"Never seen you afore."

Jess pulled his bowie lightly across the man's throat. Sharp as he kept it, he knew it didn't cut deep, and even though he couldn't see it, he knew it brought a trickle of blood. "I can still leave you out here to feed the coyotes."

A sigh sounded from above Jess's knife. "Yeah, we're them."

Jess had found out what he wanted to know. He and his men most likely faced only three men—now only two. But they could have gotten more men to share their fun, and Sanford had no doubt but what they intended to, in some way, try to kill the sheep.

Before leaving, he tied the puncher's bandanna around his mouth.

Back at camp, Sanford looked at the bedding spread around the fire. Each blanket had a hump under it as though it covered a sleeping man. He sidled up to the wagon. "Hope, y'all ready?"

"Yeah, Jess. You still think they're gonna attack us?"

"Think they'll try for the sheep, honey. You an' Bessie stay down. Don't want you gettin' hurt."

A soft "I know, Jess," came from the wagon. He went to his horse, saddled it, and rode toward the flock. "It's me, men," he called softly before riding up on them. "It's like I thought; them men in town. I figger only two o' them, but might be more if they had friends."

None of the hands knew anything about sheep, so they treated them like cows. They rode a loose circle around them, each singing softly. Every man had his rifle in hand. Midnight passed, and each time Sanford passed one of his men, they asked the same question. "You reckon they're comin', boss?"

His answer, too, was the same. "They'll be here. Shoot straight."

By Jess's best reckoning, the sun was not far from rising when out of the dark, yells, shouts, and shots erupted. And the noise came from more than two attackers.

The sheep were instantly on their feet and running. Sanford picked gun flashes to fire at. In the murky light, he missed on his first two shots, but with his third, a man fell from his horse. A fiery streak burned Jess's cheek. He fired at another shadow. It fell off the far side of his horse. Suddenly the only sound was of bleating sheep, pounding hooves, and yells. Sanford figured the voices he heard were his own men.

The sheep headed straight for the ravine and certain de-

struction. Horses ran all out; the riders, heedless of the risk
their horses might step in a prairie-dog hole, urged them
faster. Far ahead, Sanford heard a long, thin yell, and even
from where he rode, he recognized the kid's voice. He was
doing his job, trying to turn the sheep from the lip of the
ravine.

Jess prayed he got the job done before the sheep, the kid,
and his horse went over the lip of the ravine. Another hundred yards or so and the flock curved into Sanford's path.
The curve tightened, throwing the stampede back on itself.
Sanford reined his horse to the side and watched the sea of
wool slow, then stop. Quaid had done his job.

Jess rode toward where he knew the kid had to have been
to turn the sheep. "Quaid . . . Quaid? You all right?"

The kid's voice sounded from below where Sanford rode.
"Boss? Yeah, I b'lieve I'm okay, but I done killed my
horse. Broke his neck when we went over the bank of this
here gully." The sound of Quaid trying to climb the steep
sides, then the sound of rocks sliding and tumbling down
the sides of the ravine, intruded on the pounding of Jess's
heart.

"Kid, I'm gonna throw you a rope. When you find the
end of it, give me a yell an' I'll pull you up. We'll get your
saddle, bridle, an' other gear in the morning."

Sanford soon had the kid up, and gave him a hand to sit
behind him on his gelding. Quaid acted like he'd only been
for a quiet ride on a Sunday morning. He chuckled. " 'Cept
for the smell, boss, this ain't much different from cow-
boyin'." He sobered. "Shore did hate to lose that horse,
though. He was one o' the best cuttin' horses I ever rode."

Sanford cleared his throat. "Kid, when we get home you
can take yore pick of any horse I got in my string."

"Uh, boss? That there dog deserves a lot o' credit. Without him, I wouldn'ta got the job done. Don't know where

he ended up after I went over the rim o' that gully. Hope he's all right. I done took a likin' to 'im.''

"Reckon we'll have to wait till mornin' to find that out, kid.'' Sanford chuckled. "Speakin' o' mornin', reckon it's here.'' The horizon to the east showed a tint of gray, promising more light soon.

Back at the fire, Sanford slid tiredly from the saddle. Hope and Bessie were busy doctoring cuts and bruises. Her glance toward him showed worry, then relief. "You all right, Jess?''

He nodded. "Yep. Take a look at Quaid here. He fell in that ravine I wuz tellin' y'all 'bout.'' He wiped at his cheek with the back of his hand and brought it away smudged with blood. "Somebody come mighty near to gettin' in a good shot.'' He walked to the fire and poured himself a cup of coffee. "We gonna have to wait 'till full daylight 'fore we can tell what kind o' damage we done to them what attacked us—an' what they done to us.''

By the time they'd eaten, the sun sat at seven o'clock in the brassy, cloudless sky. A quick search of the gunfight area found three dead punchers, two others shot up pretty bad, and fifteen sheep crippled or dead. Sanford stared at the human bodies a moment, his face a frozen, hard mask. "Throw 'em in the ravine and push rocks over 'em.'' He looked at Hope. "You an' Bessie bandage them what's still breathin', the men can put 'em on their horses and cut 'em loose.'' He still sat his saddle. "I gotta go turn that waddy loose what I tied up last night—if the coyotes ain't made a supper of 'im by now.''

"Jess Sanford, the way you talk!'' Hope's words caught up with him when he rode away.

Sanford found the man and untied him. "Don't know where yore horse is, but that's your problem. Reckon you gonna walk home. Them friends o' your'n wasn't lucky as you.'' Before he toed the stirrup, he shucked the shells from the puncher's rifle and six-shooter he'd taken the night before. ''Gonna give your weapons back, an' gonna give you somethin' else, cowboy, a few words of advice. You an' yore friends stay away from my ranch. I run cows, an' now sheep, an' my crew's salty as any bunch you gonna find anywhere. You can save yoreself a whole bunch o' misery by ridin' a wide circle around us. *Comprende?*''

The waddy gave him a sullen nod and walked back toward Miles Town.

By ten o'clock, with not the slightest breeze, the sun felt as though it would fry Sanford's brain, and heat from the baked earth pushed into his face. The sheep smelled even worse, but the dog had come back and was doing most of the work keeping them bunched and moving.

By noon, Sanford worried about Hope and Bessie. The heat, dust, and bounce and shock of the wagon hitting rocks and ruts might do harm to them, or the babies they carried within. Every half mile or so, he rode back to the wagon and checked on them. They assured him every time they were doing fine.

Riding ahead of the flock to check the best route, he turned around and headed back. It was then a puff of breeze cooled his face. He raised his dust-caked eyelids and stared toward the west. Dark, ominous clouds lined the horizon. He swung his gaze to the southwest, following the line of dark gray. The cloud bank was heavier there, and sent streamers from the tops of the buildups out ahead of the storm. He urged the gelding to a faster pace.

When at the rear of the column of woollies, he yelled to the nearest rider. ''Push 'em harder. Don't kill 'em, but get 'em movin'. We got some real weather comin'.''

He studied the storm clouds a moment. There might be hail, flash-flood waters, twisters—almost anything buried in the belly of the black, rolling mass. If they could get the sheep across the Powder before it hit, they could make a run for the dugout.

He again yelled at his men. "If they's lightnin' in that storm, get off yore horse. Get close to the ground as you can, an' pull your horses down with you."

He kneed his horse toward the wagon. "If it hails, get under the wagon. Lightnin', do the same. I'll unhitch the team an' pull 'em to ground. Gonna try an' make it across the river 'fore this hits." He kneed the gelding toward the river, now less than a mile ahead.

22

SITTING HIS HORSE on the bank of the Powder, Sanford studied the water. It looked no higher than when they had headed for Miles Town a couple days ago. He dismounted, ground-reined the gelding, walked down the bank to the water's edge, and stuck a twig into the bank where the water lapped. He stood there, watching the twig and the water. In less than a minute, water covered the twig. Rising.

He wondered if he had time to get the wagon with its precious cargo across before the river became a roaring, roiling monster.

He raced for the wagon. The storm still stood a few miles to the southwest, but runoff from land bordering the river, as well as creeks feeding it, would get here before the storm.

At the wagon, Sanford reined alongside and jumped to the wagon bed, crawled to the boot, and pushed between Hope and Bessie. "Gonna get y'all across the river 'fore it gets too high—I hope." He slapped the reins along the horses' backs. They broke into a lope. A few more slaps of the reins and they were running.

They passed the flock, also being pushed into a run. When Jess pulled the wagon to a halt at the top of the bank, the water had risen a couple feet more than when he last looked at it. He might float the buckboard across, but it carried a pretty heavy load. He looked at Hope, at the river, then tuned his gaze on the fast-approaching storm. "Ain't gonna try it. Hope, you an' Bessie get under the wagon while I unhitch the team."

Without question, they stood in the boot, and reached for him to help them to the ground. Then he turned the horses loose. "Stay under there 'til the storm passes. This bluff here is about the highest land around. If the river rises, it shouldn't get this high. Gonna tell the men to hold the sheep on this side."

Sanford reined toward his men, now about three hundred yards away. A glance toward the approaching storm showed a white wall of almost solid water preceding the midnight-dark, turbulent buildups behind it. Lightning split the heavens in constant jagged streaks, crackling and hissing across and through the clouds, then exploding in a deafening crescendo.

Sanford waved the men off their horses, let the sheep fend for themselves, then turned his horse. The gelding ran all out for the wagon. Still holding the reins, he left the saddle at a dead run. Trying to stop his headlong pace, he bounced against the side of the wagon, pulled his horse to the ground, and crawled under the bed next to Hope and Bessie.

Hail pelted the ground, the wagon, everything about them. In minutes, the marble-sized missiles covered the terrain to a depth of several inches. Lying next to his gelding, Sanford watched the icy layer build, thanking every deity he'd ever heard of the ice chunks weren't the size of his fist. He'd seen horses, cattle, and men killed by large shards of ice in Texas.

His eyes shifted from the ground to study the sky, looking for, yet hoping not to see, a long funnel shape dip toward the earth. He looked from the sky to the two women under the wagon, both now large with child, and again felt remorse that he'd let Hope talk him into getting married when they did. The only thing he could offer her was a life of hardship. Then, still thinking on it, despite the weather, he smiled to himself. The thought of trying to leave her behind would've started a war to make the War Between the States seem like a Sunday-school picnic.

The hail ceased, and behind it the downpour continued. In only minutes, the earth became a quagmire. The incessant bleating of sheep, the pounding of rain against the earth, the crash of thunder, and crackle of lightning hammered at Sanford's skull. A half hour passed, the thunder drew away to the northwest, but the rain continued. Jess stood, pulled his horse to his feet, climbed aboard, and rode toward the Powder.

Water, muddy, rushing, turbulent, tore at the trees and brush along the top of the river's bank. Jess sighed. "Reckon I done at least one smart thing today, an' not tryin' to cross that stream was it." Wind tore the words from his lips. Water spilled over the bank, still rising. He studied it, then glanced at the bluff, gaging its height and the land around, making sure the river had plenty of lower space to spread before climbing the hill. Satisfied the women and men were in no danger, he turned back. Before he reached the wagon, the rain slacked to a steady but gentle soaking.

Joe Bob met him as he climbed from the saddle. "How's it look, Jess?"

Sanford grinned. "'Less you mind sleepin' wet, eatin' hardtack, an' smellin' them damned sheep, reckon it looks pretty good."

"We gonna stay on this side tonight?"

Jess nodded. "Tonight, an' maybe a couple more. Don't know how long it takes this river to dump its overflow." The men had gathered around by now. Sanford swept them with a glance. " 'Course, if we have to stay here long, we can slaughter one o' them woollies for food."

One of the hands sniffed. "I ain't eatin' no stinkin' sheep. Why, hell. I quit ridin' fer a man once what wanted to feed us sheep. They smelled worse cookin' than they did on the hoof."

Sanford let his eyes crinkle in a slight smile. "Don't worry, men, I dislike 'em as much as you do, but there's them what don't mind eatin' 'em—or wearin' wool clothes. I bought sheep in case we need 'em to keep this ranch alive after a hard winter. Hear tell woollies winter better'n cows. Reckon we gonna find out."

He looked at the women huddled under the wagon. " 'Sides bein' wet, how y'all doin'?"

Hope smiled. "Better'n I figure we look—stringy hair, dirty faces, swollen stomachs, sure not the women you and Joe Bob married."

Jess grinned, scratched his head, and looked at Joe Bob. "How you figger it, partner? If they look bad as I just heard, they might not be the same beautiful women we married. Me an' you might oughta ride back to Miles Town, see if we left our ladies behind, an' if they ain't in town, maybe we can find a coupla better-lookin' ones to replace 'em."

Sober-faced, Joe Bob frowned, nodded, and said, "Why now, Jess, that sounds like a mighty fine idea. Wait'll I catch up my horse and we'll ride in together."

Hope and Bessie scrambled from under the wagon bed. Hope, trying to hide a smile, looked her man up and down. "You even make a move to climb on that gelding an' I'll fix you like you fixed him—then I'll help Bessie take care of Joe Bob the same way.''

Joe Bob shook his head. ''Uuuuh-uh. Jess, sounds like them women we married up with, but shore don't look like 'em.'' He nodded. ''Yep, reckon you're right. We better head back to Miles, see maybe we lost 'em 'long the way somewhere.''

Hope slogged through the mud to one of the men standing just out of earshot. ''Ben, lend me your bowie for a few minutes. Bring it right back.''

The lanky puncher reached behind his belt, pulled his knife, and handed it to her. ''Why shore, ma'am, is it anything I can do for you?''

''Nope, this is something I'll take care of myself.''

Slapping the broad, heavy blade on the palm of her hand, she walked to stand in front of Jess, pinning him with that straight-on look. Before she could say anything, Bessie stepped close to them. ''Hope, I got a better idea. Let's you an' me write our pas and tell them how we bein' mistreated by these two critters. They'd saddle up an' be here 'fore snow flies.''

Joe Bob slapped his thigh. ''Gosh ding it, Jess, now you done done it. Figger I could stand whatever them two women wuz gonna do to us, but danged if I'm gonna face them two men from down Texas way.''

Jess couldn't hold it in any longer, he laughed until tears rolled down his cheeks. Borrowed bowie and all, he pulled Hope into his arms, held her close, wiped a muddy smudge off her cheek, and kissed her soundly.

When he turned her loose, a little breathless, Hope stepped back, a smile crinkling the corners of her lips. She again tapped the knife blade against her palm. ''So you thought you'd find another couple of women better looking than us?''

Jess again pulled her to him. "Honey, I'm s'prised you didn't call my bluff. They ain't no woman in the whole world prettier'n you." He stood back and looked at her. "You an' Bessie got dry clothes wrapped in your ground-sheets, you better get outta them you got on 'fore you catch your death of cold. I'm gonna see can I find somethin' dry that'll burn. We need a fire."

From long habit, Sanford kept a couple of old bird's nests in the bottom of his saddlebags to use as tinder for starting fires. He had the men find twigs and limbs and peel the bark off to the dry wood underneath.

They moved the wagon to the highest part of the bluff, soon had a fire going, and the ladies went about preparing supper, using some of the canned goods they'd brought from Miles Town. The men stood close to the fire letting their clothes dry. The rain had long since moved on to the west.

During the night, Sanford checked the edge of the water. It continued to rise, and the higher it got, the closer the sheep drew in toward camp, until about midnight, when the water rise began to hold steady. By daylight, the river level dropped enough that it was struggling to get back in its banks. After again checking the stream about noon, Jess told them they'd sleep at home that night.

Still a half mile from the dugouts, Jess heard Ransome ringing the supper bell. He hurried his party along.

Around the fire that night, he told all the men about the sheep, why he'd bought them, and the fight they'd had on the way home. "Any o' y'all cain't see yore way clear to herdin' sheep, I'll pay you off now. You might be smart to draw your time anyway. I figger we gonna have some gun trouble because of them."

The kid, Quaid, grinned. "Hell, boss, I wuz jest 'bout ready to step forward for my wages till you promised us some fun. You say we probably gonna have to fight 'bout them woollies? I'll stick around.''

Sanford gave him a sour look. ''Kid, you been quittin' this crew ever since the day you hired on. I figger I'll watch you grow white hair, wrinkles, an' get stove up from old age 'fore you ride outta here.''

''I been thinkin' to see you get solid on yore feet, boss, then I might go downstream from here and start me a outfit.''

Jess nodded. ''Good thinkin'. Gonna take that sort o' thing to build this country. I'll help you when the time comes.'' He swept his crew with a glance. ''That goes for all o' you.''

Twilley jabbed a thumb toward the two dugouts. ''In order to finish the fronts and insides of them half soddy, half dugouts, we stripped the creek banks for a quarter mile upstream an' downstream of us, but we left trees standin' here close to us. Don't think we left a tree standin' no-where, but we got our sleepin' places finished.'' He grinned. ''Bet them sod roofs keeps snow out better'n they shed rain.''

Sanford nodded. ''They will. And this time next year we'll have a house, bunkhouse, an' outbuildings. I figger our first calf crop's gonna take care o' the cost an' still leave us enough to live high on the hog—if the cold don't wipe us out.''

They sat there longer than usual that night, drinking coffee and trying to see the future. When the last embers burned to a dull glow, all were in their blankets.

The next day, Jess and Joe Bob went looking for pasture for the sheep. They wanted to keep them separate from the cattle since the sheep would eat the grass down to the roots. Hope watched them ride out, then went about fixing the dugout to be more comfortable. They'd eaten only a cold biscuit and bacon for their nooning, and then gone back to work.

She and Bessie worked steadily until about midafternoon, when Bessie held up her hand for silence. "Horses comin'. It's too early for the men folks to be back."

Hope went to a rack on the wall, took down a Winchester, handed it to Bessie, then took one for herself. "Stay in here out of sight. If it's trouble they bring, be ready to empty saddles." At the same time she hoped the cook stood inside his dugout with a rifle.

Bessie nodded.

Hope stepped outside to see four men draw rein about ten yards in front of the dugout. A large, burly man swung his leg across his horse's rump to dismount. "Hold it right there, mister. Where I come from, a body don't step from his horse till invited to do so. Sit back in your saddle easy like."

The man settled back into his saddle. "You ain't very neighborly, missy. Where's your man?"

"Working. Why?"

The man's face hardened. "Want you to tell 'im somethin'. Tell 'im Brad Burnstall wants to see him."

Hope eared the hammer back. "That name supposed to scare 'im?"

Burnstall's face hardened. "Only after I take 'im down a notch and kill them stinkin' sheep he put on this range."

The Winchester Hope pointed at him didn't waver. "Mister, I'm gonna do you a favor. Gonna explain some things 'bout my husband to you. First off, he can whip you with guns, knives, or fists, and he don't take kindly to threats. You kill one o' them sheep an' he'll swap you even; one man—one sheep. If you don't want to face him, I'll take you on. Right now. Any of your men make a move for their weapons, I empty your saddle first. If you don't want it that way, ride out and don't come back.'' Hope brought the rifle to her shoulder. ''An' I'll tell you something else, mister, our crew, without exception, is 'bout as salty as any you'll find anywhere, so whatever way you want it, you got your work cut out for you.''

Burnstall glared at her a moment. ''Ma'am, I never fought a woman, don't intend to start now. Tell your man I'll be back.'' He neck-reined his horse toward the river and rode off.

Hope watched Burnstall and his crew until their horses were swimming the stream, then let her pent-up breath escape in a gust. Her muscles turned to water. She bent her knees slowly and sat on the ground by the entrance to the dugout. Not until then did she gently let the hammer down on her rifle.

Bessie came from behind the door and sat opposite her. ''Hope, I never been so scared in my life, but I wuz shore glad when you said as how you wuz gonna shoot that Burnstall man first. I jest eased my sight a bit to cover the man right next to him.''

Hope stared into the eyes of her friend. ''You know what, Bessie? I figure we could of whipped them.''

Bessie stared back at her, then her lips quivered, and she broke into gales of laughter. Hope joined her. Finally Bessie swallowed her humor enough to say, ''I ain't never had one doubt about that. We woulda whipped 'em good.'' It was then Sanford pulled his horse to a stop alongside of them.

''What in the name of hell y'all sittin' there in the mud for?''

Hope choked back her laughter and eyed her man. ''Jess Sanford, Bessie and me just found out we can do without you and Joe Bob right nicely.''

Jess frowned. ''What brought that idea about?''

Both women started talking at once, then Bessie looked at Hope and said, "You tell 'im."

Hope started at the beginning and didn't leave a word or action untold. While she talked she and Bessie giggled every few words.

Jess knew much of their laughter was the release of nervous tension. And while they talked, blood forced its way to his head. His back muscles tightened, and his jaws clenched. He pulled his horse toward the Powder.

"Where you goin', Jess?"

"Gonna catch up with him an' read to 'im from the book."

"Jess, he said he'd be back. Don't go out there alone to face him. That'd play right into his hands."

He sat there a moment, frowning, thinking. Finally, he nodded. "You're right. But if I stay here, it'll put you an' Bessie in danger."

Still cradling the Winchester in the crook of her arm, Bessie stared from Jess to where Burnstall crossed the river. "Mr. Jess, if he comes back 'fore the men get in from work, me an' Hope standin' behind the door, an' our cook, Mr. Ransome, behind the door of the crew's dugout—the three o' us with rifles ain't gonna hurt yore chances none o' winnin' out over him."

Jess stared at the ground a moment, then feeling his eyes crinkle at the corners, looked up and smiled. "Reckon you're right, Bessie." He stepped from the saddle. "Don't want to fight this man Burnstall, 'less I have to. The fact he didn't try to rough you ladies up none says to me he's a Westerner. Maybe I can talk to him." It was then Ransome walked up, also carrying a rifle.

"Long's Miss Hope had things under control, I stayed hid. Figured a ace in the hole wasn't gonna hurt none."

Sanford nodded. "You did good, Ransome. If he comes

back, I'll handle it. Stay hid, but keep your weapons handy.''

Jess stayed close to headquarters the next two days. The morning of the third day, he and Joe Bob assigned the men their chores, watched them ride out, then walked back to their shelter. Sanford stopped just outside, frowned, and looked at his partner. "You know what? Don't seem like that man Burnstall's gonna come back. We're wastin' a whole lot o' work hours, an' I figure he's done showed he ain't gonna hurt our womenfolk. He wants to see *us,* so let's get to work."

Sanford toed the stirrup and reined his buckskin to leave when he heard horses. "Joe Bob, tell Ransome to stay put where he is, an' get the women folks in the shelter with rifles. I'll talk to this man."

Sanford stood in front of the soddy when Burnstall reined in, eight men siding him. "This your place?" The question came out hard, and the eyes behind the words were even harder.

Sanford studied the man a long moment, then nodded.

"You figure to stay here?" Again the words showed no softness.

Sanford pinned the man with a look. "Mister, I figure to be here the rest of my life. An' from the way you an' your men rode in here, showing no friendliness, the rest o' my life's gonna be a considerable while after I drop you from that saddle." He stepped toward the riders one step. "Suppose you tell me what's on your mind—then head out. 'Sides that, I like to know who I'm talkin' to." He knew the man's name but wanted to hear him say it.

"Name's Burnstall. I'm here to tell you to get rid of those sheep you bought in Miles Town and you can stay."

Sanford let a cold smile crease the corners of his eyes. "All right, Burnstall, reckon I know where you stand, an'

I'm gonna tell you where I stand. First off—I don't like you. Second, I'm keepin' the sheep *an'* stayin'. Third, I got the men an' guns to back my play. I don't want no range war, but if you bring it to me, you gonna lose. You leave me alone and I'll leave you alone. That's how it is. Call my bet or throw in your hand.''

The burly rancher's look traveled the length of Jess, top to bottom. He reined his horse as though to leave, then turned back. ''You wanta talk about this?''

Sanford's eyes never left Burnstall's. ''Fight or talk—makes me no nevermind. You call it.''

23

A HARD SMILE creased the burly rancher's face. "Yore wife tells me it's customary where you come from to be *invited* to step from your horse. We going to talk from where I sit?"

"Climb down. Your men stay where they are."

Burnstall stepped from the saddle, walked to within a few feet of Sanford, and stopped. He measured Jess again, from head to toe. "You don't look like a damned sheepherder, and I hear tell you got a few thousand head o' cattle spread out on this range. Why the sheep? You didn't come in here with 'em, so raisin' them woollies wasn't your intent to begin with."

Sanford wondered how reasonable the rancher might be, especially considering that those men they'd shot coming in from Miles were probably Burnstall's. He hooked his thumbs behind his belt, his hand close to his six-shooter. "Mister, I ain't one to explain my actions to others, but with you I'm gonna make an exception. First off, don't none o' my men, or me, likes sheep any better'n you do, but you can damn well believe we're gonna keep 'em."

He watched those words sink in. He wanted a pipe to finish this powwow with, but wondered if he dared get his hands busy packing the bowl. Still, with four rifles aimed square at Burnstall and his bunch, he decided he'd take the chance. He could think better with his pipe in his hand.

"Burnstall, they's several rifles pointed at you an' yore men, so I'm gonna have a pipe. Join me in a smoke if you want."

Jess busied himself with his pipe, seeing that the rancher did the same. After putting fire to the bowl, he pinned Burnstall with a head-on look. "Keepin' them sheep sounds unfriendly, but like I done told you, I figure to stay in this country, an' I had it 'splained to me that one hard winter up here could wipe a cattleman out. I decided to hedge my bet. Them woollies'll be here when all the cows die from the cold—an' I'll be right here with 'em."

Burnstall took a long drag at his pipe, blew the smoke out in a cloud quickly snatched away by the wind, and studied the dust at his boot toe. He looked up. "Sanford, I come in here from Oregon only a year ago. What you're tellin' me sounds plausible. I figure to stay in this country, too. Those men of mine you shot the other night were acting on their own. I gave them no orders to attack you." Abruptly, his stern features broke into a smile. "Sanford, you reckon we could be friends? After hearing you talk, seems I gotta think about gettin' some sheep. Don't know that I will, but I'm sure gonna think on it."

Jess studied Burnstall's smile, decided it was in earnest, and held out his hand. "Have your men step down. We'll have a cup o' coffee."

Despite Burnstall's acceptance of his explanation, Sanford couldn't help wondering at the easy way he accepted the deaths of his men. A Texan would already be fighting.

About the time Sanford offered coffee to Burnstall and his men, Marshal Bruns, fifty miles away, drank the last swallow of the two-day-old mud he called coffee, listened a moment to the sound of a lone horse in the powdery street dust, put the letter from Tennessee, addressed only to "The Miles Town Marshal" back on his scarred old, cigarette-burned desk without reading it, and walked to the window. He liked to know who came and went in his town.

The horseman must have stood six feet four inches, a big man, given to a soft, fatty-looking roll around the middle. He wore two six-shooters, not the usual thing. Two scabbards on his saddle carried what Bruns guessed to be a rifle and scattergun. He studied the man a moment, running what he saw through his mind, playing it against the wanted notices in his desk. The man's appearance didn't match any of the descriptions given in the notices, but he looked to be a man looking for trouble, and ready for it.

The rider reined in to the front of the End of Trail saloon across the street and went inside. Bruns settled his handgun against his thigh, sighed, and went out the door. Might as well find what business the rider had in Miles Town.

Inside the saloon, Bruns walked directly to the bar and stood next to the stranger, who glanced at the star on the marshal's chest, picked up his drink, knocked it back, and held his glass for another. He looked from his full drink to the marshal. "I just rode into your town, lawman. I've not done anything wrong, and don't take kindly to being bird-dogged, so leave me alone."

Bruns felt bile rise into his throat, but pushed the sudden anger to the back of his mind. He looked into the stranger's eyes. "Gonna tell you something, mister. It's my job to 'bird-dog' heavily armed strangers. Now, I want to know your name and what business you have in my town."

The man eyed Bruns a moment, and obviously figured the marshal would not stand for any nonsense. "I'm lookin' for a man I once knew, and my name's Simon Bauman."

He knocked back his drink and held his glass for another. "Now, Marshal, if you've done your duty, leave me alone."

Bruns nodded. "Remember somethin', Bauman. I don't stand for trouble in my town. Be sure you don't start any." He looked at the redheaded bartender. "I'll take my daily drink now, Red—down at the end of the bar."

Bruns stood there sipping his bourbon, occasionally eyeing Bauman, wondering who it was he looked for. His gut feel told him the big man meant harm to the person when he found him. He finished his drink and headed for his office. It would soon be time to start his rounds of the saloons, twenty of them and more building every day. The seven brothels usually didn't cause him trouble. Those patrons had things other than fighting on their minds.

In his office, Bruns reached for the letter, stared at it a moment, and figuring to read it later, stuffed it back in its envelope and put it in the desk drawer. He went to the gun rack on the wall, took down a twelve-gauge Greener, and went out to start his rounds.

While Burnstall and his crew drank coffee with Jess, Joe Bob, their wives, and Ransome, the rest of the crew drifted in, obviously wary. Each rested his rifle across the saddle in front of him, until determining the visiting riders were friendly.

Sanford drank the last of his coffee, threw the grounds out, and swept Burnstall's men with a glance. "Y'all welcome to stay for supper."

Burnstall shook his head. "Much obliged, Sanford, but we got a long ride. Won't get home till 'bout midnight, and my missus'll be getting worried." He stood, signaling his men they better get gone, and held out his hand. "Glad our visit ended friendly." He nodded. "Gonna give sheep some thought. You folks come visit when you can. My place is 'bout thirty miles straight west of here.''

A few minutes later Jess stood, his arm around Hope's shoulders, and watched their visitors ford the Powder. He looked down at Hope. ''Glad Burnstall turned out to be a reasonable man. We gonna need good neighbors.''

Hope snuggled closer under his arm. ''I'm glad he made the offer for his wife to help when my birthing time comes. Bessie's time'll be mighty close an' it might not be good for her to go through that with me. Besides, he said they have four children, so his wife'll know more what to do.''

Jess smiled. ''Don't need to tell you, honey, it took a load off my shoulders.'' He nodded. ''Yeah, we'd of made do, but I figure you an' Bessie gonna feel a lot better havin' another woman around.''

The next three weeks passed quietly, but at least once a week Joe Bob said he had to go to town. ''I writ some folks a letter, an' I'm 'spectin' a answer. Told 'em I'd pick it up in Miles Town.''

Sanford eyed his partner. ''Joe Bob, if you didn't already have such a pretty lady, I'd suspect you wuz goin' sparkin'.''

Joe Bob shuffled his feet a moment, then looked straight on at Jess. ''Partner, Bessie knows why I'm takin' these long rides, an' she's all for it. I'll tell you 'bout it someday.''

Sanford frowned. ''You got trouble, remember we done shared the good an' the bad.'' He nodded. ''I'll wait till you figure to talk to me 'bout it.''

24

THE DAYS GREW shorter. The prevailing winds shifted to the north, and put a chill on the land, and in mid-October the first snow dusted the frost-killed grass. Each day, Hope and Bessie bundled up and took long walks by the river. Jess and Joe Bob had long since put a stop to their riding. Christmas came and went and the partners and their wives tried to have something special for each of the hands.

Jess became more impatient. He checked on Hope so often that by mid-January she stepped solidly in front of him, hands on hips. "Jess, if you don't stop worrying about me, I—I'll . . ."

Jess didn't give an inch. "Tell you what, woman, by our figurin' that baby's gonna be here in 'bout two weeks. One week from today, I'm goin' to Burnstall's place and bring back his missus.

"You an' Bessie ain't slowed down none. Both o' you walk, wash clothes, help Ransome, and anything else needs doin' 'round here." He scratched his head, paced the floor, came back, and looked her in the eye. "Hell, woman, neither one o' you act like you're carryin' a baby."

Hope smiled into his face. "Oh Jess, I know you're worried because you love me, but Bessie and I've talked a lot and we figure the healthier we are when our time comes, the healthier the baby will be, and it'll make for an easier time for us. We're careful not to strain any woman parts what might be harmful to us *or* our babies.''

Hope's words didn't lessen Jess's worry, and in a week he saddled up and headed for Burnstall's ranch, taking the kid and Twilley with him in case of an outlaw attack.

When they arrived, Mrs. Burnstall told him she was about ready to take the buggy and come see how things were going. ''You know, young man, with a first baby, it's no tellin' when the little devil'll want to see the light of day, so I was gonna come and wait it out.''

Four days later Ma Burnstall—he'd taken to calling her ''Ma''—came out of the shelter with a red, wet, squalling baby boy. She looked at Jess and Joe Bob, who despite the freezing temperature continuously wiped sweat from their necks and brows. ''Done checked him all over an' he's got everything a baby boy ought to have. Here, Jess, hold your son a minute 'fore I take 'im in outta this cold.''

Jess tentatively held out his big hands, worry creasing his forehead. ''Might drop 'im, Ma. You keep 'im.''

''Oh pshaw. Take 'im, he ain't gonna break.''

Jess took him like he was juggling eggs and looked down at the wrinkled little face. He hoped his son would someday shed some of the ugly. Damn, the kid sure wasn't pretty as Hope; maybe he got his ugly from him. He looked at Mrs. Burnstall. ''Ma, you reckon he's gonna look like this all his life?''

She laughed. ''Jess, in a couple of days he'll lose the red, and the wrinkles. He's a fine-looking boy.''

That took some of the worry from Jess's shoulders. He sighed.

Ma stayed another week before she told Jess she ought

to be getting home to her own brood and, before she left, promised Joe Bob she'd be back to help Bessie.

Two months later Jess and Joe Bob packed up their wives and two baby boys and headed for Miles Town. Jess and the women had not been to town for months, but despite the cold, Joe Bob had been in every week. On occasion he took the wagon and a few of the crew with him to bring back supplies. The letter he'd been looking for never arrived.

Jess cut the men loose at the outskirts of town and told them to be ready to ride in two days. He wanted to give them more time in town, but the heifers were dropping calves in numbers that promised a bumper crop. Some of the cows would need help in their delivery. It had been a mild winter—for Montana. Very few subzero days.

Jess drove down the row of unpainted buildings to the same rooming house where they stayed the last visit, helped take the bags in, waited for the ladies to freshen up and change the babies, then they went to Leighton's. "Figure you girls need some stuff to make dresses from, an' if they got any store-bought things that'll fit, you oughta get some.

"Joe Bob an' me gotta see 'bout orderin' dressed lumber to build our houses outta. Captain Grant Marsh can bring it on the *Eclipse*. He's supposed to bring his boat up the Yellowstone on the June rise sometime between mid-May and mid-June; that's when the river'll be at its highest from snowmelt and spring rains. We'll get our rough-sawn lumber for our outbuildings from the sawmill up on Government Hill. Give us time to sell off what steers we need to in order to pay for it all." He looked toward the door, then back to Hope. "Figure y'all gonna need us for the next hour or so?"

Hope ran her fingers over a bolt of cloth, then looked at

Joe Bob. "How much can we afford to spend, Joe Bob?"

He pulled a small book from his shirt pocket, studied it a moment, then looked at the two women. "We got the crew paid to date, but we need supplies." He scratched his head. "Then again, Mr. Leighton wuz jest tellin' me an' Jess beef's bringin' a pretty good price this spring. Reckon y'all can make do on fifty dollars apiece?"

Hope looked at Bessie. "That's more'n I figured to spend. How 'bout you?"

Bessie grinned. "That's more'n I spent in the last three years, an' if it seems we gonna run short, we'll just leave off some of the foofaraw."

Hope nodded. "Sounds good to me. You men leave us while we shop for women things. Better buy for the babies first, though."

Joe Bob headed for the post office to see if he had an answer to his long-ago letter. Sanford crossed the street to visit with Marshal Bruns, stopped in the middle of the road to let a freight wagon pass, frowned, and walked on. Something was wrong. A knot settled in between his shoulder blades—a signal of danger. He shook his head. Wrong signal, he thought. Right here in the middle of town, what could happen?

As soon as Jess walked through the doorway, Bruns swung his feet off the desk, stood, and came to shake hands. "Damn, boy, figured you got lost out yonder somewhere. Where you been?"

Jess grinned. "Been hidin' out like a old bear, Marshal. I hear tell this's been a mild winter, but back home in Tennessee it would've been called pure-dee *cold*."

As soon as Sanford mentioned being from Tennessee, he wished he could call the words back. It might cause Bruns to look in that direction for wanted posters.

They talked awhile. Bruns offered Jess a cup of coffee

with the promise he'd made it only that morning. Sanford took a swallow, eyed the marshal, and raised an eyebrow. "Bruns, if I lined postholes with this stuff, them posts would be there forever, or this stuff'd eat the bottoms off them. Even bet which it'd be. Damn, man. If you have to pay for yore own coffee grounds, you gonna go broke."

"Nah, now, Jess, you just gotta learn to drink coffee with character. Now, I admit you young fellows down Texas way don't have any reason to put body into your drinkin', but up here, in bad winters, you need something like this to line your stomach."

Sanford looked over the rim of his cup. "Marshal, this stuff won't line your stomach, it'll strip what linin's there right outta it."

They joshed back and forth until Sanford stood. "Gotta go out to Government Hill. Need some rough-cut timber for outbuildings, then I need to order building materials for two homes, Hope's an' Bessie's."

"Sure glad to see you settling in permanent like, Jess. We need your kind up here."

Out on the street, Jess sighed. Bruns hadn't said anything about him being wanted. He looked for Joe Bob and saw him come out of a store down the street. He climbed on his gelding and rode toward him. "Get yore horse. We got enough time 'fore supper to ride out to the sawmill and order our outbuilding lumber."

The knot hadn't left the middle of his back; in fact, it had become downright painful.

Two hours later they were back in town with a promise that the lumber would be delivered in about a month.

They went from store to store until they found Hope and Bessie in the Broadwater, Hubbel and Company general merchandise store, babies under one arm and packages under the other.

Jess reached for the baby. "You got anything we need to collect from the other stores?"

"Nope. We brought it all with us. We better go back to our rooms so we can change and feed the babies." Hope shifted some of the packages to her free arm. "While we take care of the babies and let them get a nap, you and Joe Bob might want to go down to the Cattleman's Saloon. Mr. Leighton says there're some cattle buyers in town and they sort of make headquarters in there."

Jess nodded. "Sounds good. We'll have most o' our business taken care of, then tomorrow we can see the town."

At their room, Sanford unbuckled his gun belt to leave his Colt in the room, but the knot between his shoulders changed his mind. He buckled his belt again.

Sitting in a rocker nursing the baby, Hope frowned. "You got trouble, Jess?"

He shook his head. "None I know 'bout, but somethin' tells me it's sittin' out there waitin'. I been listenin' to my hunches too long to pay 'em no mind now."

Hope frowned and shifted the baby to her other breast. "Whatever it is, Jess, be careful."

With a quick, jerky nod, he said, "Figure on it."

Before leaving the rooming house, Sanford thought to take Joe Bob with him, then decided to let him spend some time with Bessie. He headed for the Cattleman's Saloon.

Standing at the window of his office, Bruns watched Sanford push through the big solid doors of the saloon. He frowned, trying to remember if Jess had mentioned something about Tennessee. Seemed like he had. He thought on it a few moments and convinced himself Sanford said he was from there.

Tennessee. What was there he should remember about

that state? He poured himself a cup of coffee and pondered the question. Then he remembered the letter he'd never read.

Sanford walked to the bar, thinking to ask the bartender to point out any cattle buyers in the room. At the long polished surface, Jess figured first things first. "Bourbon and branchwater, bartender, an' when you get time, I need to talk to you."

The bartender poured Jess's drink, brought it down the bar to him, and looked across Sanford's shoulder. "What'll you have, mister?"

"Gonna talk to the man you just brought that drink."

Sanford hooked his thumbs in his belt and looked over his shoulder. He didn't recognize the huge man standing there. "What can I do for you, stranger?"

The big man hunched his shoulders, dropped his hands to his side to brush the holstered six-shooters, and glared at Sanford. "You Jess Sanford?"

Jess studied the man a moment, something trying to stir his memory. "That's what they call me. Why?"

The stranger pulled his neck farther down between his shoulders. "I been waitin' in this hick town four months to see you. Heard you were comin' this way with a herd of those Texas cattle."

"You heard right. I been here, or a few miles east o' here, 'bout five months. What brings you to wait for me that long?"

The brute of a man grinned. "Oh hell yeah, Jess Sanford, I'da waited one hell of a lot longer. I rode many a mile to find you. You don't recognize me, but I'm here to kill you. I'm Simon Bauman."

Every nerve in Sanford quieted. He studied the man. Yes, the pudgy hulk was Bauman. He saw what the ravages of

whiskey, soft living, and hate had done to the man he'd
left for dead in those Tennessee woods years ago. The only
emotion he felt was relief. He wasn't a wanted man—never
had been. A cold calm gripped him. "Why do want to do
harm to me, Bauman? That fight happened years ago. I beat
you fairly and squarely, even though you tried to kill me
with a posthole digger."

Bauman's eyeballs reddened, his face flushed, he gripped
his hands at his sides. "Nobody, not even my father, ever
put a hand on me until you. I've lived for the day I'd meet
you."

Sanford stared at the big man. "You gonna try to whip
me? You do, you'll lose." He wanted to make Bauman
angry enough to swing at him. "In the years past, you've
gotten soft. I beat the hell outta you back then. It'll be easier
this time." He shrugged. "But if you gotta have it, shuck
yore hardware an' we'll get at it."

Bauman shook his head, his mottled jowls turning even
redder. "We're not fightin' with fists this time, Sanford. I
heard down the trail a ways you bragged about not being
fast with your six-shooter. Well, I been practicing. Think
there are few who can match me—and you damned sure
aren't one of them."

Sanford didn't feel anything; not anger, not fear, not re-
gret. He might as well have been facing a bale of hay. He
had to try to avoid this if he could, but knowing it was
useless, he said, "Bauman, we don't have to do this. You
could crawl on your horse and head for Tennessee. You
forget it, an' I'll do the same."

Bauman, obviously getting more angry by the moment,
stood trembling. "They accused *me* of killing *you,* and
burying your body; then, when they couldn't find your re-
mains, they had to let me go. Now I'm gonna do what they

accused me of. You can pull that six-shooter you're wearing anytime.''

Sanford shook his head. An icy calm had settled in his
brain. ''Bauman, you want me dead, you better go for your
gun. I ain't drawin' on you. I'd rather see you live, 'cause
you've turned out to be the white trash you once accused
me of. I'd like to see you wallow in your self-pity, an' then
when yore pa spends his last cent supportin' you, I'll see
you ride the grub line bummin' meals. No, I ain't drawin'
on you, but I want you to reach for yore gun, then *I'm*
gonna blow *you* in two.''

Bauman stepped back, then took four more quick steps
backward, widening the distance between them. He
stopped. ''Draw, damn you, draw!''

Sanford stood there, thumbs hooked in his gun belt,
never taking his eyes from Bauman's.

Bauman's lips split in a snarl and his hands swept his
sides. Sanford waited until the big man's weapons were
almost clear of their holsters, then pulled his belt gun. Bauman pulled triggers as fast as his fingers would work. He
got off four shots, two of them through the sides of his
holsters and another that creased Sanford's shoulder before
Sanford brought his Colt level and fired.

A black hole opened in Bauman's chest. Sanford took a
step toward his enemy and fired again. A second hole
opened beside the first one. Each shot knocked the big man
back on his heels. He wouldn't go down. Hate had control
of his brain and his body. Sanford stepped toward him
again, brought his arm straight out, aimed, pulled the trigger, and watched Bauman's head explode, brains, skull, and
hair flying out the back. He moved out of the way when
Bauman fell toward him, watched his archenemy stiffen,
pull his legs to his stomach, straighten them, twitch a couple of times, and lie still.

Sanford stood over the body, the room so quiet the breathing of the men present was audible. "You heard I wuz slow, Bauman, but you didn't listen good enough. The whole sentence was, 'I'm slow, but I don't miss.' " He turned to the bar, picked up his drink, and knocked it back. "Think I'll have another, bartender." His voice was still the only sound in the graveyard-quiet, smoke-filled room. He held his glass out for a refill before the crowd let out their breath. Then the noise vibrated the walls, everyone talking at once.

Sanford raised his second drink to his lips before Bruns came through the doors. The marshal stopped in midstride, looked at Bauman's body sprawled in the middle of the floor, then swept the roomful of men with a glance. "What the hell happened here?"

A tall soldier, a captain, stepped forward. "Mr. Sanford was forced to defend himself, Mr. Bruns. He tried every way possible to avoid trouble, but that man lying there wouldn't have it that way. After Mr. Sanford tried to talk the dead man into going back to Tennessee, he drew and, I believe, fired at least two shots before Mr. Sanford fired."

"That's 'zactly the way it happened, Marshal," a man in overalls said. Then others stepped forward and vouched for the soldier's statement.

Bruns again swept those present with a glance, gave a jerky nod, and walked to the bar. "Buy you a drink, Jess? I owe you one."

Jess asked, "Why you owe me a drink, Marshal?" The killing had not yet overpowered the relief of knowing the law wasn't looking for him.

Bruns held up two fingers to the bartender, waited for him to set their drinks in front of them, even though Jess hadn't yet finished his second one, picked up his drink, and eyed the big Texan. "Owe you a drink for two reasons, boy. First off, I was gonna have to run that man outta town, or kill 'im myself. He's been stirrin' trouble ever since he hit town." He took a swallow of his drink.

"Second reason, Jess, is I done you a great disservice, you an' Joe Bob both. Several months ago I got a letter from Tennessee. I don't read so well. Readin's a chore for me, so I put the letter in my desk drawer figurin' to read it later. I forgot it was there until you mentioned bein' from Tennessee earlier today. Watchin' the street from my window, I seen you come in this saloon. It was then I took it out an' read it." He took out his pipe, packed and lit it, then took another swallow of his drink. "I mighta been able to stop this killin' if I'd read it sooner."

Jess shook his head. "Bruns, you couldn't of stopped it. That man yonder wuz eat up with hate—hate that'd been festerin' in his gut for years." He stared into the bottom of his glass. "No, friend, it wuz gonna happen no matter what. Don't blame yourself." The smoke from Bruns's pipe kindled the desire to smoke his own pipe. He pulled it out, packed and lit it with steady hands, then looked into Bruns's eyes. "How you figure that letter from Tennessee might of caused you to try to stop this killin'?"

Bruns looked at the blood soaking Jess's sleeve above his elbow. "Ain't bad, or you woulda said somethin' 'fore now."

Jess grinned. "Hell, Marshal, I could of bled to death if I waited for you to say somethin' 'bout it." He shook his head. "Naw, it's only a scratch." Then the marshal surprised him. Bruns asked the bartender for a bottle of his best bourbon.

"Gonna take this young fellow over to my office an' get 'im soused. I owe 'im that." He looked at Sanford. "C'mon, gonna tell you 'bout that letter."

In his office, Bruns poured each of them a coffee cup

full of bourbon. Jess stared at his cup, his eyes wide. "Great heavens, Marshal, I drink that an' you'll have to put me to bed. I ain't never drunk that much."

"Sit, I got some things to tell you."

Jess spun a chair around and straddled it. "Start tellin'."

Bruns told Jess the letter he'd received had been written by his mother. She'd had a letter from a man by the name of Joe Bob Brown implying he knew where you were, and if she wanted to get in touch with you to write him and he'd see you wrote her a letter.

Brown told her you thought you'd beaten to death a man by the name of Simon Bauman.

Her letter said Bauman hadn't died, but instead had been suspected of killing you, and that she, too, thought all this time you lay in an unmarked grave somewhere.

She said she wrote her letter to the law knowing Bauman left home saying he would kill you—if he could find you. She thought it was a ruse of Bauman's and Brown's to flush you into the open if you were, in fact, still alive.

Bruns picked up the letter. "She finished off her letter like this: 'Mr. Marshal, if my son, Jess Sanford, is in your town, please caution him he's in great danger from Simon Bauman and this man Joe Bob Brown. Tell him his father and I are doing fine since the war—we got into raising horses and we want for nothing nowdays. And, Mr. Marshal, please tell him we love him and to write us.' "

The crusty old marshal looked up from the letter, his eyes misty, and apparently to hide his emotion, picked up his drink and took a swallow. "Son, now you know why I said I owe you a drink. I coulda saved you an' your folks several months of heartbreak if I'd read your ma's letter earlier.

"Might not of been able to keep Bauman alive; don't think he was worth savin' anyway."

Jess stood, a little unsteady, twisted the chair around, and sat in it. In the last hour, things had happened too fast for him to comprehend. He took another swallow of his drink, then tilted the cup of raw bourbon and drained it. Bruns poured another. They talked, each drinking their second cupful. After a while Jess looked at his friend.

"Am I free to go to my wife, Bruns? She's gonna give me hell for drinkin' like this, so might as well get on with it."

"You need help gettin' to your room, son? I got you like this, but I figure it's a time to celebrate."

Jess stood. "Nope. I'll make it."

A few minutes later Jess hesitantly pushed open the door to his and Hope's room.

Hope looked up from rocking the baby, then her eyes opened wide. "Jess Sanford! You're drunk."

"Yep. Get Joe Bob an' Bessie. Got somethin' to tell y'all."

When Hope brought them into the room, Jess, knowing he grinned stupidly, said, "Ain't wanted by the law. Bauman's dead, an' a lot o' other things I gotta tell ya when I wake up. Gotta write my folks, too." Then, with a lopsided, sloppy grin, he said, "Marshal got me drunk. Figure it's legal—'cept for Hope."

With that, he fell across the bed—out cold.

J. L. REASONER

AUTHOR OF *RIVERS OF GOLD*

__*Healer's Calling*   0-425-15487-4/$5.99

On the bloody battlefields of the Civil War,
Sara Black had proven her courage and skill
as a medic. Now, the war had ended, but she
had found her true calling: to become one of
America's first woman doctors.

__*The Healer's Road*   0-515-11762-5/$5.99

When his parents died because of a lack of
proper medicine, Thomas Black vowed to
become a doctor and better people's lives.
Now, with the advent of war, he is challenged
to provide better care than ever before–in a
fraction of the time. During the savage conflict
of the Civil War, Thomas Black, and his two
children who follow in his footsteps, will embody
the true nobility of the American spirit.